THE ...
BARR...

THE
GOD BOX

Barry B. Longyear

A SIGNET BOOK

NEW AMERICAN LIBRARY

PUBLISHED BY
PENGUIN BOOKS CANADA LIMITED

NAL BOOKS ARE AVAILABLE AT QUANTITY DISCOUNTS
WHEN USED TO PROMOTE PRODUCTS OR SERVICES.
FOR INFORMATION PLEASE WRITE TO PREMIUM MARKETING DIVISION,
NEW AMERICAN LIBRARY, 1633 BROADWAY,
NEW YORK, NEW YORK 10019.

First Printing, April, 1989

2 3 4 5 6 7 8 9

SIGNET TRADEMARK REG. U.S. PAT. OFF. AND FOREIGN COUNTRIES
REGISTERED TRADEMARK — MARCA REGISTRADA
HECHO EN WINNIPEG, CANADA

SIGNET, SIGNET CLASSIC, MENTOR, ONYX, PLUME,
MERIDIAN and NAL BOOKS are published in Canada by Penguin
Books Canada Limited, 2801 John Street, Markham, Ontario,
L3R 1B4
PRINTED IN CANADA
COVER PRINTED IN U.S.A.

To Jean for being there,
to Georgius of Lydda for making it work,
and
to Paula for the suggestion.

A special thanks to
Emma Bull, Will Shetterly
and the Liavekians

FOREWORD

Allow me to introduce myself. My name is Korvas. K-o-r-v-a-s. There are no throat-clearing or tongue-bending exercises here: my name is pronounced just the way it is spelled.

Ah, I see a skeptical eyebrow or two. They appear to ask, "Korvas the what? Why does this fellow not identify himself as Korvas the rug merchant, Korvas the magician, or, at the very least, Korvas of Iskandar or whatever city or village it is from which he comes?" What nefarious personage is this, you whisper to yourselves, who must hide his rank, trade, and place of origin in the manner of a thief or assassin?

Be calm. I give only my name because time is valuable. I have only these few moments with you, and it would burden our time together to list all of my accomplishments, occupations, ranks, and places of origin. For I have been all of these: rug merchant, magician, thief, soldier, assassin, and more. I have been pauper, priest, and prince, and I have been and have been from everywhere.

I see your lips moving. They say, "If nothing else, he is certainly a great liar." Perhaps you are correct. I have been that, too, and nothing less than that has rescued my giblets on more than one occasion. However, should I introduce myself as Korvas the Liar, don't you think it might put a shade on my social standing? When I offer my counsel at court, which on occasion I do, can you not picture His Majesty, the king, asking, "And who offers me this vital wisdom?" That bloodsucking parasite at the royal family's elbow, Tretia the bloody horror, would take a moment from picking her teeth with the raw bones of newly born babies to inform the king, "Why, that is merely Korvas the Liar. Pay you no attention to his words."

Look at how restless you've become! Several of you are thinking, "He is not such a great liar at that if he is so clumsy as to claim an advisory relationship with the king. I can stand and listen to lies cut from whole cloth, but lies still on the spindle or still growing on the sheep's back are not worthy of attention."

"Yet," says another, "hear what he openly calls Her Blessed Self, Tretia, First Priestess of the Heterins. How can he do this without fear of spies or the vengeance of the fanatic Heterin Guard?"

"Bah, it's just that he's a liar *and* a fool. Smell for camel piss on his breath. He looks drunk. Perhaps he is only mad and will start drooling and twitching in a moment. Already he gibbers."

I see I have already strained your patience. Perhaps I should show you my bottles. These huge, black, silk-covered flasks are my treasures, and please do not be startled by what you see. Just let me pull the drawstring, and—

Oh dear, did it startle you? You must forgive me. A headless corpse viewed so close to mealtime is unsettling, isn't it? Before I cover it again, though, please note the well-developed musculature, the huge, gold-studded sword still gripped by the corpse's massive left hand, and the red tattoo over the heart of the corpse. For those of you who cannot see it clearly, it is of a great red flame. Of course you recognize the insignia of the Heterin Guard's elite fraternity, Soldiers of the Fire. Look at that sword, those muscles, that tattoo, and can you have any doubt that these are the remains of Captain Shadows?

I heard a few gasps. I certainly did. There are those here who know of Captain Shadows, and to know him is to fear him. But I hear another whisper—no point in denying it, fellow. I heard you and I will answer your question. What if this is just a corpse snatched from some graveyard, beheaded, tattooed, and dropped into a jug along with a sword? Does it have no head because too many know the real face of Captain Shadows?

First, please notice the etching on this magnificent bottle. Those of you who can recognize the mark of the king's household will see it here. Now, let me draw the silk from this smaller bottle—I see I have again caught you unprepared. You must forgive me. Observe this head, my friends, and look upon the face used by countless mothers to frighten countless little children. I have the pleasure of introducing to you, Pagas Shadows, Captain of the Heterin Guard.

See how the eyes blink and the jaw snaps? He's still alive in his spirit bath. Watch what happens when I knock on the bottle. There, see how the lips snarl and the jaws snap? Isn't that simply delightful?

Perhaps, now, I have your attention. Korvas, your humble servant, may not be all things; but he is something, you are thinking. Who is it that has the decapitated corpse of Captain Shadows? Who is it that can, with impunity, stand here and say that Tretia, First Priestess of the Herterin Temple, murdered her own mother? I don't say that she did and I don't say that she didn't. I do say that I can accuse her of it without fear—

Hold on there. No harm will come to you for listening to me. You are under my protection. "Oh," I hear someone ask, "and what is the protection of Korvas the Liar worth? When I stand in front of the king's magistrate accused of treasonous conspiracy, what will they say when I disclose my great trump: that I am under the protection of Korvas the Bodysnatcher? They will wear out nine whipmasters on my bleeding back."

Fear not. Let me cover these distracting bottles again, and I shall explain. —Look at him snarl! He is certainly lively tonight, isn't he? There. Perhaps the good captain can sleep beneath the silk. Perhaps not. I have never caught him napping. He might always be awake. Let me peek—yes, he's awake. Hello, hello. My, what a snarl.

He's so angry he's beside himself! Yes, please forgive me.

As I remarked, I am no bodysnatcher. These bottles and their contents were the gifts to me from none other than Tretia her bloody self. Now that my bottles are covered, I shall tell you about myself, about a great hero, a beautiful maiden, a great villain and how Captain Shadows became my present associate earning me two coppers a peek.

—What say you, sir? What do I have beneath this third piece of black silk? I was just getting to that. Are you certain you want to see? What grisly thing might it be that Korvas saves for last? Could it be another head? Perhaps it is only a bowl of intestines—

Fear not, friends, for the object that lies beneath this silk is and can be only good. It is the reason why we are all here. This object is a gift of the gods, an item invested with great powers. This is not the instrument of some mere wizard or magician, however. This is the power of the gods themselves.

—Hold your accusations back there, fellow! I do not lie and I am not about to sell you any medicines! In fact, I cannot lie. If I should tell a single lie during my following narrative, may all of the bolted fires of Heaven itself descend and strike me dead this instant—

—Now, why are you all moving away? Come back here. Please, come back. I said that to calm you, not to frighten you.

Now, where was I? Ah, yes. The power of the gods. Let me remove the silk. I see by your puzzled looks that this thing has fallen far short of your expectations. For those of you in back, the object is a small chest of four drawers build into a roundish cabinet of dark wood. It looks almost like a tiny barrel. It has some scrolling for ornamentation, and there is a carved ivory handle on top. Each drawer can be pulled open from either end, and none of the drawers looks large enough to serve any useful purpose, some of you are thinking, I'm sure. The entire thing might be nothing but a child's toy. Can this contain the power of the gods?

It is the truth. These drawers might be tiny, but what if they were filled with gold reels? What if they were filled with diamonds? That would impress you, would it not? What if I told you that what these drawers contain is something much dearer to you than either gold or diamonds? What if what these drawers hold could tap you into the wisdom and the power of the gods themselves?

More important than that, what if I told you that the magic in this object is available to anyone who chooses to use it? You do not need to seek the intervention of a priest or magician. This piece of magic is for everyone who wants it. However, to want it requires a certain degree of bravery, as well as a peculiar bent of mind. Who among you has the courage, humility, and sense of mystery to try it?

How much does one cost? What a strange question to ask. It is an even stranger question, however, to answer. It costs nothing and everything. You must invest no coin, but you will hand over much of what you are. It is not a price, my friend. The gods are not merchants beseeching you to toss them a few coppers in exchange for their favors.

Yes, fellow, I'm certain it sounds confusing. But never fear. I shall explain, for there are secrets involving the use of such a thing that you must know before building or purchasing your own.

—Yes, my friends, you heard correctly. You can buy these or build them, and they all work as well as this one, if you know the secret. Save your expressions of disbelief until after you have heard my tale and have witnessed the great powers contained in these drawers. I promised you great magic of your own. If I do not deliver, then I will willingly refund any investment you have made. So, hear me out.

I shall now retire behind this curtain to prepare my narrative. Meanwhile, my assistant Ruuter will pass among you with a cup for your coppers—I'm sorry back there. Yes, you will find the doors are all locked. Some of you may notice from Ruuter's rather powerful aura that he is of the Omergunt tribe. As most of you know, Omergunts customarily cultivate hideous body odors. In fact, it is one of their highest traditions. If you would like him to move more quickly through the rows, please have your coppers ready.

Until then, my friends.

1

My story does not start very long ago. I was then, as you see me now, a handsome figure of a man. From inclination, rather than necessity, I was always interested in the possibility of learning more efficient ways of increasing my fortune. Gold is not my sole motivation in life, I assure you, but the reasons I do things do make an occasional visit in that neighborhood. On one such an occasion was my visit to the Omergunts and Oghar the Valiant, Chief of the Omergunts. But I am getting ahead of myself.

A few days before on my piece of the square at the Iskandar market, for I could not afford a stall, there was a lesser magician named Jorkis who was shopping for a flying carpet. I had the usual weaves imported from the sleazier districts of Iskandar's blemished jewel bearing labels from as far away as the exotic kingdom of Ahmrita. What eventually transpired concerning this alleged magician, incidentally, was not entirely my fault. After all, the fellow was shopping for a carpet that any fool would expect to cost thousands of reels. Here he was in the market square with a purse holding barely enough coins to weigh down a mosquito. I believe at least a portion of the blame should rest upon his shoulders.

Be that as it may, this magician was searching among my carpets, and when his back was turned I blew upon a silent whistle. A carpet, one of the better blue designs on loan from the Zivenese, began twitching.

"Great Yhandra!" he cried as he invoked the ancient Itkahn goddess of flight. Inwardly I smiled, for I knew I already had my fingers in his purse. As I silently whistled my signals, the carpet crawled around left, then right. "Yhandra herself is in this carpet, Korvas."

"She is there, true enough," I answered. "She only awaits a great magician such as yourself, Jorkis, to bring her chariot to life."

"Then the carpet would fly?"

"Fly? That is such an ordinary word—such a feeble word." I looked toward the sky and pointed toward a cloud. "Say instead that it would soar." I pointed with the movement of my hand at an imaginary flight far above consisting of dives, loops, and great reaches of height and speed. I was about to blow the signals for the rug to roll and wrap itself when Dorc, a local fool the merchants use to send messages, ran up to us.

"Master Korvas, I have—"

I quickly hid my whistle. "Silence, Dorc! I am with a customer." I turned to the magician saying, "My apologies, Jorkis."

"What is this?" Jorkis's voice sounded quite puzzled.

"I beg your pardon?" I looked at where the magician was pointing and saw about fifty of my trained mahrzak beetles running from under the carpet pell-mell into the square. I could not spare the time to explain them away to Jorkis. It had taken me years to train those bugs, and of course I ran after them.

"Hold, sir! Madam, watch where you step!" I confess, my composure was already threadbare just wondering what Jorkis would do, but suddenly a madman from one of the stalls came at me with a horrible contrivance surely designed to be used by Quaag the Torturer in the king's dungeon.

It was a huge drum run by a handle. As the drum rolled, it rumbled like an earthquake. It quite stopped me in my tracks. Before I could get moving again, the creature had run his contraption over my precious mahrzak beetles.

I was aghast. I was ruined. Who wants to buy a carpet

that just lies there? To add more distress to my portion, I thought of the beetles I had known well enough to name.

There were Benthia and her children, Nab and Tib, that I had nursed through the croup, brave Bomba who lost a leg to a hungry mantis and who still carried his share of the rug using the tiny peg leg I had whittled for him, ancient Hadrubba who was the first to come to me after I had been cut down from the whipping post and had nothing. . . .

I was devastated. Before I could recover, the creature with the torture instrument returned, his face beaming. "There is no charge, brother, for my services."

"Charge? Charge! Charge for what, you maniac? And don't you *brother* me, you crawling, muck-sucking, son of a Vulot slug!"

The color came to the fellow's face. "I find your words a trifle offensive, ragman."

"Ragman? Ragman? I am Korvas the rug merchant, and I sell the finest magic carpets in this or any other universe. Just who and what are you?"

"I am Obushawn the Shrubber. I am a merchant, as well."

"Merchant," I sneered. "What merchant rolls about on such a torture instrument?"

He laughed at me, and I would have throttled him had he not placed that thing between himself and my aching hands. "Brother Korvas, this is no torture instrument. I sell these. This is a lawn roller."

"Lawn roller?" I looked at the thing, the surface of its drum stained with the corpses of my faithful beetles. "What is it for?"

"Why, it is for rolling lawns."

I shook my head and laughed back at him. "Do I look like I have hay in my ears, fellow? Just why, madman, would anyone want to roll a lawn? There would be nothing left but mud, and the grass would die from lack of sun."

"No, Korvas. Rolling means to flatten."

"No, it doesn't. A roller rolls; a flattener flattens."

Obushawn sighed and nodded. "Very well, it is a lawn flattener. It's for flattening lawns."

"I see no purpose in it. If I wanted a flat lawn, that's what I would have planted in the first place. I think you are a failure at business, you obviously drink to excess and beat your wife, dog, and children, you steal from the temple and blind beggars, and are most likely well on your way to being put away in a home. I do not want to talk to you anymore. Go away."

I turned back to my place of business to find the magician Jorkis, as well as his golden reels, gone. In his place was the fool Dorc. He groveled to excess. "Forgive me, Master Korvas! Forgive me!"

"Forgive you!"

He picked up a stick, handed it to me, and presented his back. "Beat me, master. I deserve it. Please beat me!"

"Make up your mind, idiot!" I broke the stick across my knee and threw the pieces into the dust. "Give me your message, Dorc, before I obtain a small piece of drainpipe and reacquaint you with the experience of birth."

"Eh?" He froze as he attempted to discern the meaning of my words.

"Never mind what I said, fool. Just give me the message."

"Message?"

"What message do you have for me?"

Dorc appeared to panic. "Forgive me, master, but it seems that I have forgotten—"

"What?" I took a step toward him and he fell backward onto my remaining rugs. As fate would have it, in the process of falling upon those rugs he also landed upon my remaining mahrzak beetles, ruining both beetles and rugs forever. I have never found a cleaner who could remove the dark purple mahrzak stains. So much for the vaunted wizardry of Iskandar.

I rubbed my eyes as I shook my head. The gods of commerce play jokes every now and then, and I do not begrudge them their recreations. However, the number of times I have been singled out as the object of their humor often gives me pause. Surely there are others who could amuse the gods for a bit.

"Master?"

I opened my eyes and Dorc was standing. He nodded toward the market's Sunset Gate. "The magician said that he was going for the King's Guard to have you flayed alive for fraud?"

"Did you have anything else to impart to brighten my day? Has the Heterin faith reopened the Unbeliever Pogroms again? Have the bug monsters of Chara's Sea attacked the city?"

"B-b-b-bug monsters?"

"I was only joking, idiot."

"You aren't laughing, master."

"It was only a joke," I shouted. "Tell me what you want now. Ruined carpets? I have a fine selection."

"This." In his outstretched hand was a piece of paper. "Here is the message I was supposed to deliver."

He dropped the piece of paper and ran. From every side of me there were snickers as my colleagues and their customers found amusement in my suffering.

I pulled out my whistle and blew assembly. Only three of my mahrzak beetles—Amram, Tiram, and Iramiram—managed to struggle out of the carnage. I put them in the pocket of my robe, wiped away a tear in memory of their faithful comrades, and picked up the paper containing the message.

It read:

Korvas, My Benefactor,

Years ago an old beggar asked you for the price of a cup of soup, and you gave him instead ten gold reels. I was that beggar, and I took that small fortune and used it to buy my way into a business. It has become quite a success, enough so that I was able to hire help in locating the family from which I was stolen as a child many decades ago.

I am dying now, and am returning to Ehyuva to be with my dear sister for my remaining days. I have left my valuables and instructions at the Nant Temple where I have found comfort these many years. Seek the priestess

*there called Syndia and give her this message as proof of
your identity.*

*When the dark closes over me, I will intercede on your
behalf with the Nant gods, and I have no doubt that they
will honor my wishes for you, for the Nant gods favor the
compassionate.*

With grateful thanks,

Olassar

After reading those words, my feelings were quite uncertain. It was warming to feel so generous, as well as so
generously remembered. However, I could not for the
life of me call to mind any beggar named Olassar, nor
indeed any beggar to whom I would have given ten gold
reels without the beggar first holding a razor at my throat.

Still, with the demise of my beetles, and the subse-
quent fouling of my carpets, I headed my footsteps past
the end of the bazaar and up the hill toward the Nant
Temple. There was little point in waiting here for the
King's Guard, and perhaps my inheritance might be
enough to purchase the indulgence of Jorkis the angry
magician. It should be at least sufficient, I thought, to
have my rugs replaced.

2

I suppose if there were a god of justice with a realistic sense of proportion regarding humor it would have been sufficient that even the thought of approaching the fearsome mercenaries who guarded the Nant Temple curdled my phlegm. Of course, I wouldn't have a tale to tell if the gods led more balanced lives. It is always wise to remember that it was the gods who put nipples on men, seeds in pomegranates, and priests in temples.

Temples make me nervous, priests and priestesses bring anxiety, conversation not concerned with making money causes stress, and my least favorite color is black. In addition, I am not fond of the dark. So there I was, in a black anteroom in the Nant Temple speaking to a Nant priestess named Syndia about a beggar whom I had no memory of ever having met, for the purpose of—

Well, I had quite forgotten the purpose. Perhaps I should also mention that the priestess Syndia was a great beauty. She was beyond beauty. She was a veritable goddess. Her beauty was such that it made me feel unworthy to look upon her.

"Your name, sir?"

"Yes! My name!" I swept my hat from my head, caught a feather from it with my teeth, and stood there looking as though I had just eaten a raw pheasant. Quickly I pulled the feather from my mouth and attempted to hide it behind my back. The swing of my hand knocked over an immense iron candle stand. The clatter was shattering, to say the least. In addition, the room was now even darker. Again, the humor of the gods. It does not take much to amuse them, for they keep playing the same tired jokes over and over.

"You appear to be a bit nervous," she said with a smile. Oh, that smile! For another such I would have taken on the entire Nant Guard with a hairpin. She nodded at a temple servant and the fellow bent to the task of restoring the candle stand to an upright position and cleaning the wax from the flagstone floor. Oh, friends, her diamond-ticked black gown was so, and contoured just so; their temple gowns are nothing like those dull rags they wear on the street, I can vouch truly.

Her face, her hair, her lips, her scent, by the Great Nasty's toenails I would have converted on the spot could I have remembered the god or gods to which I belonged. The form beneath that cobweb of a gown— Great Elass, my hair fairly smoked with imagination!

"Korvas!" I burst out.

Her lovely brow knit in a wee sign of confusion. "Korvas?"

"Yes! My name! Korvas!" I must have sounded like some pimpled whelp trembling in the parlor of a bordello for the first time. My face was so red it must have glowed in the darkened room. There was nothing left to do, so I pulled the message from my sash and held it out.

Her hands gently enclosed mine. Mine could feel the warmth of thine, and she held my hand for so long that I could see us writhing in endless passion, rearing children, growing old together. Why else would she have held my hand so gently, so long?

"Korvas, I cannot read it until you let go of it."

My fingers sprang open and quickly hid within the folds of my robe. The movement was done with such deftness and speed that I managed to punch myself right in my, eh, heritage. "Of course," I gasped. "My apologies, Syndia."

She held Olassar's message to the light of another candle stand to read it, and with her face so near the light my heart fairly burst. I turned my head and backed a step away, and tripped backwards over the servant who was cleaning the floor. I hit the flagstones with a splat—

It was a horrible time, friends. Simply horrible. I don't know why I feel compelled to put all of my warts on display. I suppose, however, that you must know the real me *then* if you are to appreciate the real me *now*. But I digress.

Between Syndia and the servant, I was placed in a chair for my own protection. While I sat there feeling like a fool, Syndia sat in another chair and read the message. "So," she said at last, "you are Olassar's benefactor." She studied me with those deep oceans she had for eyes. Her look evoked a very strange feeling within me. It was as though I, Korvas the Whatever, was a very special person to the Nant priestess.

By Angh's tender claws, the entire matter was too deeply immersed in temples, religions, and spooky weirdness for me. "Priestess Syndia, by my mother's bones, I cannot remember this Olassar." It is true, friends. I said those words before I had gotten even a single glimpse of the inheritance. I told the truth, for I could not lie to the priestess. It was a terrible pickle for a carpet dealer to be in. *I could not* lie. Not to Syndia. It must have been a spell, and it mattered not. Dear Syndia, what need have we of riches or lands? What need we of fame or power when we will have us?

"Master Korvas," she said as she folded the message, "perhaps there has been an error. Are you certain that you have no memory of Olassar?"

"None."

"Or of any beggar to whom you might have given some coin? Perhaps you simply did not remember the name."

"None."

"Are you certain? The incident might have slipped your mind."

I looked down at the floor. "I am a selfish wretch, Syndia. I hardly make an effort at paying off debts that I owe. Look at my rags. Charity is not a part of me. I can remember no such beggar."

The priestess studied my face. "Korvas is not a common name."

"My father, Rafas, was a native of Ahmrita across the great ocean Ilan. He named me."

She nodded slightly and looked again at the message. "Olassar was quite specific in his instructions as to your name, description, and where you might be found. It is important that no mistake be made."

"Oh, I agree."

"Master Korvas, we have a way to bring back darkened memories. Are you willing to undergo the ritual?"

"Yes." I would have undergone white-hot pokers thrust into my armpits to remain with her. She stood and glided from the room. I began to rise from my chair when a face from a bad dream arrived in front of me.

"My name is Iamos. You have agreed to undergo dream raking?"

"Dream raking? I think so, but I have no recollection of it being called dream raking." Keeping the humorous nature of the gods in mind, I asked, "Does this ritual have anything to do with hot pokers and armpits?"

Have you ever seen anyone who looks uglier grinning than frowning? That's Iamos. The Nant priest chuckled. "Why do you ask?"

"I made a rather hasty comment to myself a bit ago, well within the hearing of any passing spirit. If my comment were taken seriously, the remainder of my visit here could be quite unpleasant."

"The process is painless, provided that the memory itself is painless. There are memories that can cause great suffering, and other memories that can even kill."

"Where is Syndia?"

"She prepares for the dream rake. Do you have an interest in history?"

"When I can afford it."

"The dream rake is quite a historical ceremony, dating back to Itkahn times. Come."

He gestured with his hand, and I pushed myself to a standing position and followed on wobbly feet. Iamos led me through a corridor into a great hall, the back of which contained a set of large iron doors. The hall was so huge that the lights from the few candles that burned there seemed not to reach the walls or ceiling. I tugged at the priest's black robe. "This does seem like an awful fuss to make over one little memory."

He frowned, then his face assumed an expression of one who must deal with infidels. "Memories are the treasures of the goddess Raven. She decides, for reasons of her own, where a memory rests: either with Amu the light or with Horax, mist and darkness. When you think you remember something, the memory is in the possession of Amu. When we forget, Horax is the keeper."

"Horax must be the stronger of the two," I offered, "due to the burden he must carry. Certainly more is forgotten than remembered."

"Amu is the stronger," said Iamos as he placed his hand upon the huge latch of the iron doors. "Horax must only hold the raven-goddess's treasures safe. Amu must, in addition, bear the weight of what mortals do with what they remember."

"What they do?"

"Yes. What they do to themselves and to others." He nodded with the weight of many memories. "Yes, and what they do to truth."

The sound of the latch opening reverberated around the cavernous hall loudly enough to disturb the lantern spirits, who slept in the dark corners of rooms on beds of dust kitties.

The doors swung open by some unseen hand revealing an immense chamber, the floor of which was formed by the hill's natural bedrock. The room's dome reflected a dim blue light that backlit the craggy features of the floor. Each sharp rise of the floor was capped with candles waxed onto the rock. Iamos led me to one of the rises. Once we had successfully made the climb, he stood with his hands clasped in front of him, so I did the same. The heat and odor of the incense from the candles was heavy in the air.

Looking down from our perch, I could see a level area that looked much like a stage that had been cut from the living rock by the ancients. Iamos pointed at the stage and whispered, "This was our first place of ceremony and worship many centuries ago when we were called the Itkah. This," he gestured at the room's great dome, "was built much later under the Nants."

At each end of the stage coals burned in huge braziers. Perhaps it was only my imagination, but I swear there were instruments heating up in those coals. I was about to take my leave when the dreamy chords of lap harps filled the air. There were black shapes above—huge black birds! Their wings moved majestically as they circled above. There was something strange about them, however. They had the wings and heads of enormous ravens, but as my eyes adjusted fully to the dark I could see that they had the naked bodies of young men and women.

I pointed up and whispered a question to Iamos. "Wires?"

He arched an irate eyebrow at me. "Wings."

"Sorry. No offense."

One of the raven-women plunged down from the circling bird creatures, flared out as she reached the center of the stage, and came to rest as gently as a down feather. I knew I should be thinking of the inheritance, perhaps of the great religious drama before me, maybe even of those instruments heating upon the braziers. However, my attention was devoted to the naked raven-woman on the stage. I don't know how I knew, but I knew it to be Syndia.

"Tell me, Iamos, how does one go about obtaining instruction in this religion?"

"Hush."

The raven-being on the stage held out her wings, and I was certain the wings were real rather than costume. I have seen real ravens before, and that is how the wings moved; that is how the head moved. The raven's eyes sought me out. Suddenly I knew what a grasshopper in the open felt like. I turned to hide behind Iamos, but he was gone! Disappeared!

The room became filled with horrible piercing screams. The sounds were so painful that I held my hands over my ears, to no avail. The sounds were not lessened one whit. The screams were in my mind.

The ring of raven-beings dropped down until they circled me at eye level. The Syndia bird screeched louder than the rest and flew up from the stage, above the circle, then plunged to come to a landing immediately in front of me. It was quite amazing how this ritual helped to bring back memories. In an instant long-forgotten prayers from my childhood leaped to my lips.

The circle grew tighter, the Syndia-raven enclosed me with her wings, and there was a darkness I have no words to describe. Let it suffice to say that anything you might ever have called darkness was blinding light by comparison.

I felt lifted into the air, but could feel no hands or wings on me. I must have been thousands of strides above the ground, but had no sensation of height.

There was a hardly noticeable glimmer of light in my mind, for I did not see it with my eyes. It grew brighter, and at its center in a mere particle of a second I saw everything that I had ever seen, thought, or felt. It was all there, from my mother's womb to my terror before the raven-beings in the Nant Temple.

My father, my mother, my twin brother Tayu who my father had told me had died, every girl and woman I ever lusted for, every shady deal I had ever made, every wrong I had ever done, and every wrong that had ever been done to me. An entire life served up on a platter. Then it was all gone save the interior of the Red Dog Inn, the smells of fabulous cooking in the air, and before me the luscious shape of Lona.

Ah, indeed I was back in time. Those were the days of fine fat and gold, too. I had coin jingling in my purse then, a flock of darlings upon my arm, and men of culture and commerce seeking me out for my favor and advice. I traded then in precious gems, and no one in the world had such a fine life and reputation as I.

Ah, Lona. She would end up with the gems. After the judges were through with me, her husband, the draper Yothoc, wound up with my fine house and business properties, and they both wound up with each other. I wound up copperless and hanging from the flogging post in Xaxos Square, named for the god of fools.

But look at her. Look at that lovely Lona, her breasts straining against the laces of her bodice. Her fiery red hair up from that meal of a neck. Could I be blamed if I didn't notice that beggar at my elbow? I didn't even glance at him. Keeping my gaze on Lona, I reached into my purse, pinched a few coins, and held them out just to end the interruption. I didn't even count them or look to see what they were. Ten gold reels seemed like such a pittance then. Of course, after Lona, Yothoc, and the whipmaster were finished with me, I would be scrabbling for half-coppers. But she was very, very beautiful, wasn't she?

"Yes, she was."

I opened my eyes to find myself back in the Nant Temple's anteroom. Syndia was standing before me, featherless, but fully dressed. Her dress was rough, pale blue with a darker blue outer robe that also served as a veil. Beneath her arm she had a bundle wrapped in white cloth. On the floor was a small wooden box of four drawers. She pointed at the case with her free hand. "From the grateful Olassar, this is your inheritance, Korvas."

I shook my head in shame. "My generosity," I snorted in disgust. "It was hardly a thought on my part. The coins were nothing to me. I don't deserve anything."

"Korvas, with your entire being consumed by lust, your instinct when asked by Olassar for help was to give it. Another in the same situation might have given Olassar the back of his hand."

"You say then that I am a good man?"

"I did not go that far." Her lips sprouted a tiny smile. "Still, you are redeemable, Korvas. Redeemable."

"Would you say that if you knew what I have been thinking of you, priestess?"

There was a flash of dark mischief in her eyes. "I know everything that you have ever thought of me and every other woman. I have just been through every memory of your life, Korvas. If you want to have secrets from me, you had best begin gathering them now."

The blush from my face must have melted the candles. I turned to my inheritance. It was like a tiny barrel with a set of four drawers set into the end and shaped to the rounded sides. The case rested upon scrolled feet, and the top had scrolled ends as well. It was made of a very dark wood, and the highly polished case had an ornate carved ivory handle on top. I lifted it and found the case suprisingly light. There seemed to be an odor of olive wood about it.

"This is my inheritance? It is strange-looking, but it is handsome. I suppose I could trade it for one or two reels, for which I am grateful. It should replace my rugs."

Syndia pointed at one of the drawers. "Open that."

I replaced the case on the floor, squatted before it, and pulled open the lower right-hand drawer. Immediately my feet went out from beneath me and I landed on the floor with my bottom. The drawer was filled to capacity with gold ten-reel pieces. "There must be—there must be over . . . a *thousand*."

"There is no limit, actually."

I looked at the priestess. "I don't understand. This case is much too light to have— That much gold alone is heavier than this entire case!"

Syndia held her hand above the case. The drawer closed and the case rose from the floor and placed its handle in her hand. She smiled at me. "Olassar was a very special trader."

"A wizard?"

"No. This is what he purchased with your ten reels."

"In just what did Olassar trade?"

"Whatever you needed for whatever you didn't need."

"Oh no." I began shaking my head and backing away from the case. "I can see what's coming, and no thank you. This is one of those cruel magic burdens designed as an object lesson by some moralizing wizard with nothing better to do with his time than inflict his bigot's values upon everyone else, destroying those found unworthy. We both know very well just how I would measure."

"Korvas, no wizard created this object, nor did any wizard give it its power. Here in the temple we have talked about little else since Olassar entrusted us with it. Many of the priests believe it to be a god, or perhaps the home of a god. At the very least the gods touch it."

I laughed and dismissed the theory with a wave of my hand. "That would be worse, wouldn't it? As I remember, the general run of gods are more bigoted than any mortal, and the especially good gods would have me dead in an instant."

"Korvas, who you think you are, and who you are, are worlds apart. Know this: I cannot lie to you; you cannot lie to me."

"A terrible fate for a rug merchant," I commented. However, what Syndia had said was distressingly true, about not being able to lie to her. I had tried and failed. I looked again at the case and slowly shook my head, just imagining all of the wonderful things that might be in it. My greed almost vibrated with anticipation "What should I do with this wonder box, then, Syndia?"

The priestess held out the case to me and let go of it. It hovered there until I grasped it with my hand. "Your carpet business has expired along with your beetles and your toleration by the King's Guard. Even now the soldiers search for you."

"Bah. Jorkis was nothing of a magician. Why would the King's Guard jump because he almost purchased a flying carpet?"

"I believe the charge had something to do with him almost purchasing a crawling carpet."

"Still, with the hundreds of petty crimes committed each moment in Poor Town, why would the Guard find mine so heinous?"

"Have you ever heard of Pagas Shadows?"

Instantly my spine fused with fear. "The captain of the Heterin Guard?"

"Yes."

"Of course. Who hasn't heard of the fiend?" I dismissed the name with what I hoped was a fearless wave of my hand. "But I am too small to draw his attention."

"That is your hope, Korvas." Syndia placed a gentle hand upon my arm. "Jorkis is his father-in-law."

"The gods save me, I am a dead man. I am a standing dead man. I am a standing, talking dead man. There is no hole in Poor Town deep enough in which to hide." I held her hand in both of mine. "Dear Syndia, once, many years ago, a fishmonger sold Captain Shadows a bad piece of redfish. The fellow is still hanging by his big toes in some slimy, rat-infested dungeon beneath the king's palace. And I tried to shuck a few reels from the captain's father-in-law? I can see my entire life passing before my eyes, and there hasn't been anywhere near enough of it. What am I to do?"

"Perhaps what you need is to carry on Olassar's work."

I looked again at the box. "Yes, I see your point." I pointed at her bundle. "What is that?"

"My things. I am going with you."

"With me? But—I mean, you know me. How I am around you. I couldn't."

"Are you stumbling around now?"

"No. I'm not. Did you give me something? Something from this box?"

"Yes."

"What was it?"

"What you needed." She turned and began walking toward the entrance to the temple. "Come along now."

I caught up with her. "Where are we going?"

"Olassar had one outstanding contract. It is with the Omergunts in the Mystic Mountains. The chief there is not pleased with the results of Olassar's work. We must make it right."

"How did you know about this contract?"

She laughed. "I took from the box what you needed, Korvas, and that contract was it."

"Why are you coming?"

"That is my work."

"Your work? What does that mean? What is your work?"

"I witness miracles."

Her answer was as clear as coal. It was true that I
needed to get out of town, and the drawers of Olassar's
box were filled with gold. Still, I had this feeling that I
was being moved into play by an unseen hand.

I admit to having several misgivings about a trip to the
far Mystic, even with so lovely a companion as Syndia.
It's almost five hundred miles to Kienosos, and the valley
of the Omergunts is another hundred and seventy miles
north from there. My boots, what there was left of them,
seemed not up to the task. I was certain that before we
reached the old city wall I would be walking with nothing
but tops covering my toes.

Since I was carrying Olassar's case of drawers, I thought
I might avail myself of its services. If it could come up
with gold, perhaps it could do something for my ward-
robe. More than that, I could use a horse or jackass, or
at least a new pair of boots. I opened a drawer, and
found it empty.

"That's odd," I remarked, because if anything was
apparent to me it was my need for a pair of boots. I
opened another drawer and found it empty as well. Well,
I thought, I'll open the drawer I knew contained the
wealth of gold and buy myself a pair of boots—*two*
pair—two pair and a suit. That drawer was empty, as
well.

"Syndia, when I first opened this drawer the box thought
I needed gold. Now it does not?"

"That is true as far as your understanding takes it,
Korvas."

She led the way around the fountain across from the
king's palace, to a place between the Heterin Temple
and the Amuite Temple. There a caravan was assembling. It was a mad flurry of activity and sound. Camel
drivers were attempting to outbray their charges, while
magnificent horse-drawn wagons were being outfitted by
Nant priests and wagon masters. A detachment of Nant
Guards, fully armed with swords and pistols, kept watch.

Syndia paused in the midst of this clamor and faced
me. "I don't believe Olassar's case thought you needed

gold. I believe it thought you needed to *see* gold. Now that you have decided to do Olassar's work, you no longer need to see it."

I gathered that she meant the box had manipulated me to do its will by the promise of riches it had no intention of delivering. That certainly sounded like a god to me. If it hadn't been for my belief that I could find a loophole in the rules governing the contraption, I probably would have left it, except that that would also have involved leaving behind Syndia. It did little for my sense of justice to contemplate the fact that the Nants are a monastic order of celibates.

There was, as well, my unfinished bit of business with Captain Shadows urging me out of town. I seemed to have spent the better part of my life being moved by things other than my own decisions. Current events lent no evidence that this state of affairs would change any time soon.

"Well, I do need new boots if I am to be expected to talk to the Mystic."

She laughed again and held out her hands, indicating the caravan being assembled inside the remaining walls of the Elassan Temple. "Does one who rides by caravan need boots?"

I looked again at the assembling caravan. This was no one-humped affair. I saw at least thirty camels, five of those huge wagons, and more horses than I could accurately estimate. "Where did this come from? Is it yours?"

"It is the Nant Temple's. We have been preparing the caravan ever since Olassar gave us the case to hold for you. All we were waiting for was your appearance and agreement to carry the case to the Omergunts."

"Why all this? Why is the Nant faith doing this?"

"To witness miracles, a priest of any faith could do no less."

Well, my spirits lifted considerably. Nevertheless, there was a small part of my spirit that was sagging. "Syndia, do you not think it unseemly to ride in such a fine caravan wearing such shabby boots?"

"Oh, I see," laughed the priestess. "You meant to say

that you *wanted* a new pair of boots. Olassar's case contains no wants, only needs."

We have all had experiences with magic before. I wonder to this day why a spell, talisman, wand, or other magical thing cannot be up front and straight about what it is supposed to do. There always has to be a catch or a trick.

I once bought a talisman created by Redjyak, wizard of Ziven. The wearing of this talisman was supposed to proclaim to all men that I possessed great humility. However, as soon as I placed the talisman around my neck, it disappeared! Now what good is that?

In the wagon I placed Olassar's curious box in the couch across from mine. I stared at it and teetered between staying and going, that golden vision still hot in my memory, until the wagon began moving.

I suspected that, although powerful and benevolent, the gods, if they existed at all, had a mean streak.

3

I am a person who needs companionship. It's not that I find my own company disagreeable. Rather, it gets tiresome after awhile. I was left alone in my wagon with my inheritance. There was no door from the passenger compartment to where the driver sat, so that opportunity for conversation was barred. The wagon itself was very comfortable, with deep couches, drapes hanging all around, and soft lighting from sweet-smelling lamps.

From the door in the rear of the wagon I could see the train stretching behind. I could also see the walls of Iskandar far behind. That meant that the King's Guard hadn't stopped us. Perhaps they didn't wish to tangle with the Nant Guard, or maybe temple caravans are sacred. Nevertheless, I had escaped the city, and was getting quite bored.

I was just beginning to entertain thoughts of disguising myself and slipping back to Iskandar when one of the drawers on Olassar's case slid silently open. I leaned forward on my couch to have a peek inside. Instead of the gold that I had hoped to find there, I found a piece of paper. There were words upon it, and they read: *"You cannot return to where you have never left."*

I slumped back in the couch, thinking, what nonsense is this? I leaned forward and addressed the case. "You, there. What is the meaning of this?"

The first drawer closed, and as it did so the drawer next to it slid open. "More words; no gold." I reached in and picked up the slip of paper. "Let's see," I said as I began to read: *"Think."* That was it.

I was beginning to see little hope of making a profit from this bizarre curiosity. Leaving the rear door open, I leaned back and watched the ocean. The King's Highway follows the coast all of the way to Kienosos. Early into the evening, as the red and orange lights of sunset played among the clouds, I saw us pass through the gates of Fort Braw, a squalid wayside town that hundreds of years ago was an important fort.

At the time the wagon carried me into its center, however, it was little more than a way station for weary travelers and a hiding place from the King's Guard. Although the king's law rules in the road towns in theory, in practice the locals rely rather heavily upon mutual agreements and personal armaments for justice. The caravan stopped, and in a moment I saw Iamos walk up to my door.

"Master Korvas, has your ride been pleasant?"

"Lonely, but comfortable."

"Lonely?" His face crawled about until it was again carrying that loathsome smile. "It has been so many years, the thought never crossed my mind."

"What thought?"

"That anyone would find solitude lonely. It is our custom to travel alone—to live alone. We find it more conducive to meetings and conversations with the gods."

I glanced at my inheritance and back at Iamos. "Do any of your gods have ivory handles?"

"I beg your pardon?"

"Never mind. Are we going to spend the night here?"

"No. We will be here only an hour to change horses. We will travel through the night and stop at Fort Damra. Would you like me to arrange a traveling companion for you?"

"That would be pleasant." A quick thought crossed my mind. "But tomorrow. I will sleep soon. Are we to eat in the village?"

"Either that, or you are welcome to partake of our humble fare."

"My thanks, Iamos, but I think I'll have a look around town."

Iamos nodded and walked toward the front of the train. I saw a familiar face loitering in front of a local tavern. In a flash my mind was made up and I reached out my hand toward Olassar's box and snapped my fingers. "Let's go."

The box just sat there. I stood up, gripped the handle and tried to lift the thing. It weighed so much that I couldn't budge it. The strange thing was that it hardly dented the cushion upon which it was sitting. "Come on. You're mine now, and I say let's go."

Still I couldn't budge it. "Look, what I need right now is to know if you are worth anything." The box shot up. It had absolutely no weight at all. "I'm glad you changed your mind."

I took the magic box, climbed down from the wagon, and when I was certain no one was looking I tiptoed to the sidewalk and ducked between two buildings. When I glanced back, no one seemed to have noticed my going. I asked myself, why was I slinking around? I was a free man, and this object belonged to me, didn't it? "Force of habit, I imagine."

I stepped out on the sidewalk and, with the box swinging by the handle, I walked until I was in front of the tavern. I stopped in front of the familiar face. "Ker, you pirate," I greeted.

"Korvas, you thief," he responded. These were terms of endearment, I might add. They were no reflection on our community standing.

I pointed at the tavern. "Why are you standing here, my old friend?"

"As usual, Korvas, waiting for opportunity. Are you my opportunity?"

"I might be, Ker. I might be." I held up Olassar's box. "I have come into an inheritance. It is this valuable chest of drawers, each corner of it simply stuffed with magic."

He grinned through several missing teeth. "I hear the King's Guard is after you, Korvas. Is this object the reason?"

"No. That matter is unrelated to this. It had something to do with an angry customer."

"Crawling carpets again, Korvas?"

"The box is mine, and I have a letter to prove it."

"A little marketplace fraud isn't enough to bring out the entire guard. Who was your customer?"

"The father-in-law of Captain Shadows." Ker laughed out loud, shook his head, slapped his thighs, made as though he was wiping tears from his eyes, and generally made an enormous ass of himself. "Are you quite finished, Ker?"

"Yes." He looked down at the case of drawers in my hand. "Now, what would you sell to me?" He pointed at it. "What is it? A jewelry case?" Several other tough-looking characters gathered around us to look at the box.

"It is a simple chest of drawers. However, as I said, it has magical properties."

"Like what?" He still had that smirk on his face.

"It . . . the drawers contain whatever you need."

"Indeed? And if there is nothing in there, you'll tell me that I need nothing."

"In truth, Ker, it has happened to me. Just this morning, however, one of the drawers contained over two thousand gold reels." That perked up the ears of my companions. I regretted it as soon as the words left my mouth. "I'll go, then, if you're not interested."

"Wait, please." His strong hand gripped my arm. "I don't imagine you would have any objection to giving me a free sample before I buy."

"Perhaps . . ." I looked at the ugly folk gathered around. "Perhaps not." I held out the box.

"Which drawer?" asked Ker.

"Any drawer. I don't think it makes a difference."

He pulled out the lower right. "A piece of paper?"

"Sometimes that's all there is. Read it."

Ker read the note, his face went white, and he dropped to the sidewalk like a basket of wet wash.

"Here, now," said one of the uglies. He was a chunky sort with dark clothes covering an indiscreet display of muscles. He leaned over, examined Ker, picked up the note, and looked at it. " 'You die now.' " He screwed his face up into a semblance of confusion.

I was stricken with horror. "Ker isn't dead, is he?"

"Oh, yes he is," answered the tough. "I've seen dead in every great city of the world, lad, and believe me, that's genuine dead. Poor old Ker." He looked back at the note in his hand. "Now, what puzzles me is, it says 'You die now,' and Ker he up and snuffed on the spot."

"I guess that's what he needed to know right then," I offered with a wan smile.

"See here, fancy hat, that's my old friend and comrade Ker down there in the dust. You'd best make this right by me, or it'll go hard on you."

I held out my hands. "Anything."

He took Olassar's box from my hands. "Better let me take care of this, fancy hat." He held it up, looked at it, shook it as he listened, then looked at it again. "By Angh's bunion, I can't see what took out old Ker. Is there a little poison needle that pops out? Maybe rigged to a spring and a secret catch?"

"No. There's no such thing."

"Well, then, what's it do?"

"It gives you whatever it is that you need."

The ugly fellow raised his hairless eyebrows at me. "Now, did my dear friend Ker get what he needed?"

"If you were just about to die, what would you need?"

"Haw! Well answered, fancy hat. But I think I'll just have a go at this little thing. Any drawer, you say?"

I nodded, my lips rather dry. "Any drawer."

He grinned widely and pulled open the upper right-hand drawer. He looked in and frowned. "Another message?" He glanced up at me. "Hear me, fancy hat. If I should drop dead sometime within the next few seconds, my comrades here will make short work of you. Do you hear me?"

"I hear you," I answered. At the same time I prayed that the gods would water their humor with just a bit of discretion.

"Now what I need from this box," continued the tough, "is something with soft curves." He issued a low dirty laugh which was joined by his associates'. Then he opened the message. His eyes opened wide and his jaw fell open. "My wife?" he bellowed. "My wife is *what*?"

He threw the case of drawers at me. "See here, fellow, fun's fun, but this here says that my wife Kokila is bedding my best friend." He pulled a long, slender, silver-bladed knife from beneath his tunic. He reached out his knife and carved an *X* in the case's polished surface, then held the blade beneath my throat. "Make the box say it isn't so."

"My f-f-friend, if I could get the cursed thing to do my bidding, would I be trying to sell it?"

"Then make your peace, scum."

"Hold, Natos," said one of the uglies. "Give us a chance at the box first."

"The box lies, and this one," he pricked my throat with the point of his blade, "is the murderer of my dear friend Ker."

The box was pulled out of my grasp, there were shouts, and I felt the iron-strong arm of Natos beneath my chin, lifting my head far back. The blade flashed before my eyes, and I felt a scratch on my neck followed by the sensation of warm water washing down the front of my robe and trousers. I had a silly thought as the light drained from my head to be replaced with black fuzz: the box was right. I didn't need the new boots after all.

There is a fleeting feeling of having experienced something or having been someplace before. Those feelings come when a wizard or a ghost treads upon the place where one is to be buried. One such time was immediately after I died.

Leaving the rear door of the wagon open, I leaned back and watched the ocean. Early into the evening, as the red and orange light of sunset played among the clouds, I saw us pass through the gates of Fort Braw. Everything was edged with terror, for I knew that this was where my throat would be slit. The caravan stopped, and in a moment I saw Iamos walk up to my door.

"Master Korvas, has your ride been pleasant?"

"What is happening here, priest? We have had this conversation before."

"In the universe are many realities, Master Korvas. How have you been finding this one?"

I looked around at the squalid buildings and felt my throat with my hand. "Puzzling, as usual."

"Puzzling?"

" 'Lonely' is what I answered to that question in another time. Now it's puzzling."

"It surprises me to hear that you were lonely." His face crawled about until it was again carrying that loathsome smile. "It has been so many years, the thought never crossed my mind."

"That anyone could find solitude lonely?" I anticipated with more than a hint of sarcasm in my voice.

"Why, yes. You took the words right out of my mouth. You see, it is our custom to travel alone—to live alone. We find it more conducive to meetings and conversations with the gods."

I looked at Olassar's box on the couch, then back at Iamos. "Do any of your gods have ivory handles?" The question had a significantly different meaning from the first time I had asked it.

"I beg your pardon?"

"I was a fool to ask, and twice the fool for asking again." I looked again at the ocean. "Are we going soon?"

"We'll be here only an hour to change horses. We will travel through the night and stop at Fort Damra tomorrow morning. Would you like me to arrange a traveling companion for you?"

"Thank you, no."

"Will you eat in town? Of course, you are welcome to partake of our humble fare."

"My thanks, Iamos. What are you having?"

"It is a kind of dry grain loaf peculiar to our sect, I fear. Outsiders call it sawdust bread. It is gritty with cracked grains and quite dry, with only water to wash it down."

"It sounds like a feast to me."

Iamos nodded and walked toward the front of the train. I saw a familiar face loitering in front of a local tavern. It was Ker. Before much time passed he would crumple and die.

I turned and looked at the chest of drawers. The X carved in its finish stood out very clearly. The box hadn't wanted me to go into town. However, I had insisted that I needed to know whether the box was worth anything. It had provided me with an answer that I couldn't even comprehend.

4

I awakened the next morning when I realized that I was staring at the box. I don't remember opening my eyes, only realizing that my eyes were already open. Maybe it was all a dream, a hallucination, a ghost playing tricks with my mind, or perhaps an angry magician playing tricks with my eyes.

I shook my head, for that made no sense. If Jorkis was that good a magician, he wouldn't have fallen for the crawling carpet gag. And even if he had, he wouldn't have expected to find a real one in the Iskandar marketplace. Besides, Jorkis had his son-in-law to carry out his vengeance.

I sat up, stretched out a hand and felt the X cut into the box's finish for the hundredth time. My eyes are too practiced. Had that mark already existed when I was given the box, I would have noticed it. The mark was fresh, and what I had experienced had been real. Somehow Olassar's box erased time for me, moved it back, and started it over again. The box had brought me back from the dead. More than that, the box had turned back the clock of the very universe to show me what it was. And just what was it?

There seemed to be a different taste to the air, and there was a rumbling sound, different than the iron wheels of the wagons against the paving stones. I looked out of the door. This part of the King's Highway, to get around an immovable outcropping of granite, ran very close to the ocean. I settled down and let my gaze play among the waves as my thoughts played games of their own.

Why had the box moved time for me? Why was I trying so hard not to believe what I had seen with my own eyes? It made me think of when I was a boy arguing with my father about the gods. As I had done a hundred times before, I had refused to go to the temple—we were one of the few Ihtari families in Iskandar, and that faith from my father's beloved Ahmrita was very dear to him. So dear, in fact, that he insisted I share it with him.

We were arguing for the thousandth time on this matter, and I told him again that the only gods that exist are mean little spirits that run around causing trouble. My father said that the evidence of the gods was all about me. The wind, the sun, the flowers, birds, and so on.

I remember throwing at him, *"Then why did my twin brother die?"*

"Yes, Korvas," I rebuked myself, "win your argument by breaking your father's heart." It was an easy stab to make to win an argument. I knew it would shatter my father with a memory that I didn't think affected me at all. Syndia believed I was redeemable, but it was her profession to believe in miracles.

Below me I could see the white gulls skimming the tops of the breakers while dark, long-legged sandbirds picked and plucked among the seaweed washed up on the beach.

I remembered, after the argument with my father, thinking upon the subject of divine evidence. What would it take to convince me of the existence of a god or gods? My father could look at that ocean, those birds, and be convinced. The followers of Nanteria were much like my father. They believed in goodness obtained by following a path of honesty and kindness. Obviously these people have nothing worthwhile to contribute to the real world, but they do believe in these gods.

Now, I believe in magic. What fool doesn't? The streets and back alleys of Iskandar crawl with it. If one isn't salting down a witch with coppers to put a curse upon someone who deserves it, one is probably salting down

the same witch with the same coppers to have an unde-
served curse removed from one's own person. I have
rattled my share of bones and worn my share of beads
and feathers. Between the curses, spells, and spirits in
this world, it's enough to drive one to drink celery tonic.

Yes, I also believe in spirits. Mean, hateful little things
who make noises at night to keep you awake, who put
spots on clean white linen, who spoil food, split trousers,
make horses go lame, and wreck machinery. The existence of magic and spirits I acknowledged, but only because I had seen them and their works on numerous
occasions. Gods, benevolent and otherwise, were another matter altogether.

The Nants, for example, believe in a supernatural being
of great goodness named Nanteria. She is represented
only in black silhouette and is said to live in smoke and
shadows. She is the one who urges one's steps toward
the path of goodness.

On the opposite side is Heteris, who is always represented in red silhouette and is said to live in every coal
and flame. She is the one who urges one's footsteps away
from the path of good. Somehow humankind is supposed
to be free to move between these spirits. Each one of
these major gods had about a half-dozen lesser gods and
angels to assist her.

The Heterin faith, under the gentle auspices of Tretia
the Terrible, had it all turned around. For them Heteris,
the flame goddess, is the goddess of good, while Nanteria,
the being of smoke and shadow, is the evil one.

It seemed like so much storybook time for children to
me. There were things in me that urged me to do good, and
other, more powerful, things that usually won any contest. But both urgings were mine. In my heart it seemed
as though Nanteria and Heteris were thought up long ago
simply to personalize good and evil for children, or perhaps for adults of a more innocent age. But that is only
my skeptical nature, as my father would have said.

There was the old Ihtari story of Ahtma, he who
would have been emperor except for his skeptical nature. I turned my head and studied the chest of drawers

as the story of Ahtma came back to me. It was almost as though I could hear my father's voice with its strange singsong accent.

Although he had reigned for more than a hundred years, Rojuna, Emperor, Chosen of the Ihtar, had died. Since he had been regarded as veritably immortal, the question of succession had never arisen. Now no one could think of anything else.

The priests gathered from every corner of the empire to study the ancient texts, formulas, and scriptures. The stars were read and compared against the birth records of each city, town, and village. The signs seemed right, and a choice was made from the village of Akuhma. The young man, Ahtma, was brought before the ancient temple in Givida, spiritual center of Ahmrita.

The priests told Ahtma that he was next in line to be the emperor of the Ahmritans. The fellow was delighted, of course, especially when he found out that with his crown would come vast lands, personal and public treasuries, the devotion of a hundred million subjects, a harem of his own choosing, fine horses, jewels, perfumes, an army of a million at arms, and ships that commanded the oceans of the world. All he had to do would be to believe with a true heart in the existence and good will of the Ihtar, the gods peculiar to Ahmrita.

Ahtma had been as skeptical of the gods as I, but his special place in history gave him an advantage. To aid him in his quest for faith, the gods would perform a miracle at his command. Ahtma demanded to be taken up high enough to see the entire continent that then comprised the Empire of Ahmrita. That the gods did. Then Ahtma demanded the miracle: "Here is my request. With a mighty hand, Ihtar, if you do indeed exist and have power over men, cut that continent through its center with a single, swift stroke."

"If we do this, Ahtma, will you them believe?" asked the gods.

"Of course," answered the youth. He waved an impatient hand "Do get on with it, if you can."

Below his boots, to his surprise, Ahtma saw the land

part and the seas rush in, and where there had once been solid land there was now a long, narrow sea. A priest of Ihtar was brought up to Ahtma, and he asked, "After witnessing this great miracle, Ahtma, are you ready now to declare your belief and become emperor?"

Ahtma frowned, studied the split continent below, rubbed his chin, and said to the priest, "I want to see them do that again."

Ahtma, of course, did not become emperor. Instead, quite disgusted with him, the Ihtar dropped him, saying, "Ahtma, we do not exist for you; hence, you must fly on your own."

His desire not to admit that he was wrong—his stubborn pride—was much stronger than his need to have faith. To this day the inland sea between the Empire of Ahmrita and the southern kingdoms is known as the Sea of Ihtar. The fisherfolk there know from their soundings of a deep hole in the floor of the Ihtar Sea. They call it Ahtma's Fall.

I told Ahtma's story because I always related to the legend and often wondered to myself what it would take to convince me of the existence of these great wonderful gods guiding human destiny. As each new piece of filth and brutality came beneath my scrutiny, I grew ever further away from the Ihtar and ever closer to my twisted hero, Ahtma. Now here I was with Olassar's box as my split continent, and I shook my head in despair. Was my pride so bound, or would I have to see another demonstration?

I didn't know. Perhaps the box moving back time for me had been just a simple magic trick, or a spell of some kind. But I had never heard of such a thing; and even so, why? For what reason? Perhaps it was nothing more than an upset stomach or a dream. The one thing I did know was that it is very difficult to keep an open mind at the same time every particle of my being is trying to keep it shut tight.

So that it wouldn't remind me of all of my unanswered questions, I threw a pink couch blanket over the box and climbed down from the still-moving wagon to walk along-

side. Walking helps me to think, and I no longer cared
about my boots. Ahead, past the front of the train, I
could see the minarets of Fort Damra's Nant Temple.

Reed flutes were braying out their harsh music and the
sounds of hawkers and merchants made a dim hiss against
the sounds of the wagons and horses. The smell of the
salt air was laced with the scent of evergreens. Away
from the sea, to the north, I could see the majestic
Mystic Mountains.

I could, of course, see only a few of the mountains. The
entire range extended from the foothills in Iskandar, east
of the Kigev Desert, almost to the far Zivenese port of
Janira, two thousand miles away. But do the mountains I
cannot see disappear when I am not there to see them?
When I cannot see them, do I still believe they exist?

What to do, what to do? Was the box a god? Did it
contain a god? Did it make any difference what I called
it? It certainly acted like a god. I cursed, and the gods be
damned for it. It was my right to curse, and I did so. I
hadn't felt so soul-torn since I had been a child.

I heard a stifled laugh, then another and another. I
glanced over my shoulder and saw three of the turbaned
Nant guards riding alongside the train. All three were
trying very hard not to laugh and they were failing
miserably.

"What's so funny?" I demanded of the first guard.

He pointed a shaking finger and almost fell off his
horse, he was laughing so uncontrollably. His two companions were also pointing and laughing. I turned around
and saw a caricature of a pink ghost hovering behind me.
Olassar's box had followed me. I pulled the blanket from
it, my face quite hot. "You're making us both look
foolish. Get back into the wagon."

The box waited for me to climb in first, then it followed, accompanied by the sounds of laughter.

5

In Fort Damra, with the box's silent permission, I wandered around for a few hours. I found several games of dice and cards that whetted several of my baser instincts; however, no one would let me play on credit. Eventually I settled down in an outdoor restaurant and watched the caravan for the signal to return.

I kept waiting for a glimpse of Syndia, but eventually I tired of this. The wagon master was checking harness, and teamsters and camel drivers were caring for their animals and checking loads. Around the caravan stood the Nant guards, motionless and very deadly-looking.

I was wondering where the guards slept, or if they ever did sleep, when the door in the wagon in front of mine opened. A military officer and a ranking civilian stepped down. As the officer touched his hand to his hat, I could see Syndia in the open doorway. Her face looked quite troubled.

I stood next to my table and caught her attention by waving my hat. I gestured toward my table, and she nodded. Still she didn't look very happy. When the officer and the official had left, she climbed down from her wagon, spoke to one of the guards, and approached. Despite her frown, she still moved like a dream. I held out a chair for her.

"Thank you, Korvas."

I sat down across from her. "I would offer you the

finest cuisine that this place has to offer, Syndia, except I
am somewhat strapped, financially speaking."

Syndia smiled and shook her head. "The goddess
Evantia must favor you, Korvas."

"Why?"

"You actively court a sworn celibate, you offer to
purchase a wonderful midday meal with no money for a
priestess who must not break her fast until evening, the
Heterin Guard is combing the countryside trying to find
you for your crawling carpet fraud, yet you still have
plans to start up a new beetle herd from the three in your
pocket. Evantia is the patron of lost causes. By the way,
they are hungry."

"Who?"

"The beetles."

"Syndia, I know that you have seen all that I remember, but how can you know these other things?"

"Such as?"

"That the beetles are hungry, for one example."

She pointed toward my chest, and I looked and saw two
of my mahrzak beetles peeking around the edge of my
robe. They did look hungry. "You see, Korvas, what a
marvelous oracle I am?"

I shrugged a minor apology. "I tried to feed them
some of the sawdust loaf last night and they wouldn't eat
it."

"It's an acquired taste." The priestess motioned to a
waiter. The fellow came over, and he appeared as though
he observed the entire world down the length of his nose.
After arching an eyebrow and curling a lip at me, he said
to Syndia, "Yes, priestess?"

"Could we have some cheese and bread," she glanced
at me, "and wine?"

I shook my head at her. "My apologies, but wine
makes me stupid." I looked at the waiter and now both
of his eyebrows were raised. "What else do you have?"

"Ale."

"That's worse than the wine. It makes me stupid and
gives me gas, as well. Can you recommend anything
else?"

"Goat's milk?"

"No. It gives me hives and tastes like onions." I could see that Syndia's gloom was vanishing. In fact, she was laughing at me. I glared up at the waiter. "Come now, you must have some kind of juice."

"Yes, we do. Aged grape juice. We call it wine."

"How about tea?"

"We have maue. Not many care for it. It is very bitter."

"I would love a cup of maue. I was suckled on it."

The waiter looked at Syndia and she paused in her laughter long enough to say, "Nothing for me, thank you."

After the waiter left I whispered to her, "I can't stand maue."

"Then why did you order it?"

"That waiter was looking so far down his nose at me I could see the backs of his eyeballs through his nostrils. I see your gloom has left you. May I take small credit there?"

Immediately the gloom dropped back on her face. "You may take credit for the gloom, as well."

"What have I done?"

"While you were wandering the village, the Heterin guard came looking for you."

"Here?" I felt my heart beating.

"Yes, and led by Captain Shadows himself."

"Cap—"

The waiter came out with bread and cheese on a board and a cup of hot maue. I sipped on the tea, smacked my lips, and grinned at the waiter. He left and I almost vomited. Once I had regained control of my stomach, I grabbed Syndia's hand. "Captain Shadows. He must be after someone else. I am not that important. His father-in-law isn't that important."

"He is after you, Korvas, and by name. I admit he does appear to be making more out of the offense than it deserves—"

"Quite a bit more, I should say."

"I agree. His men searched the wagons and pack animals very carefully. You are fortunate that you were elsewhere."

"Oh, how fortunate." I shook my head as I looked at the cheese. "My father always said I would end my days twitching from the end of a wire tied to an uncomfortable place." I looked up at her. "Where is he now?"

"They went ahead in the belief that you had left them far behind. Once they discover that you are not ahead, they will turn back."

"I do not understand why the captain chases me with such fervor. It makes no sense . . ." A dim light dawned. "It makes no sense unless during the course of his investigation he has learned of Olassar's box."

The priestess studied me for a moment. "Of course. That is the answer."

"If it's something the captain wants for himself, couldn't I just give it to him with my compliments?"

"No."

"I didn't think so." I clasped my hands and rested my elbows upon the table. "Why?"

"Pagas Shadows is not a greedy man; he is a fanatic. He is in the service of Tretia, and I believe Tretia thinks this box threatens the Heterins."

"What should we do?"

"Now, that is something for you to ask your inheritance." She pushed back her chair. "Please, don't get up. Whatever happens, we will want to move quickly. I must speak to Iamos. Finish your cheese and bread."

"What about the box? If he searched my wagon, the box has certainly been found."

"Perhaps not. My feeling is that the box only goes with whom it chooses."

She walked quickly toward the wagons, and I almost choked on the bread and cheese, my throat was so dry. It became slightly dryer when I realized that I had no money with which to pay the waiter. Figuring I could be hung no higher, I took three-quarters of the loaf and three-quarters of the cheese and put them in my pockets. I pulled out my three mahrzak beetles and placed them on the board. They headed right for the cheese and began gnawing their way through it. "Eat heartily, my friends. This might have to last for awhile."

Once they had their fill, I stood up, bent over the table, and whispered, "Meet me back at the wagon." I stood up and shouted. "What filth! Horrible insects all over! Yechh!" Other patrons looked toward my table as the waiter came running over.

"Is there a problem?"

"No, there's no problem, unless you think eating in a bug-infested hovel is a problem. What do you serve with a full meal? Worms?"

The waiter looked at the table, and my friends did a credible job of appearing filthy and loathsome as they chirped and waved their horrible little legs. I swear the waiter lifted his apron and issued a silent "Eek!" Since that petunia was not about to harm my friends, I took my leave.

"Be assured that I will never eat in this establishment of ill health ever again!"

I assumed a posture of offended dignity, stormed toward my wagon, and climbed inside. I noted that the box was still where I had left it. I pulled out the bread and cheese and noticed that one of the box's drawers was opening. I leaned over and peeked to see what Olassar's case thought I needed. It was a full copper coin. I picked up the coin. "What for?" I asked around a mouthful of cheese and bread.

"To pay for the cheese and bread, Korvas," said Syndia's voice from the door. I looked and she was holding my three beetles in the palm of her hand.

"There's no need," I offered. "The beetles—"

"I know all about the beetles. Now there is something you *need* to do." She pointed at the coin in my hand.

"Why?"

"It is the honest thing to do."

"What's your point?"

"Korvas, I believe you are redeemable, but you must help in the redemption just a little. Go pay for the bread and cheese, then get back here. We must leave before Shadows returns."

"Where shall we go?"

"I know not."

"The box." I turned to Olassar's box and asked, "What does the caravan need?"

No drawers opened, but as I was about to open one, a fellow arrived behind Syndia. He removed his hand and, looking very much confused, he asked, "I be a guide. Does anyone here need a guide?"

"A guide?" I asked. A strange scent wafted beneath my nostrils. I checked the cheese, and even though the beetles had returned and were having a snack, it wasn't the cheese.

"Yes, a guide," said the man. "Something told me . . . I be told you need a guide."

Syndia faced the man. "Can you get us to the land of the Omergunts without traveling any farther on the King's Highway?"

"Yes. We go straight up into the mountains from here."

"I didn't think there was a road into the mountains this far to the west."

"There be not." He grinned. "That be why you need guide."

I waved my hand in front of my face in an attempt at moving along whatever it was that had befouled the air. "Fellow, what is your name?"

"Ruuter. I be Omergunt. Will I be staying here?"

"No. We value our solitude too dearly." I turned to Syndia. "Isn't that true?"

She stepped down from the wagon and said to Ruuter, "We'll find a place for you, never fear." She looked up at me and said, "Pay for the bread and cheese."

"But—"

"Pay."

I paid for the bread and cheese. I didn't like it, but I did it.

6

There were enough good reasons for staying out of the Mystic Mountains to make the route through Kienosos very attractive. In the mountains were strange flying men, wicked witches, bloodthirsty murder-worshipers, and a sufficient assortment of things that slithered, crawled, and crept to make use of the mountain roads one's last choice.

In addition to these unpleasantries, there was no road into the mountains from Fort Damra. Brief stretches of ancient logging trails were still visible, but they were too overgrown to be of any use. At the outset this meant leaving the wagons behind.

To divert Captain Shadows, Iamos took the wagons and most of the Nant Guard back toward Iskandar in an attempt at making it look as though the entire caravan had turned back, while we took Guard Commander Meru and seven of the Nant Guard, some horses and pack animals into the mountains.

This was the first time I got to see the occupants of the two other wagons. The first was a terribly ancient Nant priestess named Ahjrah. Her incredibly wrinkled face carried an expression of resignation to constant pain. A guard rode next to her.

The person who had been riding in the fifth wagon was still something of a mystery. It was so small he or she had to have been a young child or perhaps a dwarf. The person was covered from head to foot with a dark veil.

Syndia instructed me not to speak to the small one at all. Under no circumstances was I allowed to speak to the person.

The priestess said to me: "If you obey this rule in the same manner that you obey so many others, Korvas, you will die instantly at the hands of the nearest guard. There will be no appeal. Do you understand?"

I nodded, of course. However, the questions almost burned holes through my pate. Who was that person? Why was I not allowed to speak to the person? What did that person, or the old woman, have to do with Olassar's mission to the Omergunts?

Despite the lack of roads, our guide Ruuter seemed to find no trouble at all getting us so deep into the mountains that we found places where I am certain that sunlight never touched the forest floor. There were mushrooms there as tall as horses. The entire place was thickly wooded with vast tangles of huge, broad-leafed vines, and at any second I expected to see hot yellow eyes staring at me from out of the dark, or screaming tentacled horrors dropping upon me from out of the treetops.

It was about when I was entertaining thoughts of praying for the sun to rise that the Omergunt stopped us and said we must make camp. The sun was setting. I couldn't believe that it could get any darker, but I dismounted along with everyone else.

Four guards were posted while the remaining four cleared brush and servants put up the tents. Once a fire had been made and the evening's sawdust loaf consumed, I felt slightly better. Not quite enough better to make up for the constant feeling of being watched from the forest, or for the deadly silence around the campfire. Only Syndia, old Ahjrah, the veiled one, and I sat at our campfire. The guards had their own fire, and the servants had a third. Quite beyond the servants' fire was a fourth fire where Ruuter sat by himself.

From the surrounding woods came screams, hisses, growls, clicks, snaps, and the rattle of leaves. I never liked the woods. I don't like how they look, how they smell, how they sound. I don't like the color, the shape or the feel. That was why I always lived in cities.

In cities there were always cutthroats and robbers waiting for you around every corner, but these were upright men of business. They either wanted your life, your money, or both. They would take what they wanted, and leave. Beasties in the forest, however, wanted to gnaw on you and worry pieces off of you for their little beastie children. Some of them even make a point of keeping you alive for a long time. This allows pieces of you to be taken off over a period of days or weeks without spoilage.

Syndia was staring into the flames of the fire and the old priestess was, as well. I'm not certain if the veiled one even had eyes, but he, she, or it sat as motionless as a brick wall. I can get only so much entertainment from a controlled fire. Hence, after an hour or two I was closed to going "Boo!" at the veiled one just to liven up things. That's when I looked around and saw one of the guards standing in the shadows behind me, his pistol in his hand.

"Good evening," I said.

He nodded curtly and I settled down for another episode of watching the logs burn using a rolled blanket for a pillow, my arm wrapped around my inheritance and a lead-sensitive itch between my shoulder blades.

Flames do dance and move about hypnotically. The fire that night seemed to form arches that were openings into vast chasms, pits, halls, and chambers of flame.

"There!"

I jumped up at the word.

The old woman, Ahjrah, was half standing and had a gnarled finger pointed at the fire. I looked and I could see above the flames a figure; a red silhouette; the image of the flame-goddess Heteris. I was startled for a moment, but then reassured myself. I had seen flame-conjuring before. Conjurers stood on the low end of the magicians' hierarchy, but it was a good trick with which to impress the dimwitted. I resolved not to be impressed.

"Get you back to the fire," ordered old Ahjrah.

"Ahjrah," the image seemed to say, "let me show you the way."

"Back to the fire," Syndia joined in. Both of the priestesses were on their feet chanting a hymn in a tongue unfamiliar to me, although the name *Nanteria* was part of the chant.

"Come, Ahjrah." The silhouette waved its arms. "Here is a part of the new path."

This was no fire-conjuring trick. I watched with amazement as the old woman's robe fell away and her wrinkles faded until she stood there with the form and face of a girl of sixteen. She was so beautiful my heart almost cracked.

"I can give you back the youth you never had, Ahjrah. You can have the young men you had to forsake to serve Nanteria. Serve me and I will do all this."

Ahjrah's chanting continued and soon a huge black silhouette blocked the reflection of the firelight from the trees. It was Nanteria, and she placed her arms around Ahjrah and spoke to the fire. "This is my daughter, Heteris. You may not have her."

"Then the child," spoke the fire. "Only the child."

"Only Ahjrah can give you the child."

The fire-silhouette grew huge and bellowed at Ahjrah, "Look! Look at you!" The red silhouette became a red mirror, reflecting to all of us the naked image of the sixteen-year-old Ahjrah. "See what I can be for you. Instead of the constant tiredness and pain of age, I have given you youth. Instead of ugliness, you have beauty. Instead of death tugging at your sleeve, I have made the reaper something not to be considered for another eighty years." The red silhouette filled with a deep scarlet. "Let me have the child, Ahjrah."

Ahjrah in her nakedness, her youthful cheeks streaked with tears, pointed a finger at the flames and ordered, "Back to the fire, Heteris. I am the daughter of Nanteria, and I have lived the time allotted to me and have done it with honor. Back to the fire with you! Back!"

A horrible shriek split the dark and fire seemed to fill my vision as the flame-monster reached out its arms and grasped Olassar's case. Immediately I jumped up and yanked the case out of her grasp.

"No, you don't! This is mine!"

Another shriek, and I was in one instant covered with flame and the next flat on my bottom, my inheritance in my tight grasp and all my clothing soaking wet.

When I was assured that my eyebrows were not aflame, I ventured to open my eyes. The fire had died down almost to coals, Ahjrah was again dressed and was again incredibly old and wrinkled, and the veiled one hadn't budged so much as a hair.

Syndia was examining me. When I could see her face again, she was smiling. "You are singed here and there, but there is no permanent damage." She opened a drawer in Olassar's box and withdrew a tiny cup filled with some sort of evil-smelling goo. "This ointment will help with the burns."

She began rubbing the goo on my face, and to have her stroking my face, the goo didn't smell all that foul. Despite that, there was something that concerned me. "Syndia, is this going to happen every time we light a campfire?"

"Anywhere, anytime is the place and time of the gods, Korvas. But I think we shall have some rest for awhile. Heteris suffered a humiliating defeat this night—two humiliating defeats. Ahjrah cast Heteris back into the fire and you defied her. She is probably very tired."

I looked over and saw that the old priestess was weeping silently to herself. This was beginning to look like a dangerous religion. "Is there anything we can do for Ahjrah?"

Syndia shook her head. "No, but there's something you can do for me."

"Anything you wish."

The ointment was all used, and the tiny cup in Syndia's hand faded and disappeared. "Tell me why you fought with Heteris. She is Evil, Deceit, the Mother of Lies. Most persons would have been paralyzed with fear just at her sight. Yet you fought with her."

I held up my inheritance. "Your flaming goddess wanted my box!"

"And," she prompted.

"It's *my* box! Heteris can't be a very bright flame if she can't understand that. I know little of your world. To be honest, which it seems I must, I know little of my world. But this I do know: this little chest of drawers belongs to Korvas!"

The veiled one got to its feet and walked around the fire until it stood next to me.

"Remember," cautioned Syndia, "do not speak."

"Mmmm," I agreed. The figure sat next to me and cuddled into my shoulder. I put my arm around it. From the sounds of breathing, I gather it fell asleep. I raised my eyebrows, but the priestess only held her finger to her lips. After a moment I whispered to Syndia, "My clothes are soaking wet. How did they get that way?"

Syndia nodded in the direction of the old priestess. Ahjrah stood, walked around the fire, and was standing over me and the veiled one. I think there was a tiny smile on her face as she whispered a prayer over the sleeping form next to me. When she was finished, she snapped her fingers and my clothes were suddenly dry. A *very* strange sensation. She smiled at me, patted the veiled one on its shoulder, and hobbled off into the shadows beyond the reach of the firelight.

"Where is she going?" I whispered to Syndia.

"Ahjrah is going to die." Syndia sat down upon a rock and continued looking at the fire, her eyes glistening.

7

The night was filled with one horrible nightmare after another. It was almost as though the small figure sleeping next to me projected them into my mind as I slept. It was much less trouble to stay awake. However, I would drift off again and then have another nightmare.

These phantoms would often be of two children playing, and they filled me with sadness. I would start awake with my cheeks covered with tears. By the time the forest's sarcasm of a morning arrived, I was a wreck. As I suspected, however, that would not be the full extent of my problems. During the night all of the servants had fled, and four of the guards were gone in search of them. That left Syndia, the veiled one, Ruuter, four guards, and your humble servant Korvas.

While the guard commander, Meru, kept watch, two guards packed up two of the tents and loaded the pack animals, while the fourth guard cooked and served a morning repast of fried forest fungus and leaf tea. Syndia ate the stuff, and the veiled one brought it inside the veil and nothing came out. Perhaps it was edible; however, it amused me to think that at one point in my life I had been concerned about gaining too much weight. This problem was lifted from me as I contemplated my new diet of sawdust and forest litter.

I dumped my plate into Heteris's bed—the coals—and spoke to the priestess. "Syndia."

"You have questions, Master Korvas."

59

"Yes, I do. First—"

"Ahjrah is dead. We will light her funeral pyre as we leave."

"Oh." I felt stunned by the bluntness of her answer to a question I hadn't yet asked. "Secondly—"

"Her time had come. The reason no one followed her was out of respect for her solitude."

"Are you a mind reader, Syndia?"

She smiled and poked at the coals with a stick. "I have seen every memory of yours up to two days ago, Korvas. I know how you think, what bothers you, what confuses and frightens you."

"Do you know what my next question is, then?"

"Perhaps it would make you feel better to ask it yourself."

I waited for a moment, convinced she was laughing at me. "I take it you know what makes me angry, as well."

"Korvas, I know that not having all of the answers, not being in control of a situation, makes you angry. I know your anger is fear of placing your trust in someone or something other than yourself."

"People laughing at me makes me angry, Syndia."

"I am not laughing at you. Perhaps you should listen to what you are telling yourself about you."

"You are not making any sense."

"Did you have another question?"

I drummed my fingertips upon my knee. "Yes." I pointed at the coals. "This business with the gods fighting over the old priestess, then over that one," I pointed at the veiled one, "then the flame-goddess Heteris going after Olassar's box." I leaned forward and placed my elbows on my knees. "And more: the fantastic powers of this box, and Captain Shadows on my trail like a hound in heat." I held out my hand. "This expedition. We are not on a mission of mercy to carry perfume to the Omergunts, are we?"

"Not exactly." She stood up and handed her empty plate to the guard. "We must be leaving soon. Pick one question and I shall answer it."

I pursed my lips and frowned. "You will not lie or mislead me?"

"I cannot lie, Korvas, without condemning my soul to the fire."

I nodded once and pointed a finger at the veiled one. "Who is that?"

"Now that Ahjrah is dead, you may speak to him. He has chosen you for his guardian. That is your twin brother."

Syndia walked from the clearing and began talking to one of the guards. I stood there with my mouth hanging open. When I had reclaimed a minuscule portion of my composure, I turned to the veiled one and lifted its veil. It looked like a boy of no more than six or seven years old. Yet there was something very different about the face. The eyes did not stare, but they seemed to have only a baby's intelligence behind them. How could this be my twin brother? My brother had been dead for the past thirty years.

—Or at least that is what I had been told. Syndia said that she could not lie to me, but that, too, could be a lie. I sat on the log next to the boy and whispered in his ear, "What is your name?"

I saw the boy's lips move, and I whispered into his ear again, "Your name, boy. What is your name?"

I held my ear to his lips and heard him say, "Tayu." My brother's name, to be sure. But that was also a memory of mine that Syndia had at her command. I looked at Olassar's box, wondering what answers it might hold for me.

First I had need of my own kind of solitude and a tree in a quiet patch of forest. I pushed myself to my feet, but I had taken only a few steps when I felt uncomfortable leaving my inheritance behind. I turned back and saw two fingers of fire creeping out of the coals across the ground. The first was eating its way toward the chest of drawers. The second was moving toward Tayu. In haste I looked, but the bottles of water and the basin had been packed.

"Heteris," I called out, "now don't be naughty." I pulled down the front of my trousers, aimed my member at the flaming arm reaching toward Tayu, and burst forth

with a mighty stream. After extinguishing the first arm, I
doused the one reaching for Olassar's box. When that
one was chased back I turned myself upon the coals. "I
believe I warned you, Heteris: that box is mine."

"Korvas!" The shocked voice came from behind me. It
was Syndia, and her face was bright red. "Cover yourself!"

With a shake and a yank of my trousers, I was covered. "You don't understand, Syndia, the fire—"

"Were you reared in a stable? Do that sort of business
away from the camp and behind a tree!" She pulled Tayu
to his feet and led him away.

"Syndia, the fire—"

"I'm shocked, Korvas. Utterly shocked."

The coals hissed and crackled with what struck me as a
trifle too much glee at my discomfort. I shrugged and
said, "In for a copper, in for a reel." I picked up a
handful of leaves, gathered up the hem of my robe,
pulled down my trousers, and finished my business with
the flame-goddess.

Prepared to continue our journey, Syndia and Tayu
stood before the modest funeral pyre, a guard a step
behind them with a black smoking torch at the ready.
The pyre was little more than Ahjrah's frail form lying
on a three-foot-thick bed of dried evergreen branches.
Syndia anointed the old priestess's forehead with rose oil
and sang a prayer in that strange tongue used by the
Nants. As she did so, Tayu climbed up on the pyre,
kissed the old woman's cheek, and climbed down again.

When the song was finished, Syndia nodded at the
guard and the torch was touched to the pyre. In a few
seconds it was a column of black smoke, but I could see
no flames. After a few seconds the smoke had cleared
and there was nothing left but ashes. A black cloud came
over the treetops, settled on the ashes, and rose again into
the sky straight up until it faded from view. Where
Ahjrah's funeral pyre had been, the ashes were gone,
and the forest floor look undisturbed. Not a single dead
leaf was scorched.

8

The deeper we rode into the mountains, the surer I was that I was ignorant of where I was going and why I was going there. I was convinced that if the box ever did produce gold, gems, or anything else of value, it would be only on some goody-goody basis that would see me giving it all away to widows, beggars, and street urchins.

Ahead of me, riding on a horse led by a guard, was Tayu. In front of him was Syndia riding behind two guards and Ruuter, the guide. I looked back, and beyond Commander Meru's grim visage were another guard and the trail through which we had recently passed.

Did I possess the minor tracking skills necessary to find my way back to Fort Damra? Perhaps, but first there was the problem of getting around Commander Meru and his faithful companion, whose name I did not yet know. Second, there was the problem of getting around Captain Shadows, who must have made it back to Fort Damra. By now he had spread out a few coppers among the alley rats, would know what he needed, and would be hot on my trail.

I saw Meru pull up his mount, turn, and ride the way we had come to see if we had company. For the moment, it looked as though I had best go along with Syndia's plans. Of course, what were her plans? The fantastically expensive caravan, this peculiar box, the boy who called himself Tayu, the fight between the Nant gods over the boy, Heteris's lust for my inheritance, and Olassar's un-

finished contract with the Omergunts. On top of all this
was the rabid search for me led by Captain Shadows.

The leathery voices of tawbirds filled the forest as I
tried to see beyond the brush into the darknesses beyond,
looking for the monsters that lurked there. I could see
nothing. I concentrated instead on Captain Shadows.
Why was he after me? Would Olassar's box be enough to
send him sniffing into the Mystic after me? I didn't think
so. It was a clever enough contraption, but Iskandar is
filled with magic. Why must he have this particular piece?
It did not make sense.

Even the King's Guard fears the Heterin Guard. Everyone, man, woman, or child, who lived by his wits on
the streets and alleys of Iskandar knew and feared Captain Shadows. I have seen more than one head I knew
mounted on a pike along the Temple Circle as an object
lesson. Shadows was always mindful of expenses in his
disposition of our friends, too. Such frills as investiga-
tions and trials were rarely indulged. I knew of only one
fool who tried to bring a complaint about this to her
bloody self, Tretia. After he had been killed, I found his
head mounted on a Temple Circle pike the next morning.
That was all I ever had to bury of my father.

I wiped my eyes and looked ahead. Tayu was looking
back at me. There were tears in his eyes, too. Could he,
indeed, be my brother? At times he seemed to feel what I
felt. But I couldn't see how he could comprehend such
feelings. I wanted so many of these questions answered
now. I looked to Olassar's box, its ivory handle tied to
my horse's saddle. I spoke to it and asked, "What do I
need right now?"

The lower left drawer opened. Inside was a slip of
paper containing a single word: *"Patience."*

I crumpled up the paper and threw it upon the ground.
"I know that!" The drawer closed by itself. I put the
anger out of my voice and tried again. "How then do I
obtain patience?"

The same drawer opened once again. This time the
note read: *"Put your impatience in here."*

"Bah!" I was about to throw the object into the woods

when the Nant guard who had been riding in back reined up beside me and whispered out of the side of his mouth:

"Take this." He held out his hand and dropped into mine a balled-up piece of paper.

"What is this?"

"You dropped it. If Commander Meru had seen this you would have been executed on the spot. To him it would have looked like you were attempting to leave trail markings for the Heterin captain. I think you are, instead, only stupid and careless."

"Thank you, I think."

"Don't mention it. If you ever do I will slit open your belly and hang you by your own guts."

Charming. Simply charming. I gave him my best wan smile as he again fell back in the procession. Commander Meru rode up from the rear, paused to speak to the guard, then paused to speak to me. "We are picking up the pace. Shadows is only an hour behind." He continued up the line, eventually reaching Ruuter. As soon as he did we began moving first at a canter, then at a gallop.

I don't much like horses. They are unpredictable critters that cannot remember if anyone is riding them or not. Neither am I much of a rider, preferring instead the security of either four carriage wheels or my own feet beneath me. I lost my hat to one overhanging branch and almost lost my head to a second. I placed my cheek next to my horse's neck, threw my arms around it, and held on with my eyes shut.

I could feel the clods of dirt thrown up by the pair of horses ahead of me striking me in my face. There are many kinds of terror, and I had cultivated the habit of avoiding most of them. But on the back of a panting horse, running at top speed through an overgrown forest, with gods fighting overhead, who knows what waiting for me, and Captain Shadows sniffing at my heels, all of the terror in my life that I had managed to avoid visited me at the same time.

Olassar's box was jumping all around, banging the horse, my shoulder, ribs, and thigh. I gripped it with my

right hand just as my horse followed the others into a
hole in the trees, cutting off almost all of the light. "Help
me," I prayed to whatever spirits or deities might be
listening.

There was a warmth in the box. It warmed my hand,
then my arm and shoulder, then my heart. A voice came
into my head, and it said *"I am with you."*

"Great," I whispered. "So what do I do now?"

An animal screamed loudly, something swatted my
face, and the voice said, *"Turn over your fear to me."*

"I will, but how?"

"Just ask me to take it."

"Please . . . please take my fear. I would be eternally
grateful if only—"

My fear was gone. That sickness that was eating up my
heart was gone. I sat up, feeling a new sense of awe
about the box. In a flash it had changed me from a
sniveling coward to a man who could ride with pride.
That was when a branch caught me between the eyes, I
saw those marvelous stars of daylight, and as everything
went dark heard the voice say, *"I didn't say sit up!"*

9

I wandered a dreampath, and half sensed that it was a dreampath I was seeing. There were the dark beams of a ceiling above me, and there was crying coming from the right. Rolling my head to the right, I saw a baby. Its cries ceased and it looked at me. I held out my hand to it, and only when I saw my hand did I realize that I, too, was a baby.

A face came into view, and I looked to see my father. His face was younger but contorted so that I hardly recognized him. Another face came into view. Although it was thirty years younger, I recognized the face of the Nant priestess Ahjrah.

My father looked first at me, then at my brother, then back to me again. He closed his eyes and shook his head. Ahjrah put her hand on his shoulder and her lips said, "Rafas, it is written that it be a father's choice. You must choose."

My father's hand touched my cheek, then my brother's. He lifted Tayu and placed the baby in the priestess's arms. As Ahjrah moved out of view, my father cried.

I awakened and opened my eyes feeling puzzled and sad. When I could bring things into focus, I saw that I was in a crude hut of woven branches and leaves. There was a fire, a pot boiling above it, and strange odors filling the air. There was a face above me, and—

I closed my eyes again, certain that I had not yet awakened and just as certain that my dream had moved over into nightmare. The face I saw was hairless, wrinkled, gray, and looked as though its features had been arranged by the interbreeding of a bat and a road accident. It grinned at me with yellowish needle points of teeth.

"Dagata'k? Dagata'k you speak, yes?"

"Yes, I think so."

"Think so, good, eh!" It snurfled off a laugh behind its arm. The arm appeared to be webbed to its torso with a membrane. "This is pahmma. Good. Eat. Grow strong."

I sat up in panic and looked at the creature squatting before me. "Captain Shadows?"

The creature wheezed out three laughs and shook its head. "Shadows out chasing shadows." The lame joke had the ugly thing in a laughing fit. When it finally calmed, it held out a wooden bowl full of yellow guck. "Eat pahmma. Make you strong. Put you on your feet again."

The thing dipped a wooden spoon that appeared to be about the size of a shovel into the bowl and thrust it into my mouth. Although I gagged a bit at having the spoon shoved down my throat, the pahmma itself wasn't untasty. Immediately I began to feel better. I took the bowl and spoon. "Let me."

" 'Et you!"

That, too, had the creature in stitches. I swallowed another mouthful of the squash soup and pointed the spoon at the creature. "What was it you said about Captain Shadows? Where is he?"

I waited impatiently for the thing to stop laughing. When it did, it said, "Smarter you shou'd ask where you find yourse'f, yes?"

"Very well. Where am I?"

A deadly serious look came over the thing's face as it held up a clawed finger. "You be where Shadows is not. Good, yes?" Then it went into another laughing fit.

Obviously my nurse was mentally defective, and I waited somewhat uncomfortably for the thing's keeper to come with a net and drag the creature off to an asylum. Then the creature became serious again and studied my face. Reaching out one of those clawed hands, it slapped my face lightly. "Ah, you are sick, sick. You cannot 'aff?"

" 'Aff? You mean, laugh?"

"Most certain'y, 'aff. You must be very sick not to 'aff."

In a panic I remembered Olassar's box. I looked about for it and found it on the hut's floor next to me. I placed my hand on it and laughed.

"Ah," said the thing. "You 'aff. Much better, more pahmma. Put you on your feet." It pointed at the bowl, and I continued eating.

The familiar visage of Commander Meru stuck his head through the hut's doorway. "Korvas, how are you feeling?"

I felt around my ribs, head, and so on, and tallied up the results. "I feel surprisingly good, no thanks to that insane run through the forest. This is due, no doubt, to this excellent porridge." I nodded at the creature. "My thanks."

"Come out and join us when you are finished, and don't eat too much of that," cautioned Meru as his smirking face left the doorway.

What nonsense, I thought as I finished up the bowl and held it out to the creature for more. For some reason, holding out the bowl caused the creature to fall backward over itself, its winged arms wrapped around its middle, laughing so hard it could not draw a single breath.

I watched this spectacle until a sudden urgency hit my bowels with a passion unequalled in my prior experience. I dropped everything, ran out of the hut, and off the edge of a branch into thin air. My frantic grasps at a tangle of vines and Meru's grip on my collar were all that saved me. Whoever these creatures were, they lived in trees. Angh only knows where they do their business.

"Meru, I am in need—"

He pulled me up to a flat place next to him and

pointed at another hut. "In there. And don't fall in. It's a long way down."

I looked, and the massive tree trunks extended down and down until they were lost in mists.

As I closed the door of woven branches and straddled the opening in the floor, I had to agree. Pahmma certainly does put you on your feet again.

10

After completing my business and securing my inheritance, Meru led me to join the others in a huge hut cradled by the branches of a single enormous tree. Inside, the Nant guards stood near the door. In the center of the hut burned a small fire in a carved stone brazier, the pan of which was just above the woven floor. There was a circle of listeners around the fire.

Syndia and Tayu were seated there along with nine of those ugly creatures. Surrounding that circle, the edges of the hut were crammed with more than two hundred of those beings. Although my nurse's possession of any particular sex had been difficult to tell when I had first awakened, the creatures did come in male and female. The females had breasts of a sort, but the entire race struck me as something that had recently been conjured up from a nightmare.

One of the things—a male—led me to an open place in the inner circle next to Tayu. I sat cross-legged on the ground and placed Olassar's box upon my ankles. I leaned across Tayu and whispered to Syndia, "Where is Captain Shadows?"

She held her finger to her lips and nodded toward the other side of the circle. One of the creatures was huddled beneath an ornately embroidered blanket. There was an unwholesome-sounding wail, then the critters on either side of the blanketed one lifted the cover from her, for it was a female covered entirely with bright yellow paint.

She squatted before the fire and held her clawed hands
out before her, saying, "B'essings on us, this fire," she
held her palms open toward us, "and on our visitors." I
could see that there were huge eyes painted upon her
wings.

She passed her hand over the fire and the flames died
down as an image appeared above the flames. It was the
full figure of Pagas Shadows. The image was real enough
to cause my spine to tremble. My inheritance reminded
me that it was there as well, and I again gave it my fear.
As I did do, my fear left me. But there was a strange
message from the box. It cautioned me, with my newly
granted courage, to mind overhanging branches and other
enemies of false pride.

"I am Bachudowah, and my art is before you this
orrintime."

Of the box I asked, "Orrintime?"

The answer came: *"Now; the present moment."*

"Beho'd," she held her arms up toward the image of
Shadows, "Pagas Shadows, monster of Heterin Guard,
spawn of Zyrchitih, Bitch of Fire." The flames sparkled.
Bachudowah held her palms over the fire, and the flames
subsided.

"I see everything, so keep nothing from me; everything I say serves a purpose, so hear with ten ears." A
milky white membrane seemed to pull over each of her
eyeballs, giving Bachudowah a demonish look. The hut
grew very silent as a greenish blue cloud formed above
Bachudowah's head. The cloud moved until it hovered
over the image of Shadows. A piece of it separated and
settled around the captain's head.

The cloud moved on, pieces leaving the main as it
passed the Nant guards, Syndia, Tayu, myself, and the
creatures sitting with us in the inner circle. A piece of the
cloud settled on Olassar's box at the same time a piece
settled around my head. There was no sensation.

Again the main cloud circled the hut, gathering up its
pieces. It eventually came to rest above Bachudowah's
head. Slowly it settled down upon her wrinkled yellow
shoulders, enveloping her head in clouds. A *shwoosh*ing

sound filled the hut and the cloud disappeared up the creature's nostrils. Bachudowah opened her eyes. Her eyes were silver and reflected light like mirrors.

She grinned, displaying a set of vicious-looking pointed teeth. "Ah, Bachudowah sees many secrets among grounders—you outsiders. There are things each of you keeps from the others. Do you va'ue your secrets? If you do not va'ue them, then we wi' share them. If you do va'ue them, then offer a prize. You, Syndia."

The Nant priestess closed her eyes and opened them again. "My secrets have no value."

Bachudowah pointed a handful of claws at Tayu. "You, Tayu."

The boy lifted his veil. His face still had that vacant look, but he spoke out loud for the first time. "All I know is yours, Bachudowah."

"You, Korvas."

"I would keep my secrets to myself. I place a great value upon them and would charge you a great deal—"

There was a roar of laughter from the creatures in the hut. When it died, the one with the silver eyes explained, "I charge you not to use them, and great va'ue must make you very rich, yes?"

"No."

"Then you cannot pay for my quiet?"

"No—this is blackmail, you know."

"I did not take your secrets from you; you 'et them go."

She turned and pointed at the first guard. "You, Rosh." It was the guard sergeant who had warned me about tossing my trash on the trail.

"I have no secrets of value."

"You, Icen."

The large guard smiled and asked, "What do you charge?"

"Whatever they are worth to keep silent."

I thought I saw Icen moisten his lips before he shook his head. "Nothing of value here."

"You, Meru."

The guard commander threw a small leather pouch at

Bachudowah. The creature caught the pouch, opened it, and poured the contents into her hand. "There are only fifty reels."

Meru grinned through his black beard. "That's all they are worth to me."

Perhaps the sum of fifty reels was too little to impress Bachudowah or Commander Meru, but it had my gears turning. The creature nodded and tied the pouch to her string belt.

Of course, what immediately leaped to mind was, just what was it that Meru had to hide that was worth fifty golden reels?

The creature faced the fourth guard. "You, Hara."

The fourth guard looked with contempt upon Bachudowah. "You'll get no coins from me. If you can see inside me, say what you will."

Bachudowah grinned at Hara and turned her head until she faced me. She looked down at Olassar's box and stared at it for half a minute. She closed her eyes, crossed her arms over her chest and, still seated, bowed forward until her forehead touched the floor. "As a'ways, I honor you." I stared at the box as I wondered who Bachudowah saw there.

She sat upright and looked to the image of Captain Shadows. "You, Pagas Shadows. Do you va'ue your secrets?"

The image looked up, turned left then right, then over its shoulder. The figure bellowed, "Where are you?"

"I am above the clouds over your head, yet I am in your dreams."

The image of Shadows lurched above the fire, looking high and low. "Why can't I see you?"

"Accept that it is so, Pagas. Now, to your secrets."

"If I value them, what then? I cannot pay you in a dream."

Bachudowah let go with a shrill laugh that chilled my blood. "Captain, the manner in which you spend your dream go'd is much more important than how you spend your go'd awake."

"I pay you, then, nothing." His hideous face broke into a grin.

"So be it, Pagas."

Bachudowah swirled her hands above the fire, and the inside of the hut seemed to disappear and was replaced by a swirl of multicolored clouds. The sounds of a terrible windstorm filled the hut. The image of Shadows moved above us all until only his face looked down at us. The bright light muted, then grew dimmer and dimmer until all we could see was Bachudowah and her silver eyes.

I leaned across Tayu and poked Syndia in her arm. "Don't we have a few secrets we'd like to keep from the good captain?" I pointed up where Shadows's face had been.

"There are no real secrets, Korvas."

There was a long silence, then Bachudowah stood. "This, then, is your story. Pay c'ose mind, for in it are answers you seek, and more mysteries. Now I begin."

11

The haunting notes of a strange flute filled my hearing as the voices of the outer circle wailed an unfamiliar refrain. As the voices became very quiet, Bachudowah began:

"Know you of Books of Fayn, scriptures of ancient Itkahn faith before it shattered, its pieces becoming the many faiths. Hundred Books of Fayn contain mysteries, truths, untruths, and many prophecies written and saved for over thousand years.

"Orrintime, have your mind fi' with image of baby grounder gir' carried by great man grounder of wea'th and power, Nabas, His Exce'ency, Sheva of Desivida." An image of the wealthily berobed governor holding a baby turned above the fire. "See? He cries, for chi'd's mother, sheva's sister, died in chi'dbirth from assassin's dart. Father was dead, executed as traitor by Pherris, then first priest of Heterin Temp'e. Nabas, himse'f, was unwed. With baby in his arms he swore to his spirit, goddess of smoke, Akitaia, who Nants called Nanteria, that he wou'd give the chi'd affection, education, wea'th, power, and position.

"Howso, no grounder man in Desivida cou'd mind baby." There were snickers and wheezy laughs in the darkness. "Nabas he went to Nant Temp'e in Desivida to hire woman grounder to mind baby. Howso, Somas, first priest of Desivida temp'e, had magic eyes. He saw in that baby First One prophesied in ancient Books of Fayn: First One who wi' find Second One who wi' find great-

hearted Warrior who, with his faithfu' Guide, wi' war
with Hadyuzia, Destroyer of Wor'ds. . . ."

I listened to the Dagas storyteller and the years peeled
away. When I was very young my father had me attend
instruction at the Nant Temple in Iskandar. That was
something I ceased doing as a child when I left my
father's house. Although Bachudowah called the Destroyer Hadyuzia instead of Manku, the story of the
destruction was familiar to every child who had ever
gone to any temple, for the prophecy had been handed
down from the Itkahn religion through all of the off-
shoots of the parent religion that still existed.

At a time selected by the stars, there would come upon
the world a great destroyer, Manku. He would challenge
the world to put forward a hero who would fight for all
the world's races. If the hero that was selected won the
battle with Manku, the world would be spared destruction. If the hero lost, or if no hero was put forward, the
world and all that exists would become as dust.

To prepare for this time, the Itkahn priests consulted
the oracle of the flame-goddess, Heteris, in a cave on the
side of the volcano, Mount Rubih. The oracle spoke
from the flames, saying, "Guided by the Mirror of the
Second, the Hero will be found by the Second, who will
be chosen by a father's hand, kept by the First, loved by
the Mirror, and burned by the Mirror to be gathered
by the Smoke."

As legend had it, a dispute broke out among the priests
as to the meaning of the oracle and what to do about it.
This led, eventually, to the splintering of the Itkahn
religion and the establishment of all of the religions, each
one claiming is have the truth of the prophecy and its
fulfillment. I didn't know anyone who took the prophecy
seriously. Current dogma was believed, but the story of
the hero and the coming of the destroyer bordered on
mythology. However, there were some things to consider.

I remember the same year that I left my father's house
the Mankua Temple and all its followers were destroyed
by a bolt of lighting that appeared out of a cloudless
night sky. The streets of Iskandar were filled with terror

as those who feared Angh the god of ghosts dusted off
their prayers, asked directions to the nearest temple, and
attempted to make last-minute deals with the powers of
the universe. Not long afterward, just as the fear was
subsiding by being explained away time after time, the
Elassan Temple was swallowed by the ground.

The Amuites and Nants kept silent about the destruction, but the Heterins were pigs up to their snouts in slop
with pointing fingers and making moralistic comments
about the wrath of Heteris, who was still a goddess of
good to the Heterins.

I remember the dangerous little jokes that implicated
the Amuite priests in the destruction, and other jokes,
more dangerous, that implicated the Heterins. The sense
of all of the jokes and unspoken fears was that, in fighting to destroy each other, the splintered remains of Itkahn
would leave Manku's challenge go unanswered.

According to Bachudowah, the Nant priest Somas somehow determined that the baby brought to him by Sheva
Nabas was the First One mentioned in the prophecy.
Late one night the baby was stolen from her cradle in the
sheva's palace. Nabas had the nurse and house servants
tortured, sent his guard forth upon the city to frighten
and bully the citizens, and offered a reward of one hundred thousand reels for the return of the child.

When babies as far away as Shu'ei were either being
stolen or traded in by their parents in hopes of getting the
reward, Nabas realized the folly of his actions and called
off the reward. The search continued for some time, but
eventually it, too, ended. Nabas died alone in his grief.

The image above Bachudowah's fire became that of a
baby girl, who rapidly advanced in age as the storyteller
talked. "Somas entered chi'd into temp'e where she 'earned
Nant faith and became daughter of Akitaia. Then she
was sent to temp'e in Iskandar to study fourteen Books
of Fayn kept in secret chamber."

The image grew older and more familiar. We were told
how she entered the Amuite faith and studied the twenty-
one Books of Fayn secretly held in the Amuite Temple.
Then she entered the Heterin faith and studied the eleven

Books of Fayn held in the Heterin Temple. I watched as a new image filled the space above Bachudowah's fire. It was the ancient Nant priestess, Ahjrah.

"O'd woman, Nant priestess, Ahjrah, was First One." Bachudowah held out her clawed hands toward the boy, Tayu. "Second." She held her hands out toward me. "Mirror of Second, the Guide."

A bolt of panic streaked through my heart followed immediately by a laugh at how silly it all was. This was a legend from my childhood. How could it be about me?

"Shhhhooooo!" The storyteller hissed as a frown crowded her brow. She studied Syndia and said, "Ah." She turned, examined the four Nant guards, and said, "Ah." She conjured down the face of Captain Shadows from above, studied it, and said, "Hu." She seemed to draw in upon herself, her arms folded, bending forward upon squatting legs until her head touched her knees.

Just then a curious thing happened. Olassar's box rose from the floor, crossed through the fire, and came to rest next to Bachudowah. A drawer opened and the story-teller lifted her head and looked in. Her fingers went into the tiny drawer and withdrew holding a magnificently faceted diamond the size of a plum. It was on a golden chain, and she put the chain around her neck, that lovely gem coming to rest between her two leathery flaps of breasts. The humor of the gods did not escape me as the box returned through the fire to me, all drawers empty as I soon discovered.

As she held the diamond in her claws, the storyteller's eyes went from silver to black. As they did so, the bright room of clouds and Shadows's face vanished, the dark hut returned, and a sigh of disappointment came from the Dagas in the assembly. Bachudowah stood and held out her hands for silence, which she immediately received. "Story is not finished. If I ta'k too much orrintime, without knowing end, I ruin it for you." She looked at me. "Mirror, named Korvas?"

"Yes," I answered warily.

She held up that magnificent diamond that was worth half a million reels if it was worth a half-copper, and said to me, "Bring me back end to story. If you bring me back end to story, stone is yours."

Now that's what I call curiosity. "How will I know I've reached the end of the story?"

"God box will tell you. Do you agree?"

"Of course—" Before I could finish my sentence I was back on my horse, galloping like greased insanity through the gloomily dark forest. I wanted to feel my forehead to see if I had indeed been struck by the branch, I wanted to ask the others if they had been where I had been, but flying through the underbrush with Shadows barking at my heels, all I could do was hold the god box as it spoke to me saying, *"I am with you; and keep down."*

12

The horses were frothed with sweat and close to dropping that chilly evening as we came upon the crest of the trail overlooking the mountain village of Nita. The road we would follow to the land of the Omergunts could be seen weaving through the mountains toward the northwest. Meru pulled up his mount beside me and spoke to Syndia.

"If we can get fresh horses there, we should be able to put plenty of distance between us and the Heterin captain." He turned around in his saddle, examined the trail we had made, and said to his sergeant, "Rosh, go ahead into the village with the party. I'll take Icen and Hara back the way we came and leave a few surprises for Shadows. The more we can delay him, the better our chances."

Rosh's face had a hint of an objection to it, but he only said, "After we get the fresh horses, should we wait for you?"

"No. If we haven't joined you within two hours, we aren't coming back."

Rosh nodded, and Meru gathered up Icen and Hara and rode back down the trail. My head was still in the clouds with the Dagas, Bachudowah's diamond, and a half-million questions. I was too tired to think of any of them right then. As we crossed a stream and walked our horses into Nita, it was all I could do to keep my stumbling feet from pitching me onto my face.

As we came onto the dusty village street, the smells of cooking mixed with those of smoke and freshly milled lumber filled my nose, awakening me to the reality of my empty stomach. I remembered that the last thing I had eaten was the pahmma given to me by my Dagas nurse. It had cleaned me out—always supposing that we had even been with the Dagas at all. In any event, from whatever reality we had recently hailed, I was hungry. As I was about to ask about food, Syndia handed the reins to Tayu and her horses to Rosh.

"Ruuter. Korvas," she said, "both of you hand your reins to Sergeant Rosh." She faced the sergeant as we handed him our reins, and I rescued my god box from my saddle. "Arrange for fresh horses and meet us at the inn."

"Should I arrange horses for Commander Meru, Icen, and Hara?" The sergeant's eyes were hooded and his voice was devoid of emotion. There was an overly long silence that spoke volumes about the fact that more was going on than had been made clear to me.

Syndia stared at Rosh with unblinking eyes until she finally said, "Of course."

"I will need gold for the fresh mounts."

The priestess handed the sergeant a small pouch. Rosh turned away and, pulling the horses by their reins, continued down the street past a sawmill. I looked around, and Syndia was leading Tayu toward a building. Ruuter and I followed. Since he was upwind, I felt obligated to mention, tactfully, his body-odor problem.

"Ruuter, my friend?"

"Yes, Master Korvas?"

"You stink."

"Thank you, Master Korvas."

He had a big proud grin on his face as Syndia and Tayu entered the inn. I had the feeling that I hadn't quite gotten through to the Omergunt when I looked up at the sign above the inn's door. There was a picture of a club. Its business end was spattered with red. Beneath the picture were the words THE BLOOD AND BLUDGEON.

Charming, I thought. Simply charming.

I followed Syndia through the door, and the atmosphere in the room was very close. It was a combination of loud noises and a smoky fireplace, with every inch of floor space being taken up by drunken teamsters, loggers, miners, or their mates of the moment. The innkeeper was a scrawny man with a long, sad face. Syndia spoke to him, crossed his palm with a bit of silver, and he ushered us all into a private room where the noise level was considerably diminished.

We sat down at the plank table, and soon plates of rolls, cheese, fruit, and meats arrived. Syndia took a roll and a small piece of cheese, Tayu took a single apple, Ruuter opened a pouch at his belt and withdrew some nuts that he put on his plate. With all of this disgusting moderation about me, I hardly knew what limits I should place or where to place them.

I was about to take a lot of everything when the god box next to my plate clouded my vision. The only things I could see clearly were a plum, a small piece of fowl, a single breadroll, and a piece of cheese.

"This is not enough," I whispered to the box.

"It is what you need," answered the box. *"Give me the rest of your hunger."*

I glanced at Syndia, and she was watching me. "Why do you watch me?"

"To see what you do."

I looked at the box. "I would not be a man if I allowed myself to be ruled by a piece of furniture."

"A god box does not rule, Korvas. It only suggests."

I laughed. "Yes, but if I do not follow the suggestion, what punishment will the box issue?"

"None. The box only suggests what you need to avoid calamity. If you ignore the suggestion, reality supplies the calamity, not the box."

I thought of the times I had stuffed myself until my ribs ached. There were the physical pains, of course. But more than that, there were sleepy feelings of discouragement, confusion, disgust. It was a feeling almost that something other than myself was doing the eating—as though, instead of me eating the food, the food was devouring me. That was the calamity.

I took the pieces of food indicated and put them on my plate. It didn't look like much. "What do I do if this isn't enough?"

Syndia smiled. "It's enough, but if you still feel hungry, give the hunger to the god box."

"That's what the god box told me to do."

"It's good advice. Only a fool has to hear the same good advice a second time."

I silently gave my hunger to the god box and took a bite of the cheese and bread and chewed them as I watched my companions feast. Syndia drank from a cup, and I checked to see what forbidden potion had been poured into mine. It was sweet water.

Ruuter was gnawing upon those black nuts of his, and I asked him, "Are you turning back now?"

He shook his head and grinned. "I go on with you to the land of the Omergunts."

He still smelled terrible. I took another bite of cheese and glared at Syndia. "Well?"

"Well what, Korvas?"

"What's really happening?"

A sly smile of pure mischief spread across her face. "You are becoming very philosophical. Armies of great thinkers have worked out their entire lives trying to answer that question."

"You know what I meant."

"Perhaps you could narrow down your inquiry just a trifle."

She was still making fun of me. I pointed at Tayu. "How can this be my twin brother?"

"You were born from the same womb on the same day. That makes you twins."

"I am bigger, older-looking. He looks nothing like me."

"You and Tayu have traveled different paths to get to this table, Korvas. The voyages have affected you differently. Accept that this is so and find peace. Was there something else?"

"The Dagas."

"Yes?"

"Were we there? Were we with them? Was there a storyteller—"

"There are many realities, Korvas. Yes, we were with them, and no, we weren't. There was and there wasn't a storyteller who spoke of the prophecy of the Hero and the Destroyer."

"Thank you for clearing up that matter."

"You're welcome."

"You are choosing to ignore my sarcasm."

"What do you want to know, Korvas?"

"Am I the mirror? The guide? Will Tayu find the hero who I will guide to war with Manku?"

"I thought that was very clear."

"I find this all quite improbable."

"Ah," she laughed, "doubting Ahtma."

"I am no such thing. I would not have to see the continent twice split. And how do you know—of course. You have strolled through my mind. That's how you know of the Ihtari and Ahtma."

"True, I have been through your memories, but I knew of Ihtari long before I met you, Korvas." She clasped her hands and placed them gently upon the edge of the table. "You have seen any number of miracles this day, yet you still doubt."

"I have seen no continent split."

"You have seen time turned back and changed. Given enough time and shovels, mere men could split a continent. Who but the gods could turn back time?"

"How did you know about that? I thought I was alone."

"I am here to witness miracles." Again she smiled that maddening smile of hers. "And none of us are ever alone."

I shook my head and pushed back from the table. "All of it can be explained away as magic, confusion, hallucination, naughty little powders."

"As I said, doubting Ahtma."

"It would be a different matter if these gods would make themselves clear. I would believe if they would show themselves and do things that were honest and useful."

"I see," said Syndia as she nodded her head, that sly smile still on her lips. "The only gods you will believe in, then, are gods that you can make do what you want them to do. Korvas, don't you see that you have things turned around just a little? The gods do what the gods themselves want to do, just as you do. If you are lucky, perhaps you might be allowed to do a little of what the gods want you to do."

I pushed my plate away and silently pondered the things Syndia had said. I had come to no conclusions when the door to the room opened and Rosh entered, a strangely cold look in his eyes. "We have fresh horses and they are being saddled and packed now." He reached out his hand and dropped the little leather pouch on the table in front of Syndia. "They were more than satisfied with the four horses in exchange for seven. However, I fear we will get our money's worth."

Syndia took the pouch and held it in her hand. "What of Commander Meru?"

"Nothing. The light from the sky is all gone, revealing the stars; so it has been over two hours."

Syndia nodded at the table. "As soon as you have eaten, we will be going."

Rosh sat down and reached for the cheese while I turned two curious things over in my mind. Rosh had as much as said that Meru, Icen, and Hara were dead or captured, yet it seemed to have no effect upon either him or Syndia. The other thing might have been a miracle. I had eaten only half of my food, and I was full.

13

We rode through the cold night, and before the frost elves began painting the early dawn sky, we reached a fork in the road. The road south led to the wayside town of Narvi on the King's Highway. The northern road led into the tall mountain country where lived the Serkers, the Tchakas, and the Omergunts. We rode north for a few miles. Before reaching the settlement of Abunih, we moved off of the road into the deep forest to rest. Rosh and Ruuter backtracked to cover our trail.

I stood next to my horse, observing his breath and mine, rubbing my arms trying to get warm. Syndia walked by me carrying a bundle. "You'd best try and get some rest. You'll need it."

"Why are we traveling during the night and stopping by day?"

"It's too cold to stop at night."

I snorted in disgust. "It's too cold right now."

"It will warm up soon."

"Why didn't we stop in that settlement ahead? At least it's civilized."

"The only thing civilized about Abunih is that a number of the residents think money is something for which it is worth killing and dying." She took a new hold on her bundle. "We won't be stopping there. Get some rest."

There was only a little fire, but I cuddled as close as I could to it without giving Heteris her revenge by setting myself aflame. Syndia was across the fire from me and

Tayu was on my left. For some perverse reason, this night Tayu didn't want to sleep on my arm. I looked at Syndia, and she pulled up her blanket and rolled over. I looked at Rosh, and he pulled up his blanket and closed his eyes. Once he got off guard I suppose the Omergunt, Ruuter, might be more hospitable, but that would be when I pulled up my blanket and rolled over.

I had never been more tired, but I couldn't sleep. I stared into the flames, thinking about the Oracle of Heteris.

Guided by the Mirror of the Second, the Hero will be found by the Second, who will be chosen by a father's hand, kept by the First, loved by the Mirror, and burned by the Mirror to be gathered by the Smoke.

I had never had any more trust in meanings of words than I had in horses. If I was the Mirror of Tayu, then I would guide the hero. But what does "guide" mean to gods who seem forever unable to express themselves with precision? The only places I knew really well, and hence the only places in which I felt competent to pose as a guide, were some of the sleazier back streets and alleys of Iskandar. Unless the battle with Manku was going to be in a less fashionable neighborhood of Iskandar, I couldn't see what use I would be as a guide.

I rolled over on my right shoulder and faced the god box. Its honey-and-burnt-sugar finish glowed warmly. I pulled one of the drawers completely out of the case and examined the construction. It was well made, but nothing special. A strange spider-shaped symbol had been stamped on the bottom of the drawer, along with a name: Capys of Port Vuba.

No god had made this. Instead, some cabinetmaker in distant Port Vuba on the west coast of the Empire of Ziven had fashioned it. I lifted the box and was about to replace the drawer when I peered through the opening. For a brief moment I caught sight of Rosh through the opening and was swept away by a flood of strange feelings. Once I had achieved some kind of balance, I again looked through the opening at the sergeant—

I saw his life pass before me. As a child he entered himself into the Nant Temple for instruction with every intention of finishing his education, entering the Nant Guard, and going on to take his vows, becoming a priest.

Shortly after his eighteenth birthday he paused upon the steps of the Nant Temple to watch the changing of the Heterin Guard in front of their temple on the opposite side of the square.

There was a crowd that day, but it was not for the purpose of seeing the sights. The Heterin Guard was decked out in golden robes and polished halberds, for the bloody horror Tretia, First Priestess, was to personally conduct the changing of the guard from a specially constructed platform before the square's massive water fountain. This was the Hrontine, a special holiday in honor of the deity Hrontii, the asexual creature admired by the Heterins. It was rumored that even the king would attend the ceremony.

The square was packed. Most citizens were there to participate in the service that would be offered by the first priestess prior to the actual change of the guard. Many were there to witness the grand spectacle. A few were there to make trouble.

The priestess Tretia had no sooner taken her position on the platform than catcalls and hoots began coming from different places within the crowd. Several of those doing the heckling were quickly pounded to the pavement by the fists of the faithful, but others had time to launch rocks and bricks at her divine magnificence. The full Heterin Guard was turned out and they began indiscriminately to hack through the crowd.

Young Rosh's first instinct was to flee to the safety of the Nant Temple, but an elderly woman had been knocked down and a man was struggling to help her to her feet. In the panic and confusion, she was being trampled and kicked to death. Rosh bullied his way to her and, with the help of the older man, they had almost gotten her to her feet when a guard swung a ceremonial halberd at them, catching the old woman in the neck and killing her. The older man exploded in rage, drew his knife, and flew at the guard. Just in time the guard managed to draw his pistol and blow a hole in the man's chest.

In a rage of his own, Rosh saw the guard fall backward from the force of the man's momentum. The lad rushed over, picked up the man's knife, and plunged it through the guard's left temple. For a moment everything became still as what he had done announced itself. Then the lad sprang to his feet and ran.

First he fled to the Mystic Mountains. He lived for awhile among the bloodthirsty Tchakas, then he traveled throughout the mountains, ending eventually in the huge city of Port Vey, five hundred miles northeast of Kienosos.

In Vey he signed on a ship and spent the next eleven years in one navy or army after another. Then at the age of twenty-nine he stepped off of a ship in the port of Iskandar and returned to the Nant Temple. After much consideration, the clergy of the temple decided to take Rosh into the Nant Guard. There he served with quiet distinction until the present, burdened by the knowledge that he could never take his vows and become a priest.

A priest must be rigorously honest, and Rosh could not afford honesty. Killing the Heterin guard on that holiday so long before was one of the things he neglected to tell the temple priests when they were considering his entrance to the guard.

I lowered the god box and replaced the drawer as I leaned back my head and listened to the gentle wind. I would not turn him in, I knew, for I remembered that Hrontine so many years ago. When the thing was over, they said a thousand heads were piked around the circle surrounding the temples and the king's palace. That was where I found my father's head. He had been the older man whose knife Rosh had used to kill the Heterin guard.

Between Rosh, myself, the late priestess Ahjrah, and my alleged twin Tayu, separately and together, we had quite a score to settle with first priests and priestesses of the Heterin faith. I withdrew the drawer again and looked at Tayu. He was indeed my twin brother. Under the care and guidance of Ahjrah, upon his seventh birthday he was shown the scriptures and the prophecy. She also told him that he was the Second of the prophecy. He was asked and Tayu willingly submitted to what had to be done.

Employing spells drawn from the combined Books of Fayn, Tayu was placed into the deepest of deep sleeps and his form was reduced to the size of a pea. Ahjrah then placed my brother into a golden locket where he continued to sleep and where it was always his seventh birthday. He had been made whole again for this mission into the Mystic. Once he had chosen me for his new guardian, the old priestess could finally let go, and she died.

I looked through the opening at Syndia, and I could see no one there. I tried several times, and checked with my own eyes that her sleeping form was across the fire from me. But when I looked through the special window of my god box, there was no one there.

I replaced the drawer and pondered. I didn't know how I felt about much of anything, except that outrageous coincidence seemed to be dogging my heels. A drawer in the god box opened and I looked in to find a slip of paper. It said: *"There are no coincidences."* As I tried to sleep, I found the thought both comforting and troubling.

14

By early afternoon we were rested and there had been no sight of Captain Shadows. We ate, packed up, and headed north through Abunih. As our tiny caravan moved through the main street and only road, I watched the locals. There were enough toughs, thieves, and killers to man half the ocean of Ilan's entire pirate fleet. Here and there would be an exile clad in rags of shame, and there were renegade Dagas, an outcast Serker, and outcasts from other tribes I didn't recognize.

Sidewalk hawkers and street urchins filled the air with lies, while a heavy smell of incense was everywhere. At the north edge of town was a pass, and next to the road was a shrine which turned out to be the source of the incense.

An ancient man in a ragged blue robe knelt before the shrine and added an orange stick to the fire that smoldered deep within the stone-and-mortar monument. As she came abreast of the shrine, Syndia turned in her saddle and called to the rest of us, "We stop here."

We pulled up our horses and dismounted, and the man in the blue robe stood and walked toward us. Syndia handed him her reins and a coin and headed for the shrine. As he gathered the reins from the others, I removed a drawer from the god box and looked at the man in the blue robe. Almost immediately I jerked back my head and replaced the drawer. He was a priest of the Mankua faith! But he couldn't be. All of the Mankuas had been killed when the temple was destroyed, or so went the story. I caught only a glimpse of his life, but he had been arrested and tortured by Pherris, the previous First Priest of the Heterin faith, the same fiend who had executed Ahjrah's father.

A sudden thought crossed my mind about the murder of Ahjrah's mother while she was still pregnant with Ahjrah. I could only guess at the spells and black forces that must have been used to keep her breathing until Ahjrah, called the First, had been born. If mother and child had died, then the prophecy could not be filled and the Destroyer would make the world and all existence as dust. Bald mythology or not, it certainly must have given some believer an interest in seeing that Ahjrah never breathed her first breath. Pherris again? Likely.

I handed the old man my reins and tried to read his cloudy eyes. "Greetings to you, brother."

"All of my brothers are dead, stranger."

"Sorry. I didn't mean to dilute your resentment." I held out my hand toward his garb. "I thought this might be the robe of a Mañkua priest. I haven't seen one since I was a child."

"The Mankua temple is destroyed, the Mankua faith is gone, the Mankua priests and their followers are all dead."

"You look remarkably fit for a dead man." He seemed to stare at me with blank eyes, which is when I realized that he was blind. "I am Korvas, recently of Iskandar. What is your name?"

The old man dropped all of the reins he was holding. The horses started, but he snapped his fingers and the horses immediately calmed and gathered next to him. He placed his gnarled hands upon my cheeks and pulled my face close to his. His hands were very strong. "So," he said, then he released me.

"So?"

"You who call yourself Korvas, are the Guide." He grabbed my arm with his wiry claw of a right hand. "Is the Warrior here? Will the battle take place here?"

"No. We haven't tracked down any Hero yet—"

"Then the Child is with you?" He faced toward the shrine, still holding onto my arm. "Is he here?"

"Do you mean the Second?"

"Yes, yes."

I pulled the man's hand from my arm. "I suppose so." There were tears in the old man's eyes.

"It will come! I will be here, and it will come!"

I looked past the old man's shoulder at the shrine. "To whom is this shrine dedicated, old fellow?"

"Sabis."

"Who is Sabis?"

"I am. That is my name." The old man's face grinned, displaying the stumps of the few teeth that remained in his mouth. "The shrine is dedicated to Manku, the Destroyer."

I looked up and saw Syndia, Rosh, and Tayu praying at the shrine while Ruuter looked on. Why would they be praying to the Destroyer? I pulled a drawer from the god box and looked through the opening at the three praying at the Shrine. Syndia was still not there. Rosh and Tayu were committing themselves to whatever the results of the contest might be. Lifting the box a bit, I looked at the shrine itself.

There seemed to be endless rows of teeth, serpent coils, slime, ooze, blood, fire, and storm. Beneath it all, filling the underworld, I saw ancient instruments, scrolls, and endless shelves and piles of volumes. Then I saw a face above a vast field of skeletons. The face was strong, but it possessed compassion, which was more than I could say for the Mankua priest Sabis, the keeper of Manku's shrine. Sabis carried more hate within him than I thought was possible. It gave me a strange feeling to know this, and to know the degree of pain it caused the old man.

With the god box in my hands, I asked it what Sabis needed. *"What Sabis needs,"* answered the box, *"is to ask for himself."* I supposed that the box had just told me to mind my own business.

Once on the other side of the pass, we came to where the road forked again. North would take us to the land of the green-painted Serkers, whose warriors, it was rumored, rode upon the backs of giant lizards. We took the east fork toward the Omergunts.

Late in the evening, after stopping to eat and rest the horses, I asked Syndia what the box meant about Sabis needing to ask for himself.

"It could mean nothing more than what the Mankua priest needs is to admit that he needs help. Until he admits that, his hatred will either sustain or consume him."

"It doesn't seem fair, Syndia. After all, enormous wrongs were committed against him. His teeth were broken out with a club, burning pitch was dripped on his back—terrible things."

"True. And it seems that for the past eighteen years Sabis has been completing the work started by the Heterin priests. No one can bring quite the same degree of subtle pain to the task of torturing another as one can to one's self-torture."

"How do you mean?"

Syndia put her plate aside and looked at me. "No torturer in the world can keep a man in wretched agony from one sunrise to the next for more than a few months. A year, at most. It is a matter of stamina, both of the victim and of the torturer. The person who tortures himself, however, can keep the agony alive for a lifetime. For example, the hate you have for your father."

"Hate?"

"Yes, hate. You grew up believing your father allowed your brother to die. Now you know differently. Yet you cannot let go of the hate even though you do not enjoy it. Why is it, do you suppose?"

"Are you working your way around to saying that I need the same thing as Sabis? I need my hate?"

"Possibly." She smiled. "After all, I am only guessing. You are the one with the god box."

"How do you let go of hate?"

"Forgiveness."

Rosh almost gagged on his food, he was so angry.

After coughing, he faced Syndia. "Why should I forgive my enemies? Why should I do that for them?"

Syndia stood up and brushed off her robe. "Forgiveness isn't something you do for someone else's benefit, Sergeant Rosh. It's something you do for yourself. Hate can eat you alive, as you well know."

The Nant priestess walked toward the horses, and we all prepared to ride. As Rosh ate he stared at the fire, his eyes very intense. I was about to pack up my own horse when the sergeant looked at me and said, "Korvas?"

"Yes?"

"Give me what I need from your box."

I opened a drawer, and inside was a piece of paper with many folds. It seemed obvious to me that only Rosh was supposed to read it. I handed it to the sergeant; he opened it, read it, and said nothing.

That night, as we rode higher into the mountains, it snowed.

15

I half slept in my saddle as the horses felt their way through the blizzard. I could see little from deep within my saddle robe. At best I would catch a glimpse of Tayu on his horse in front of me against a snow-covered hill or rock, but then he would be lost in a dark swirl of flakes. There was little to do but try to keep warm and awake. I began having horrible nightmares of falling from my horse asleep and freezing to death before anyone discovered I was missing.

On one such venture into dreamland, I awakened to find myself buried in snow. I dug my way out and stood on the road, the snow so deep that it was almost to my knees. The road was empty and I called out to the others time and time again, but I was left with nothing but echoes muffled by the snow. The road was unfamiliar to me, and I could not make up my mind which way was east and which way was west. I looked to consult my god box, but I remembered that it was tied to my saddle.

My heart was nearly bursting with panic, and I picked a direction out of desperation and ran through the snow, calling for Syndia. I fell, and as I pulled my face from the snow, I opened my eyes to a great light. It was so bright it made the night day. I was suddenly very hot, and the snow melted and the water vaporized. Soon the trees and brush were aflame, then there was nothing but the parched surface of the road.

I fell to my knees, held out my hands, and addressed

the center of the light, saying, "Great Lord, who are you?"

"I am Manku," came an answer that rocked the mountains. "I am the Destroyer. Do you bring me the one who would stand against me?"

My god box was gone, but I was in such desperate fear, I opened a pocket of my robe. "God of this pocket, please grant me what I need—"

"Korvas!"

There was a rough arm shaking my shoulder. I looked and it was Sergeant Rosh, both of us riding through a blizzard. "What?"

"You were asleep."

"Sorry."

"Don't fall asleep again. I cannot watch you all of the time."

"I said I was sorry. It won't happen again."

As Rosh fell back, I noticed that my heart was still pounding from the terrible fear of my dream. I reached down and assured myself that the god box was still tied to my saddle. Not finding that comfort enough, I took the tie-down strap and slung it over my head and shoulder, allowing the god box to hang at my waist. I pulled my saddle robe around me and tried to quiet my heart.

In a few moments we turned north and followed a much narrower road—little more than a trail that snaked higher and higher until at every turn we risked falling to our deaths. The wind shrieked through the rocks and crags, and all I could hang onto was the god box as it told me that everything has an end. I didn't pry into the possibility of my end preceding the snowstorm's, for the answer might be somewhat less than agreeable.

The storm deepened and soon it was no darker with my eyes closed than open, and a great deal less painful. I covered my face with my saddle robe and sighed as feeling came back to my nose. I jogged back and forth in my saddle like this for an immeasurable time until I was jerked out of my half-slumber by a voice.

"Look! Look up there!"

I pulled the robe from my face and saw that the gray

light of dawn had chased away the shadows. It was still snowing, but not as heavily. I lifted my head, and a bright light came to my eyes. High above us was a brilliant reddish yellow glare from a towering wall of white and blue ice.

Our progress on the trail seemed to inch up toward the light, but soon our horses were next to the ice wall, the light high above us shining on the top. The wall formed part of a narrow pass that wound between two very tall peaks. We were still in the shade, but the sky was becoming pink and it gave me hope.

We eventually reached a place in the pass where a huge slab of black rock was perched high upon a pillar of ice, making it look like a giant mushroom. Our guide, Ruuter, dismounted and stood before the ice-pillar, immediately beneath the greatest overhang of that slab. He seemed to take things from his pockets and throw them at the base of the pillar, which must have been a shrine. I picked up the god box, withdrew a drawer, and took a peek.

Ruuter's deity appeared to be a mother-goddess of great kindness and compassion named Ebell. When he had last come this way, Ruuter had asked for the privilege of returning. He was now thanking her. The face of this mother-goddess for some reason bore a striking resemblance to Manku the Destroyer. I replaced the drawer in the god box and waited with the others for Ruuter to finish.

Moments after we had resumed our travel, we rounded a turn in the ice canyon, and the scene that opened before me took away my breath. Far below us, the sunlight just touching it, was a wide valley of the richest green. Winding through its center was a large blue river with tiny fishing boats visible on its surface. The floor of the valley was divided up into crops of various kinds. Higher on the gentle slopes of the foothills were waterfalls and row after row of terraces planted with all sorts of flowering plants.

As much as I disliked horses, I patted mine on its neck and, with the same sincerity that Ruuter thanked his mother-goddess, whispered my thanks to my horse. We had made it out of the ice.

With each mile down I removed another layer of clothing until we reached a misty place near the valley floor. Ruuter led us more deeply into the mists until all about me I saw steaming pools of bubbling water, hissing steam vents, and the sounds of mud pools glopping.

Ruuter stopped next to a very large pool of steaming water and began undressing as we dismounted. Before I had managed to figure out what he was doing, he jumped into the water.

"A hot bath! Another miracle," I cried as I began shucking my own togs, which were rather ripe. I fell into the water and let it close over my head as the smell of sulphur filled my nose. I scrubbed and sighed like a spent lover as I felt the icy hand of the mountain chill release my bones.

My head broke the surface, and I pushed the wet hair out of my eyes and called to Ruuter, "Will we be here long enough to wash and dry our clothes?"

"Yes. There be hot stones for drying clothes. It takes very little time." He pointed at the water. "The smell, does it offend you?"

"No, but . . ." As much as it distressed me to believe it, Ruuter still stank. "By Angh's bum, Ruuter, you still have quite an aroma."

"Thank you very much." He grinned and went back to his bathing. I heard a splash to my left and saw Syndia bobbing up in the water while Rosh stood guard. Out of her robe she looked like a young girl of voluptuous persuasions. It nearly broke my heart when we climbed out of the pool to dry our clothes on the hot rocks and our bodies in the sun. I could not look at her.

It was like a bottle of water to a man dying of thirst. If he couldn't have it, better he shouldn't see it. Still, my imagination combined with a mental committee of demons and angels to urge me to do everything from enjoy the sunshine to rape half the countryside. It was exhausting.

"Korvas?"

"What!?" I turned to see Sergeant Rosh.

"Will you stand guard while I bathe?"

"I'd be pleased to!" I put on my half-dry clothing and decrepitating boots, slung my god box, and aimed my feet for the trail. While I stormed into position, my mind was ripped by an additional anger—that special anger of mine called fear. How was I supposed to aid in some great heroic challenge when I couldn't even wrestle my appetites to the ground? Obviously I needed something. I held out the god box and said, rather loudly, "Then what do I need?"

The box said nothing, but I heard happy giggling and splashing coming from behind some huge boulders. I followed the path around and found three naked maidens with raven hair splashing in a hot-water pond. One of them saw me and she stood and motioned for me to join them. I patted my god box, for it truly had known what I needed. The gods were, indeed, above us. If Ahtma the Doubter had only asked for this miracle, he would have become a believer for life. The water nymph's two friends stood and waved at me as they giggled. It was enough to make one grateful to be a mammal.

"Come," one of the maidens said, "come play with us."

As my eyes feasted, my tongue was tied into a knot, my mind mired in confusion. Ahead of us lay the Destroyer and behind us, Captain Shadows. In between were who knew how many dangers? The situation—

What I was trying to remember was that I was on guard. My comrades depended upon me to send up the alarm if danger approached. Feeling just a little jellied in the kneecaps, I made my decision and turned away from the maidens. When I glanced back for just one more visual taste, the three maidens, and their pool of steaming water, were gone.

"Eh?" I walked back and examined the area. There was nothing there but rocks. I scratched my head and picked up the god box. "Perhaps you are having fun at my expense? I asked you for what I needed. What did I get?"

"*A test,*" answered the box.

"Who tests me?"

"You do."

That was when I concluded that the principal symptom of godhood is smugness. I took my place at the entrance to the hot springs and examined the trail. It was deserted. I sat on a rock, bent over, and looked at my reflection in a puddle. As I examined that lying, lecherous countenance, it became clear to me why I found preposterous the proposition that I was the Guide of the ancient prophecy. The Guide must do the work of the gods, and I did not feel worthy to do divine work.

Part of me argued that I had chosen to stand guard rather than leap into the middle of that press of pulchritude. I must be at least a little responsible. I shook my head in disgust. What is one little profit against my wealth of losses? To do the work of gods, one must be considerably closer to sainthood than was I.

A strange idea found its way into my awareness, and I took a drawer out of the god box, held it over the puddle, and looked at myself through the opening.

What I saw was not a judgment upon myself, but an image of my greatest fear. Shadows and his men, their red uniforms like spots of blood against the snow, were coming to the mountain road branch that would bring them to the Pass of Ebell. In another ten hours they would be at the hot springs.

"Shadows," I called to the image.

The captain pulled up his huge black horse and looked to the left, right, behind, and above, his breath steaming in the cold. "Damn your tongue! Come out where I can see you! No more tricks, Bachudowah!"

He thought my voice in his head belonged to the Dagas storyteller. "I am not Bachudowah, Captain. My name is Korvas."

An entirely different look came over Shadows's face. It was something sly, wicked. "Yes? What do you want? I was not told you were a magician."

"Captain, why do you chase me?"

He withdrew a black and silver sword from its scabbard and brandished the point in the air. "To bring your head back on this."

"Why? What have I done?"

I took another drawer out of the box and saw more of Shadows. I saw inside, the way he thought of himself. He was on a mission for the gods, to slay me and Tayu for the preservation of the Heterin faith. I removed another drawer and saw even more: his hates, loves, fears, his entire life, as though he were standing before me. I removed the fourth drawer and again saw a face that had a resemblance to Manku the Destroyer.

I sat up and replaced the drawers, my heart fairly sick with fear. What if Shadows, instead of I, was doing the work of the gods? If so, what was I doing?

"Korvas!" It was Ruuter's voice. I turned and looked back at him. He cupped his hands around his mouth and hollered, "Come! We must find butnuts."

"Butnuts?"

16

We followed a stream that formed from the hot springs down to where the trail came to a bridge. The bridge crossed the river that we had seen from the Pass of Ebell. Ruuter informed us that the river was named the Great Serpent. There we saw our first natives.

There were two boys, one a head taller than the other, and they were fishing from the bridge. The shorter of the two looked our way and dropped his fishing pole, he was so excited. He ran to Ruuter's side, while the taller of the two shouted and ran across the wooden bridge to spread the news.

"Hoo!"

"Hoo, Tolly. Where be Coul?"

"Coul be at his grove, Ruuter. Good see you."

"Good see you, Tolly. Want present?"

"Hoo, Ruuter!"

Ruuter reached into his saddlebag and tossed a bright orange ball at the boy. He turned back to tell us, "My sister Marana's boy, Tolly. He's a fine boy. He missed me a lot." He pointed across the bridge. "Coul's butnut grove be on the other side."

He led the way, and before we were a third of the way across, a crowd of perhaps ten or fifteen Omergunts came running across the bridge to meet us. Great Ehbot, the stench! It was like wearing a mask made from a dung-layer's old stockings. In fact it was worse than that. In other societies I might have appeared rude, but the greener

I got and the more vocal I became, the more complimented were the natives.

"You stink!"

"Thank you."

Impossible. After a few minutes of this aromatic horror, we managed to struggle to the northern bank of the river. We stopped at a hut next to a grove of very tall trees. A very sad-looking man was standing in front of the hut. Ruuter called to him, "Hoo, Coul! Outsiders here need butnuts."

"When?"

Ruuter looked at Syndia, but the priestess shook her head and looked back at me. "It can't take too long," I gasped. "Aside from our breathing problems, the good captain is about ten hours behind us."

Ruuter faced Coul. "We need them very soon."

"Ruuter," I called. "Why can't we simply dispense with the nuts and gallop somewhere else in one big hurry-hurry?"

Ruuter laughed and pointed back at me with his thumb. "Outsider."

Coul nodded, but never cracked a smile. "It be a long time 'til dry season, Ruuter. Extra work."

Ruuter handed the sad-looking man an entire reel, and I would have protested if I wouldn't have had to inhale to feed my words. Half of the tribe must have been gathered around by then, and I was near to passing out from the stench. It did me just a little good to see that Syndia and Rosh weren't faring any better. The only ones who didn't seem bothered by the bone-cracking aroma were Ruuter and Tayu.

I couldn't hold my breath any longer and I rode up next to Ruuter and grabbed him by the collar. "We've got to go. Got to get out of here!"

Ruuter reached into a pocket and pulled out something. "Eat these."

"Food? Are you insane? I'm not hungry, you walking dung heap! With this foul odor, I can hardly keep down my sawdust loaf!"

"Butnuts," he offered. "For the smell."

"What?" I looked into his hand and saw several crescent-shaped black nuts. I took one and ate it. As I did so, the smell decreased about fifty percent. "Amazing!"

I took another while Ruuter passed them around to Rosh and Syndia. The smell wasn't gone, exactly, but it was as if it was coming through a set of nostrils that approved. Even more than the smell, was the taste. The more I ate, the more I craved. "Ruuter, these are terrific. I see why we need them. Let me have another."

"They be gone, Korvas. That's why Coul must cry for us."

I looked, and approximately two hundred Omergunts were in the grove seated in a circle with one of the tall trees in the center. Our party sat in the circle with the natives while Coul approached the tree and the surrounding voices fell silent.

"Is he going to climb all of the way up there and get the nuts?" I asked Ruuter.

"No. The trees are too tall, the bark too slick. He must cry them down."

The one called Coul wrapped his arms about the tree and let loose with a wail that made my toes sweat. "Oh, great tree, hear me," he cried. "I be alone, for my wife left me for another. She took my belongings and all of my money." He wailed some more. "She took my three children." Two objects fell from the branches a hundred feet up. Coul wailed as they struck the ground and burst open. They were filled with the black nuts. I began to get up to retrieve them, but Ruuter motioned me down.

"We cannot risk any happiness near the tree."

"Great tree," Coul cried, "before she left, she killed my dog!" The grove keeper pounded on the tree's trunk as several more pods fell from the branches and struck the ground.

"You see," said Ruuter, "all plants have spirits, and the spirit of the mother tree constantly looks how happy the spirits beneath it be so its seedlings can be fed when food be scarce. When the seedlings do not eat enough they feel bad. The mother tree feels the sadness and drops the food."

Coul was lying at the base of the tree, kicking his feet and pounding the roots of the tree with his fist. "She placed a poison snake in my bed, gave my hut to her mother, and asked to borrow money from *my* mother for a new hut for herself! And my mother gave her the money!" There was a wail from the entire circle of onlookers. Several other trees in the area were dropping pods as well. "My mother gave her the money out of what she was holding for me!" An even greater wail arose from the circle. The pods fairly rained on us as Coul screamed, "Why me!?"

Later, as our party walked our horses through the village toward the chief's compound, I munched upon the tasty little nuts and said to Ruuter, "That is quite an act your friend Coul performs."

"Oh, that be no act. If he only pretended, the trees wouldn't be fooled. Coul be a very sad man."

"Why doesn't he do something about it besides wallow in self-pity? Why doesn't he get a new wife, build a new hut, have more children, get another dog? At a reel per performance he can certainly afford it."

"If he did, he would no longer be sad, and that would be the end of his living."

"Ruuter, if I asked my god box what Coul needed, what would it say?"

"It would say Coul really needs a first-rate calamity for and put the edge back on his misery. His harvest performance today be pitiful, and I apologize for him."

"No need." I ate another nut and inhaled, and the startling thing was that I could smell everything else, the flowers, the dust, the sweaty horses. I just couldn't smell the people. "Ruuter, it's incredible how these nuts make it impossible to smell those horrid odors you people give off."

"It works out especially well," answered our guide, "when you consider that eating those nuts causes the smell you find so repulsive."

I stopped dead in the road. "I stink?"

"Please do not brag," said Ruuter as he pulled his mount ahead. "It be very rude."

17

After we entered Oghar the Valiant's lodge, the air was so thick with incense that my nose ran and my eyes burned. Syndia stood before our band and began to address the chief of the Omergunts. He held out a hand and commanded, "Silence!" Syndia stepped back and glanced at Ruuter, whose only answer was an enigmatic smile.

Oghar was a very old man, clad in skins and wearing a crown made of human bones. The face of the skull set into the front of the crown had rubies for eyes. His wooden throne was on a raised platform surrounded by many fierce-looking weapons, and his several attendants were standing about him, sneezing, blowing their noses, and rubbing their eyes. The ones near the hut's walls would, when Oghar wasn't looking, stick their heads through holes in the walls and take a quick breath of fresh air.

Oghar turned to an attendant and barked, "Get Kosi in here!"

The attendant faced the chief, fell prostrate to the floor, said, "Your command, Great Oghar," and leaped up and ran from the hut.

"Great Chief," began Syndia, "we have come—"

"Wait for Kosi," Oghar interrupted.

An older, heavier man streaked into the lodge and skidded to a halt on his face in front of his chief. "You asked for me, Great Chief?"

"Scum," Oghar answered. "Filth! Dog! Sewage! Garbage! Bottom wipings!"

The one called Kosi appeared to be in bad odor. He held out his hands, his face still on the floor. "Great Oghar, how may I make amends for my horrible wrongs?"

"Once you are out of my sight, Kosi, deal with these outsiders!" Oghar pointed at us. "Do not fail me again, Kosi!"

Kosi somehow managed to scrabble out of the hut on his face, pausing only once to say to Syndia, "Follow me or die."

Once outside, Kosi was on his feet and filled with anger. "Where be that devil Olassar and his evil box?"

Syndia held out her hand toward me. "Our friend Korvas is the heir to Olassar's business."

Kosi glanced at the god box slung at my waist. "There it be! There be the wicked thing!" He lifted his glance until he was looking at my face. The look in his own face was something wild.

"I take it you were less than pleased with my predecessor's performance."

Kosi spat on the ground. "I stood next to the throne as Oghar's first advisor and general of his army. I had wealth, and the respect of my chief. All of this before Olassar and his cursed box came into the valley. Now there be no more army, my chief be ashamed of his people, and he blames me!"

Ruuter spat in disgust and pointed south toward the butnut groves. "Are you after Coul's position?"

"Talk clear, Ruuter!"

The guide shook his head. "If you want and cry butnuts off trees, then act like this. If you want answers, ask for them."

"Ask?"

"Yes, ask."

"You mean that thing?" Kosi pointed at the god box. His glower deepened a few dozen degrees as he aimed it in my direction. "My current dilemma be the result of the most recent time that box helped the Omergunts. I would sooner crawl into bed with a hundred pit vipers."

"That's odd," I answered as the heat came to my face. "I didn't know your mother was still in business."

In a flash Kosi had a fighting knife at the ready, I had mine out, and Syndia stepped between us. "Gentlemen, there are no solutions to be found along the current path."

Kosi shook his knife in my direction. "He will apologize about my mother!"

Syndia looked at me. "Korvas?"

"Very well."

"Very well, what?" demanded Kosi.

"I spoke in haste, Kosi. I apologize."

Kosi slowly returned his knife to its sheath. He took a deep breath, looked into the distance, and said, "Years ago Olassar came here carrying that box. Before he came we be a proud warrior people feared throughout the Mystic." Kosi folded his arms. "Our gentle king—not I—sought an end to our wars with the Dagas, Tchakas, and Serkers. No sooner had he uttered those words to me and prayed to his god, than children brought the news of a stranger in the valley. It be Olassar. My chief commanded Olassar's presence in the lodge, and the old fraud appeared with his box and explained its use. If the chief and his people *needed* an end to war, the box would find a way."

"You have no army," I said. "Your valley seems prosperous and at peace. Obviously Olassar and this box ended your wars for you."

"All too well." Kosi was silent for a long time, then he sadly shook his head. "The box said for all of us to eat the fruit of the butnut tree, and it explained how the nuts could be obtained and groves planted. We planted them, cried them off the trees, ate them, and we began to stink. Soon attacking us no one wanted, and the Omergunts became a laughingstock. Because of the smell, everyone thinks we are a stupid and dirty people. You've heard the jokes, haven't you? Why are the beaches of the Ocean of Ilan black? Because an Omergunt swam there and left a ring."

"No," I gasped, "never heard that one. Sorry."

Syndia gently pushed me aside as she spoke to Kosi. "Oghar got what he wanted, didn't he?"

"Priestess, he didn't want his tribe a laughingstock!"

"Pardon me," I interrupted, "but why does Oghar keep his lodge so heavily smoked with incense? I could hardly breathe in there."

"As an example for others," Kosi answered, "my chief has sworn off eating butnuts. However, no one will take the example. As a whole the people be satisfied with not having any wars or supporting an army. Hence, Oghar needs another way of countering the smell."

"Why doesn't he simply order his people to stop eating the butnuts, and execute those who will not comply?"

"Oghar be, after all, our gentle king."

I looked at Ruuter. "I can understand eating the nuts here in the valley, but why do you eat them outside the valley?"

The man smiled. "In none of the wayside towns, not even in Iskandar itself, have I ever been robbed. When I shop in the bazaar, I never fight crowds, and the merchants wait on me with dispatch. When I haggle over a price, the merchant's resolve melts."

"Don't you care what people must think of you?"

He shook his head. "Never."

"Outrageous," I said in admiration as I turned back to face Kosi. "What about you? Do you still eat the nuts?"

"Do I look like a fool? Of course I eat them. If I didn't I'd die in this valley."

Syndia looked toward the lodge. "Does he want his wars back?"

"No, but he wants his people be feared again."

Ah, yes, I thought as I looked at the god box. That's what he *wants*. But what does he *need*?

18

Oghar the Valiant's face glowered with every bit of the intensity of the skull on his crown. He gestured with his left hand. "Kosi says he has dealt with you. What does your evil contraption suggest I need?"

"Nuts."

The chief's glower deepened into absolute menace. "Make yourself clear, stranger."

"Eat the nuts." I held out the slip of paper that I had gotten from the god box. "I asked it what you needed, and it said 'Nuts.' " I felt something nudging the inside of my right arm. I looked down, and one of the box's drawers was opening and closing again and again. I bowed toward the chief. "Forgive me, Oghar." I picked up the box and looked into the open drawer.

"It seems there was a second part to the message. Before getting to it, however, the box suggests that you eat the nuts and air out your lodge."

The chief stood and pointed a finger down at me. "This better work, Korvas. I know I have a reputation for being gentle, but it probably wouldn't violate my nature having you tied in the village market on public display—*without any butnuts*!"

While I contemplated that grisly fate, the chief ate some of the nuts and the attendants extinguished the incense burners and opened the lodge's doors. When the smoke had cleared, I bowed toward the chief and said,

"Witness, Great Oghar, that the god box has already been like a breath of fresh air."

"Get on with it. Show me how you change a world's opinion about my people."

"As I interpret the messages, Great Oghar, it is not the world's opinion that *needs* to be changed. The world is happy believing the way it believes, and so are your people, with the possible exceptions of Kosi and your butnut harvesters. The butnut harvesters are happy not being happy, for that is their living. This leaves only you and Kosi."

"You say that *I* be the one who needs changing?"

"You and Kosi, Great Chief."

"I see a binding post in the village market with your name on it, Korvas." Oghar folded his arms. "Very well, how do you propose changing me?"

"I cannot change you, Oghar. Only a great chief may change a great chief."

"Which means what, Korvas? Make yourself clear; you be gibbering after the manner of an oracle."

That was true enough. "I think it simply means that only you can change you, Oghar." I moistened my lips, for I was not terribly certain that what the box had suggested would really work. I looked at Kosi. "The chief will need to write."

"Paper and charcoal," he shouted at one of the attendants. In a blur the attendant secured the items, skidded to a halt on his knees before the throne and held up the pen and paper. The chief took them, placed the paper on the wide armrest of this throne, and looked at me, his eyebrows raised.

"Put the shame you feel for yourself and your people on the paper."

"Eh?"

"Write it down, Great Chief. Write down all of the bad things you feel."

For a very long time there was the sound of the stick of charcoal scratching against the paper. The scratching ceased. "Very well."

I felt a little dizzy about the next part. "Put your injured false pride on the paper."

There was a silence, followed at last by the scratching of the charcoal. When the Chief had finished writing, he raised his head, looked at me, and asked, "Have you ever seen a blister raised beneath a toenail with a white-hot iron?"

"No. I don't think I ever have."

"Very painful. It be especially so when the process is repeated upon all of the nails of the toes and the fingers. You see, the blister raises fluid, but the nail prevents the blister from rising, creating a considerable amount of pressure."

"Fascinating."

Oghar held up his pen. "Next?"

I glanced at Ruuter, swallowed, and looked back at Oghar. "Put—put your desire to have the approval and respect of others on the . . . on the . . ."

"On the paper?"

I nodded and silently mouthed the word "Yes."

Oghar leaned back in his throne. "Korvas, I do not know what you thought you might accomplish by this exercise, but right now you be a tiny morsel—a crumb—on the dragon's lips."

"There is one thing more, Great Oghar."

"And that be?"

I turned to Kosi and whispered, "He needs a container."

"What kind of container?"

"Any kind! Just so it closes!"

Kosi motioned to a servant who was holding a small lidded bowl. He took the bowl, emptied the candied spiders it contained into the servant's hands, replaced the lid, and held it out toward me. I asked Kosi, "What god protects this house?"

"Yulus."

I handed my knife and the lid of the bowl to Kosi. "Scratch the name on the lid in your own script."

When Kosi was done he looked at me. "What now?"

I took my knife from him, handed him the bottom of the bowl and pointed at Oghar. "Give it to him."

Kosi groveled up to the throne, handed up the bowl, and groveled back to his place.

Oghar the Valiant held up the bowl. "What now, crumb?"

"Lift the lid, ask Yulus to take the things you have written on the paper, place the paper in the bowl, and replace the lid."

The chief did so. When he had replaced the lid, he looked at me and demanded, "Well?"

"Well, Great Chief . . . the shame, the false pride, and the other things?"

"What about them?"

"You should be relieved of them."

"I must admit, Korvas, you have just said the stupidest thing I have ever heard in my many years." The chief stood, pointed a finger at me—and then a curious expression came over his face. He lowered his pointing finger and sat back down on the throne. Oghar, at last, spoke. "It appears, Korvas, that they be gone."

There was a gasp of happy surprise from the servants and attendants in the lodge. The chief glanced at Kosi, his face darkened with anger, and he shouted, "More paper!"

A servant slid up to the throne with a new supply. The chief took it, scratched down some words on a piece of paper, folded it, and put it into the bowl. As he replaced the bowl's lid, he looked up for a moment, then returned his glance to Kosi. He smiled. "I placed my anger at you into the bowl, Kosi."

The chief came down from the raised platform and stood in front of Kosi, who by now was face down on the chief's carpet. He pulled Kosi to his feet and placed a friendly hand upon his shoulder. "My old friend, I be not angry at you, yet you still be not happy."

"I still be a general without an army, my chief."

Oghar faced me. "'Korvas, what does my first advisor need?"

"The same thing that you needed, Great Chief: a god box of his own."

"Excellent." He turned to a servant. "A god box for

Kosi." As the servant ran off, the chief resumed his place upon the throne. He nodded at Syndia. "I will hear your request now."

Syndia put her arm around Tayu's shoulders. "Great Oghar, we have come here in fulfillment of a prophecy. This one is the Second who will seek out and find the Hero who will fight with Manku the Destroyer."

The chief lifted his hand and pointed his finger as he remembered. "The prophecy of the Hero and the Destroyer?"

"Yes."

"A story for children." He shrugged and held out his hands. "Yet a Nant priestess would not lie." He studied Syndia for a long time. "You seem more than a mere priestess. Will you find the Hero in this valley?"

"Tayu, the Second, led us here. I believe he will find the Hero here."

Oghar looked around his throne room for a face displaying some enlightenment. Finding none, he said to Tayu, "There be no army for years. No training in warrior skills for as long. If you seek a hero among the Omergunts, perhaps you misunderstood the oracle. Oracles be easy for misunderstandings. It be their stock in trade." He glanced at Kosi and held out an impatient hand. "These visitors lifted the chief's anger from your back, wretch. Can you not help them?"

"I be uncertain, Great Chief. With permission, I must consider."

"Oghar," interrupted Syndia.

"Yes?"

"There is one thing more. We are being followed by a unit of the Heterin Guard under Captain Shadows. They will be at the Pass of Ebell in only a few hours."

The chief's expression did not change. "And?"

"I thought you might want to prepare."

"Prepare? Do the Heterin guards eat butnuts?"

"No, Great Chief."

Oghar dismissed the subject with a wave of his hand. "We be well prepared." He looked at his advisor. "Have you ruminated enough, Kosi?"

Kosi bowed deeply. "Perhaps, Great Oghar. I think of someone who might help the outsiders. My old war chief, Shamas."

Oghar snickered. "Shamas be a good choice if this be twenty-five years ago."

"I was thinking of Abrina, daughter of Shamas."

Oghar frowned as he pondered Kosi's suggestion. He glanced at Syndia, looked away, and rubbed his chin. The Chief nodded. "Very well," he said to Kosi. Turning to Syndia he said, "My first advisor will help you. He stakes his life on it."

19

We mounted our horses and Kosi led us back into the village, then north on a heavily rutted road called the Blackwood Trail. The road led into a forest thick with tall, moss-hung trees, and as soon as we entered we began to hear the screams of a sawmill. We came upon a pond, and on its far bank sat a mill driven by a water wheel. The lumber stacked in its yard for drying was as black as pitch. Kosi motioned for us to stop at the mill, and he went inside to get directions.

When he returned he looked up at Syndia and said, "Shamas has his crew logging at the base of the North Mountains. It be a long ride from here. I mention it because of the Heterin guards chasing you."

Syndia glanced at Tayu, the boy nodded, and the priestess looked over her shoulder. "Sergeant Rosh?"

"Yes, priestess?"

"Post yourself at the entrance to the Blackwood where you can observe the trail. When you see Shadows, come and warn us."

Rosh touched his finger to his forehead, turned his horse, and rode back toward the village. Syndia turned her face toward the trail. "Lead the way, Kosi."

I rode next to Kosi in front, followed by Syndia and Tayu, with Ruuter bringing up the rear. The deeper we got into the Blackwood, the taller grew the trees. In places there would be clumps of ferns or a little patch of grass, but nothing else grew except where one of the giant trees had died and fallen leaving a great hole in the canopy above allowing the light to reach the forest floor.

As always, out of the corner of my eye I glimpsed specters, spirits, pixies, nymphs, and uncountable creatures of the imagination lurking in the shadows. To move my mind off of the fanged impossibilities of the present, I pondered the problem of our prospective warrior, Abrina, daughter of Shamas.

"Kosi?"

"Yes?"

"This woman you have in mind. Is she a warrior?"

Kosi kept his gaze on the road ahead. "What she be be anyone's guess."

That seemed rather obscure. "Kosi, the person we need must fight Manku the Destroyer, the fiercest god who has ever come into the world. We need a man with a sword, and you offer us a woman who is not even a warrior."

"That be true."

"If she's not a warrior, what is she?"

"A logger."

I reined up my horse and glared at Oghar's first advisor. "Are you telling me that this will be some wench from a lumberman's soup kitchen? Whatever were you and Oghar thinking?"

Kosi laughed loudly and shook his head. "No. She be a logger. She swings an ax."

"Even so, Kosi. What can she do against the Destroyer with an ax?"

"Wait, Korvas."

"Wait for what?"

"Wait until you see the ax."

High on the switchback trails of the Great North Mountain foothills, we dismounted before the largest blackwood that I have ever seen. As did all of those trees, it extended upward out of sight. The roots were too high for a good jumping horse, and the trunk was as thick as a mansion. Even the ripples in the great tree's bark were wide enough to hide a large man. Kosi led us around the tree until we came to a huge door set into the trunk. The door was easily twice as tall as a man. As Kosi knocked, I caught a glimpse of Tayu, brighter and more alert than I had ever seen him, staring off into the deep woods as though he expected to meet someone he had been seeking.

A tiny port set into the big door opened and an angry face covered with a fierce black beard appeared. "What?"

"It is Kosi, Shamas."

"Kosi? Why be you here?"

"We must speak with Abrina."

Shamas was a large man dressed in furs. He examined Syndia, Tayu, and me, and announced, "Abrina be not home. She works." His last comment, coupled with raised eyebrows, appeared to imply that we weren't working and ought to feel ashamed on that account. He turned to Kosi and said in a low voice filled with menace, "You know she sees no one." He jabbed Kosi's chest with a force that would have shattered anyone more brittle. "Why be you here?"

"I said—"

There were the sounds of footsteps in the distance. I peered into the darkness of the woods, my eyes straining, until I saw her. She was a magnificent beauty with short black hair and full red lips. She wore a dark brown leather vest, laced in front, over skin-tight leather trousers and boots. She had an ax over her shoulder, and its handle was almost as long as I was tall. Each step she took was easily three of mine. She was a giantess. My head wouldn't even reach her waist. A strange pain crept into my heart.

When she saw us in front of her father's home, she was still some distance away. She stopped, took down her ax from her shoulder, and held it at the ready. "Father," she called.

"I be here, child."

"Why be they here, Father?"

"They come for see you, Abrina."

She began to back warily away from us. As she took another step backwards, Tayu began walking toward her. She saw him and paused. The boy didn't do anything but walk, yet Abrina seemed fixed by his approach. Soon he was standing before her, the top of his head just above her knees. He must have said something, for she knelt down to listen. We saw her head nod once, then Tayu seemed to swoon. The giantess caught him and cradled him in her arms. Her head looked up and she called out, "Korvas."

I jumped. "Yes?"

"Come here. Tayu has something to say to you."

I crossed the space and felt my breath catch as I neared her. Even kneeling she was a full two heads taller than I. Tayu's face was ashen, and he reached out a hand toward me. I took his hand in both of mine.

"Abrina is the one, my brother. I am finished. Now you must be the Guide."

He closed his eyes and went limp before I could understand what was happening. I looked at Abrina's face. She had deep amber eyes. "What's wrong with him?"

"Is this your brother?"

I nodded, "Yes, but I never knew him."

She held him out to me and I took him in my arms. "Your brother is dead. I be sorry."

She stood, hefted her ax, and ran into the woods.

I placed my brother on the bed of evergreen branches, Syndia arranged his robe and anointed his forehead with rose oil. If I ever had doubts about him being my twin brother, they evaporated under the heat of my loss. Syndia sang that same strange hymn that she had sung over Ahjrah's pyre, while I kissed my brother's cheek.

The boy had had only one function in the grand scheme of the gods: to find a hero. I supposed some rabid temple rat might find in that fact something for which to be grateful, but I didn't have gratitude on my mind right then. I deserved whatever jokes the gods decided to play on me, but Tayu never had a moment past innocence.

"He did have a choice, Korvas."

"Eh?" Syndia was standing behind me holding the black smoking torch. "Still reading my mind, priestess?"

"Tayu had a choice."

"Bah, what kind of choice could a little boy make?"

"A very brave choice. Once you can accept that, you will be able to see the disservice you do him now." She held out the torch. "Take it."

I took the torch and faced the pyre, ashamed. "I apologize, Tayu. Tell our father, should you meet him, that I apologize to him, as well."

I waited a moment, then touched the torch to the pyre. Just as with Ahjrah's pyre, the entire thing went up in a column of flameless black smoke that lasted but a few seconds. It was followed by a black cloud that gathered up the cold ashes and disappeared into the treetops above us, leaving the forest floor as it had been before.

Syndia touched my arm and said, "Now you must go and find Abrina."

I turned and looked at the priestess. "I am to go alone?"

"Only you are the Guide."

"What about Ruuter and you?"

"We will wait for you here."

"What should I say to her, if I do find her?"

"There is no doubt that you must find her. As to answers . . ." She pointed to where my god box hung. "There are the answers you need. Korvas, whatever you say to her must be in a hurry if we are to avoid Captain Shadows."

20

I needn't have worried about finding the giantess. The sound of her ax filled the forest. Before I reached her there was a mighty creaking followed by the enormous crash of one of those monstrous blackwoods landing on the forest floor. A second later the sound of her ax resumed with a passion.

I walked my horse into the sunlight. There was a haze of dust above the northern edge of the clearing, and I led the horse around the stumps until Abrina came into view. She was standing upon a felled tree cutting the limbs from it. Some of the limbs she removed with a single stroke were thicker than whole trees I had seen grown men curse and chop at for an hour. If she ever became angry, that would see the end of anything within reach of that blade.

I wasn't certain whether she had seen me. I tied my horse to a bit of brush that had been left standing and picked up the god box, asking it what I should do.

Its answer was, *"Watch."*

I sat on a stump and watched the giantess denude the tree. She was magnificent. She was like a tireless machine of great precision as she worked her way around the huge trunk, eventually lopping off the top where the trunk was a mere three feet thick. Even though the sun was beginning to hide behind the mountains to the southwest, I felt myself getting warmer and warmer. When what was affecting me finally announced itself, I stood and angrily walked to the opposite side of the stump and sat with my back toward Abrina.

My loves and lusts have led me into some peculiar situations, not the least of which was this strange quest with the Nant priestess. First I sharpened my horns for a celibate priestess, and now had I fallen in love with a giantess? A giant logger? By the patron of lost causes, she was twice my height! I doubted if I could even lift her ax. The head of the double-edged thing looked as though it had been hammered out of two hundred pounds of iron.

Everything about her was impossible. Certainly everything about us was impossible. However, my imagination would not be convinced. Those acres of flesh spread out on a meadow-sided bed—Great Ehbot, I could run for miles and never touch linen!

"Korvas."

"Yes?" I jumped up, turned and looked back at her as she stood in front of the log.

"I am sorry about your brother."

"I didn't know him well." I turned away and became intensely interested in the progress an ant was making across the toe of my left boot. I felt guilty that she should be thinking of Tayu's recent passing while I was thinking of—well—thinking of other things. "I've been sent to find you."

"I know."

I looked back at her. "How do you know?"

"For the past few weeks I have been visited by frightening dreams. They be dreams of fighting and great suffering. In my dreams I visited the peoples of many countries and saw what they be. There be a prophecy, Korvas."

"Yes." I stood and faced her. "I don't remember it exactly, but—" I felt a drawer from the god box nudge my side. I took the paper offered by the drawer and read it. "Guided by the Mirror of the Second, the Hero will be found by the Second, who will be chosen by a father's hand, kept by the First, loved by the Mirror, and burned by the Mirror to be gathered by the Smoke."

"Korvas, I be a woman."

I nodded with enthusiasm. "I quite agree, Abrina."

"This prophecy calls for a hero, not a heroine."

I held out my hands. "Tayu seemed certain that you were the one, and the Nant priestess, Syndia, agrees. Tayu led us here all of the way from Iskandar."

Abrina swung her ax blade onto the top of a stump and left it sticking there. She sat on the edge of the stump between us and looked at the treetops. "Korvas, ever since I be a baby men and women make fun of me. They call me tower, blackwood, mountain, and freak. Tayu said that the prophecy wants me fight a god and save the ones who call me freak." She held out her hand toward the trees. "Here, alone with my ax, the trees, and the Blackwood animals, I be at peace. Why should I go with you, out of these woods, and save those who hurt me?"

"I don't know. These are questions for priests or oracles to answer. Had I the power, I would slay all of those who have hurt you." I held out my hands. "However, all I could do would be to cheat them in a carpet sale." I sat on the opposite side of the stump, the god box in my hands, and looked up at her. "One thing I know is that the ugly people of this world will never get any prettier if they're dead. You have to be alive to change."

While she pondered my words, I pondered from whence they had come. They sounded almost profound, and I had no idea that I had any capacity for such thoughts. I glanced at my god box and suspected the source.

Abrina stood, yanked her ax from the stump, and faced me. "Korvas, when you first came into the clearing and sat upon this stump, what did you think?"

My face became very red as my vision filled with the gleam from her ax's sharpened edge. "Is it important?"

"Is living important?"

"It is important to me, Abrina."

"Then tell me."

"I, uh, was thinking of . . ." I glanced at her eyes, then down at the surface of the stump. There were hundreds of rings, and I felt sad that I would not only never live that long, but that I would probably not live long enough to complain about being older than thirty. "I was thinking of making love to you. I am ashamed, but that was what I was thinking."

I expected her to either kill me or laugh at me. Instead she simply sat there looking at me with those amber eyes for the longest time. When she closed her eyes, she turned her head and sang out a strange cry toward the trees. A similar cry answered her.

I saw it, whatever it was, coming over the treetops. At first I thought it was a huge bird, or perhaps that famous beast of legend, a dragon. It was neither. Instead it was a huge winged lion. At the shoulder he must have come to Abrina's waist, and his golden wings had a span wider than ten horses end to end.

The giantess held her hand, palm up, high above her head. The creature landed on it and immediately began diminishing in size until it was smaller than my thumb. She tucked the creature in beneath her hair at the nape of her neck and looked down at me.

"I will go with you, Korvas. And please do not be ashamed about feelings of desire for me."

As I untied my horse and mounted, I glanced at her and asked, "Someday are you going to tell me about that creature?"

"Perhaps even today. Where will the contest with the Destroyer take place?"

"I don't know." I urged my horse forward, and Abrina followed on foot. "I expect to be told at any time, however." I glanced at the god box and whispered, "The sooner the better."

Just before we reached the edge of the clearing we heard the sounds of horses galloping. Syndia came riding into the clearing shouting, "Flee! Captain Shadows is right behind me!"

I dug in my heels and soon we were riding along together with Abrina running behind us. "What happened?"

"Rosh never warned us. I assume he is dead."

"Ruuter?"

"I think the guard captured him at Shamas's house."

We heard a great crash behind us. We pulled up and looked back to see that Abrina had tipped over a dead standing tree across the trail. It would only slow Shadows a bit. The giantess turned and asked Syndia, "What of my father?"

"He died, child, giving me a chance to escape."

Abrina ripped another dead blackwood out by its roots and threw it onto the trail. There were tears in her eyes when she looked back. "Priestess, where do we go?"

"I don't know."

"You don't know?" I cried.

"After all, Korvas, you are the Guide," the priestess answered. "Where do we go now?"

I pointed up into the mountains. "Away from Shadows." Abrina took the lead, and it was all our horses could do to keep up with her.

21

Higher we went into the mountains until we ran out of logging roads. We continued through the woods and brush, for the trees were getting smaller. In time we came to a sheer cliff that extended upwards far enough to dwarf even the tallest of the blackwoods. At the bottom of the cliff the ground was covered with loose rocks, and the horses kept stumbling on them. I motioned to Syndia to dismount. With both of us standing and keeping our horses quiet, we could just make out the sounds of the Heterin guards. Abrina was listening, as well.

"They'll be here within a few minutes, Korvas."

"Syndia, if Abrina and her ax can take on a particularly mean and powerful god, is it possible that she could take on Shadows and kill him?"

"Perhaps, but what if our pursuer has magic at his command? His superior, Tretia, has the king's ear. Anything that exists she can command to her use, and that includes every kind and degree of sorcery in Iskandar. With the speed and ease Shadows has employed in chasing us, I'd say he's using something more effective than a Serker scout."

"It was just a thought."

"Think your thoughts before you voice them, Korvas. It will save time."

"Where do we go now?" asked Abrina.

I looked at Syndia. "Have you no idea where the contest with the Destroyer is supposed to take place?"

"No."

"Didn't Ahjrah tell you?"

"She believed the answer to be in one of the unrecovered Books of Fayn. What about your god box? Have you tried asking it for directions?"

"I don't feel good about trusting this thing."

"Do you have a choice?"

I swallowed as I picked up the thing and shook it. "What do I need right now?"

A drawer opened and there was a note that said, *"A quiet place."*

"Now is not the time for meditation, box!" But the god box said nothing more. "Well," I said to the others in exasperation, "I guess I'll go find me a quiet place."

I climbed closer to the bottom of the cliff, and among the boulders there I found a spot in between four great stones. In there were three small evergreen trees, a little grass, and a spring. I went in and stood there, my arms folded, my left foot tapping against the ground. "Certainly this must be quiet enough!"

A drawer on the box opened, and the gist of the note it contained was that the place was quiet enough, but that I had brought too much noise in with me. I sat down by the pool, leaned against one of the evergreens, and closed my eyes.

This was foolish. With Captain Shadows hot on my tail feathers, here I was taking a little poolside lie-down. I opened an eye, took a quick look at the box, noted that it had opened no drawers, and went back to trying to be quiet.

"This is ridiculous," I said as I began to get back on my feet. I froze as one of the god box's drawers shot into my side, then went to the other side of the box and opened. "Ouch."

I took out the note and read it. It said, *"Sit down, shut up, and listen."*

So I sat down, I shut up, and I listened, not really knowing what it was that I was supposed to hear. There was a slight breeze, a bit of bubbling in the spring, the distant voices of Abrina and Syndia . . . the face of that

incredibly old and unhappy man, the Mankua priest that
cared for the shrine of Manku at the edge of that one
town—Abunih. The priest's name was Sabis, and why
was I thinking of him?

What do I need? I need to know where to go to meet
the Destroyer. I seemed to have all of the pieces to
something in my head. Somehow the Manku priest—when
I turned the god box on the Shrine of Manku I saw rows
of teeth, snakes, slime . . . fire, and storm. A face of
strength and compassion, and ancient instruments, *scrolls,
and books—*

"Ho! Stay fast there and no one'll harm you!"

I heard the unfamiliar voice and bounded to my feet. I
ran around the boulders until I could see the sunlight on
Abrina's hair. Three hundred feet downhill a single Heterin
guard was leading his horse up to where we were. A few
seconds later the trail behind him was filled with red
uniforms.

I stood next to Syndia. "We have to get to the Shrine
of Manku in Abunih. The answers are there."

Syndia smiled as she pointed downhill at the advancing
Heterin guards. "What about the good captain?"

I turned my head and looked up. "Abrina, it's time to
call your creature out of your hair. We need a flight to
Abunih. You've ridden him before, haven't you?"

"Only by myself. Url might not like having more
passengers."

"Given a choice between Captain Shadows and your
lion-monster, I'll take my chances with the lion-monster."

"His name is Url."

"Url, then. But hurry."

Abrina reached to her neck. While she was about that,
I turned to Syndia. "Get your things from your horse."

"I have nothing. All of my things are back at the house
of Shamas on the pack animals."

"The same is true for me." I shook my head as Abrina
held out her hand and whispered to him. All at once, the
lion-creature appeared above her hand, its huge wings
raising the dust from the ground. He growled and lowered himself to the ground.

A Heterin guard below raised a pistol, took aim, and shot at the beast. Since he missed a creature the size of three oxen, is it any wonder the King's Guard makes jokes about the marksmanship of the Heterins?

Abrina picked up a boulder weighing perhaps five hundred pounds and threw it at the guard who had fired the pistol, knocking him from his horse and into the next world. "Come," she said to me, holding out her hands. I let her pick me up and place me on the neck of the beast. She placed Syndia behind me, and Abrina climbed on last.

She gave that strange cry and the lion bounded over the rocks and boulders until it had climbed to the top of the cliff. Syndia had her arms around my waist, and I had my fingers dug into Url's coarse hair. My eyes, of course, were frozen open. At the top of the cliff, Abrina gave another call, and the lion-bird ran and jumped off of the cliff, dove down, then swooped out above the blackwoods. Soon we were high above the valley floor, heading south toward Abunih.

I felt Syndia's lips near my left ear. "Korvas, are you afraid?"

"Of course, I'm afraid!"

"Give your fear to your god box."

"But what if the creature drops us or shakes us off?"

"Will being frightened help you to fly?"

I thought upon it and decided that, given I am going to die anyway, I'd prefer to enjoy the trip. I released the lion's mane with my right hand, placed it upon the god box, and turned over my fears to the box. As the fear lifted from my heart, I looked down. Where the Blackwood Trail entered the forest was a black-uniformed man leaning against a tree. His horse was hidden in the shadows. I turned, looked over my shoulder, and pointed toward the ground. "Look."

Syndia looked down. "That's Sergeant Rosh."

I nodded in agreement. The implications were devastating enough. There was no need for further conversation. Url the lion-bird took us higher, and the air became chilly as the great creature climbed toward the Pass of Ebell.

22

"Perhaps there's something to recommend flying as a means of travel, but I can't see it."

Syndia laughed and squeezed my middle. "Quit complaining, Korvas, or you'll be harvesting butnuts."

"It's almost dark, I'm a mile from the ground, hungry, freezing to death, with nature making a very desperate call. If you squeeze my middle again, we are going to get to find out just how even-tempered a great winged lion is."

"We'll be down soon."

"I hope flying never becomes popular."

"We are almost at Abunih," said Abrina. "Like for see a trick Url and I do?"

"Like what?"

"We'd love to," answered Syndia.

Abrina let loose with one of those strange cries, and the winged lion began climbing for the clouds. When it was so high I could hardly catch my breath, the trick happened. One second my fingers were gripping the mane of a giant lion while my legs straddled its back. The next second the winged lion had vanished and the three of us were tumbling through the sky, a very tiny winged lion yapping as it chased us down through the sky.

I never thought it unmanly to show emotion, which is why I began screaming and didn't stop until Url returned to his original size, caught up with us, and allowed us to climb aboard. Abrina pulled up her beast next to the pass where the Shrine to Manku stood.

It was past evening, the torches at the shrine providing a spot of light in an otherwise dark universe. I climbed down from Url, found a tree, and watered it and half the countryside with a shaking hand. When I was finished I managed to make it to the shrine. I sat down upon the steps with a sigh. Abrina had commanded Url to become small again, and as she was placing the creature in her hair, Syndia studied the shrine.

"Korvas?"

"What?"

"We are here."

"I'm waiting for my stomach." I looked up at Syndia. "Have you seen Sabis?"

"No."

Something horrible occurred to me and I looked at Abrina. "The butnuts! What do we do about the smell? Sabis will die before he allows us within speaking distance."

"When was the last time you had some?"

I thought upon it. "I believe it was while I was at your father's house, before I first laid eyes on you."

"The smell has worn off. It only takes two or three hours. In another day you will again be able to smell the odor."

"I count the minutes." I got to my feet, leaned against the shrine, and looked around. "Sabis! Sabis!" My voice echoed from the near mountains.

The Nant priestess looked at me and said, "Korvas, you said our answers would be here."

I turned to Syndia. "In this shrine are some of the Books of Fayn. In them should be where the contest with Manku takes place. How do we get in?"

The shrine was a set of four steps leading to an obelisk made from local stone and mortar. There was an alcove set into the obelisk where one could burn incense before a crudely carved likeness of Manku. I studied the face of the likeness and it was the face I had seen through the open god box.

Abrina bent over and pointed at the shrine. "Are you

certain there is something in here? It just looks like a pile of rocks." She stood up, pulled one of the torches from its receptacle, and walked behind the structure.

I looked at Syndia, and she held out her hands. "What makes you think something is here?"

"I saw it. I sort of saw it." I pointed at the steps. "Down there. There has to be a room of some kind down there. Sabis knows how to get in."

Abrina's voice came from behind the monument. "Sabis is dead."

Syndia and I ran around the shrine to see Abrina kneeling next to some brush. She pulled away the loosened brush, revealing the Mankua priest's bloodied form. Syndia knelt next to the old man and examined him in the torchlight. "See the nails? The burns in his ears? His eyes? Sabis was tortured to death."

"Shadows." The name fell from my mouth. "He must not have gotten what he wanted."

"Unless information about us was what he wanted." Syndia stood up and looked toward the shrine. "You are the Guide. Get us in, Korvas."

I walked to the shrine, pulled out the second torch, and examined the carving of Manku. It wore a draped robe. It looked as if it was just set into the alcove, but it was anchored fast and wouldn't budge. Besides, using an image of your god for a door latch would be disrespectful. I moved around the shrine, poking every likely-looking rock. The torches were close to burning out and I was preparing to give up. "What if we just turn Abrina and her ax loose on the shrine? Sooner or later we'll get down to the room."

Abrina raised herself to her full height, which definitely made a statement all by itself. "Destroy a shrine? That would be disrespectful. My gods would not be pleased if I desecrated the shrine of another."

I scratched my head. "Disrespectful." I looked at Syndia. "The very last thing a priest would be expected to do would be something disrespectful toward his god, yes?" I went back to the statue of Manku. I tried again to wiggle it, turn it, twist its head, all for nothing.

"Why don't you use the god box?"

I couldn't think of a good reason except that I wanted to solve the problem myself. That wouldn't have sounded like much of a reason out loud, so I asked the box. Its answer was *"Keep trying."*

Again I stared at the statue of Manku. The god's face had an expression of calmness about it, and that bit of compassion I kept seeing. What would be the most inappropriate thing I could do—

I took out my knife and scratched at the carving. I pushed the blade in between two of the carved folds in the robe's drape and ran the point down the length of the drape. I accomplished nothing but the need to resharpen my knife. I moved the blade to the next fold and began running the blade down the length of the drape. When the point was directly over the god's heart it sank in.

I pushed the blade in as far as it would go, and the stairs beneath my feet began sinking down. They kept going down until the former stairs up to the statue were now part of a set of stairs that extended downward farther than the light from my torch could reach. There were extinguished torches in holders every few steps.

"Well?"

I turned around and saw Syndia standing behind me. "This appears to be what we were seeking." I looked back at that staircase. It was certainly the darkest and most forbidding-looking entrance to the underworld that I had ever seen. I reached out my torch, lit the first of the staircase torches, and gave my fear to the god box.

23

There was a smell of damp and mildew in the air as well as the sounds of tiny claws scratching at the masonry. After what seemed to be an eternity, we came to what looked to be a natural cave. There were torches set into the walls which we lit. As the light coaxed the shadows from the corners, we began to appraise the room's contents. There were leather trunks, shelves filled with dusty old volumes, leather buckets filled with scrolls, and tables crowded with ancient mystical charts and instruments.

"This is all that is left of the Mankuas," said Syndia as she caressed the leather binding of a book.

I shook my head. "We could search in here for days and not find what we want." I held my torch near one of the shelves and tried to read the titles. "Syndia, what is this? I can't read any of these."

Syndia came up beside me and studied the titles. "That's ancient Itkah, the script and language of the people who inhabited Iskandar before the tribes fleeing from Ziven settled there. It was the language used by the Itkahn religion."

"I can't read it, which means that you have to do the searching by yourself."

"Korvas?" Abrina's voice echoed from the back.

"Yes?" I looked around the corner of the shelf and saw a reflection of her torch on a wall far ahead. "What is it?"

"Come here."

I walked around a stack of leather cases and down a corridor that turned sharply to the right. As I turned I saw Abrina leaning on her ax, holding a torch high above her head. It was a huge cavern, its walls lined with shelves containing more books and scrolls.

"By Angh's bleeding piles. There must be thousands—hundreds of thousands."

"Look," she pointed with her torch straight ahead.

There was another entrance. I walked to it, stuck in my torch, and gasped. It was an even larger cavern, its walls lined with even more scrolls and books.

"How many of these rooms are there?" I picked up my god box and asked, "What do I need right now?"

A drawer opened, and I read the note it contained by the light of my torch. "Again, the humor of the gods."

"What does it say?" asked Syndia.

"It says I need a plan." I fumed as I looked around. "Well, I guess we had best find out how many rooms are in this labyrinth, how big they are and in what relation to each other."

"You mean make a map," said Abrina.

"Yes. We make a map."

Using one of the larger cavern rooms for a base, we found parchment and pen and began sketching out a map. When we had been at it for some time, I was reaching what I thought was the end of a corridor when it opened up into yet another room. This room, however, was different than the rest in one respect. Its floor was crowded with cut-stone coffins. I counted them and there were forty-two. All but one were closed. The open one was empty.

This was what had happened to the remnants of the Mankuan priesthood. In the midst of this treasure of forbidden knowledge, Sabis had entombed his brothers one by one until only he remained to tend the shrine of Manku and the revenge of the Mankuas. Sabis had ached to live long enough to see Manku bring down his judgment upon the world for the sins of the Heterin faith.

Yet the old priest had died at the hands of the Heterin Guard.

I felt uneasy prowling among the dead priests, especially since we had left the last of his kind on the ground above like a sack of oats. Before continuing with any kind of plan, there was something that needed doing.

I carried Sabis's body down the stairs and through the many chambers, reaching at last the burial chamber. Abrina had cleaned out the empty stone coffin while Syndia searched among the nearest shelves for the Mankuan burial ritual. I lowered the old man into the coffin and arranged his hands. It made my skin squirm to look at his hands and imagine the pain Sabis must have endured before he died.

"I couldn't find the ritual, Korvas."

I shook my head as I picked up the god box. "Perhaps we've done all we can do."

There was a loud sound of stone striking stone. "Korvas," said Abrina, "this coffin be empty." I watched as she lifted the lid of the coffin next to the one she had just examined. I held my torch over it, and it too was empty. The inside of the coffin was lined with black glass. Sabis's coffin was lined with nothing but stone.

I looked back at Syndia. "Well?"

"I don't know." She shook her head and stood at the head of Sabis's coffin. I returned to the old priest's side and withdrew a drawer from the god box. Looking through the opening, I surveyed the body of the dead priest. Beneath his beard there was a bright blue glow.

"Syndia, what does he have hanging around his neck?"

The priestess leaned over the side of the coffin as I held the torch over the corpse. Her fingers reached to his neck and found a silver chain. She pulled on it and withdrew what was attached to the chain. It was a sapphire. She looked up at me with her eyebrows raised. I nodded. "Remove it."

As Syndia worked the chain over the old priest's head, another crash signified one more closed coffin examined by Abrina. She walked over to Sabis's coffin and loomed over us. "Korvas, all of the coffins be empty and lined with black glass. Perhaps there be no others."

"Nonsense. It would take more than one man to do all of the work that's been done down here."

"Look!" Syndia was pointing at the corpse. I held the torch high and watched in horror as Sabis began to melt. He melted as if he were a piece of wax thrown into a hot furnace. As the liquid puddled at the bottom of the coffin, it turned black and began bleeding up the sides.

"There's your black glass, Abrina. Let's get the lid on this thing before we get covered with the stuff."

Abrina picked up the coffin's stone lid and fitted it into place. There were markings on the lid, but they made no sense to me. "Syndia, what do these markings say?"

She looked at them. "Also Itkah. This," she indicated a line, "is Sabis's name in Itkah. This," she indicated the next line, "says 'All Hail Day of . . .' This last word is pronounced *kahnalru*, and it means land beyond the sunrise."

"Ahmrita," I said.

"Are you certain?"

"Ahmrita is the only Ahmritan word I know, and it means Land-beyond-the-Sunrise." I studied the Itkah phrase carved into the coffin's lid. " 'All hail day of Ahmrita.' Syndia, with this old man's desire to have the whole world pay for what happened to the Mankuas, this can mean only one thing."

"The Day of Judgment; when the Hero will fight Manku the Destroyer with the fate of the world hanging in the balance. It will happen in Ahmrita."

I shook my head. "We can't be certain. Back when Ahmrita was called by this name, the empire was twice as large as it is now. The contest could well take place in one of the kingdoms to the south—"

I noticed something strange. As Syndia turned away from the coffin, the sapphire dangling from its chain began to glow. When she turned back, the amulet went dark again. "Look at the amulet."

Syndia looked at the sapphire dangling from the end of its chain. "What is it, Korvas?"

"Turn to your right."

As she did so, the stone glowed until it achieved a brilliant white-blue color. There was a passageway behind her, and the priestess entered it with Abrina and I close behind. The passage opened onto yet another cave with shelves stacked with books. The stone began to dim, and Syndia paused. She turned to her left and the stone grew very dim. She turned to her right and the sapphire grew bright. She continued walking in that direction until we stood before a book-lined cavern wall that extended well up out of sight.

"Korvas, hold the torch near the books." I did so and watched as Syndia held out the stone. She moved it up, and the stone dimmed. She lowered it and the stone grew bright, then dimmed as she pointed it at a lower shelf. She did the same thing to the left and to the right. The amulet was the brightest when it was pointed at one particular book.

I held the torch steady while Syndia read the title out loud. "*Mortimann's Book of Locks.* It's a relatively new book, twenty or thirty years old." She pulled the volume off of the shelf and began paging through it. She turned to catch my torch's light on her reading. As she did so, Sabis's amulet went dark.

I handed my torch to Abrina. "Hold this while I investigate something." I reached into the place where the book had been and felt around with my fingers. I touched a handle. "There's a handle in my grasp. I'm going to pull it."

I did so and withdrew my arm from the shelf as the entire wall rumbled. When the rumbling stopped, the shelves had parted, revealing a tiny cavern with but one entrance. Abrina stood outside due to the closeness of the space. Inside the small room were many candles and a single shelf containing nineteen leather-bound volumes. As I lit some candles, Syndia took one and passed it before the books as she silently moved her lips from volume to volume. "Korvas, these are nineteen volumes of the Books of Fayn."

She passed the amulet down the row of books. Near the center of the row the sapphire glowed brightly enough to hurt the eyes. She took down the volume and opened it with trembling fingers. Perhaps it was only my fingers that were trembling. Inside the cover was the hand-illuminated title in Itkah.

Syndia leafed through the pages. "This is *The Book of Choice*. It is concerned with the mechanics and the ethics of choice." The amulet grew very bright. "Here is the prophecy. The original form of the Oracle of Heteris!" She read a bit, then shook her head. "This can't be right."

"What do you mean?"

"It's almost nothing like the oracle we know. Listen:" and Syndia translated the words. " 'The child, orphaned by the cult,/ Is charged by the smoke/ To protect the seeker from harm/ Until the smoke releases the child/ To hand the seeker to its reflection.' "

"Ahjrah is the child," I said, "Tayu is the seeker, Nanteria is the smoke, and I am the seeker's reflection."

"Correct so far. Now listen: 'The seeker shall find the blade,/ and more, himself, beside the one/ Before Manku in Land-beyond-the Sunrise/ All is Manku.' "

Abrina folded her arms and said, "There be no mention of a hero. No mention of a man-warrior. They called it 'the one' and 'the blade.' "

"By using the word blade, a warrior was assumed, and the men who did the assuming assumed the warrior would be a man." Syndia tapped on the page with her finger. "This closing, 'All is Manku,' is what the old translators took to mean everything is destroyed. But that same phrase is used as a 'so be it' in the Nant faith, as in 'All is Nanteria.' This could be nothing more than a prayer closing. No wonder there was a fight over its meaning."

"Is there more?"

"Yes. The meeting between the Blade and Manku; this might narrow it down. 'At the tip of Ihtar's hand,/

Where float the lavender leaves,/ The Destroyer shall meet the blade,/ Leaving only one.' "

I glanced at Abrina. She was looking back at me. "That certainly sounds like a fight to the death to me."

Syndia tugged on my sleeve. "What about the tip of Ihtar's hand?"

"The Ahmritan gods are called the Ihtar, and the print of Ihtar's hand is the Sea of Ihtar. It's a narrow body of water that splits the old Ahmritan Empire in two."

"The tip?"

"At the end of the Sea of Ihtar is a smaller sea called the Sea of Manku—Givida is on the Sea of Manku. Givida is the religious center of the empire."

"The lavender leaves?"

I shook my head. "I don't know, but at least we have a direction to travel. Let's make for Kienosos. We can get a ship there."

Syndia looked at me for a moment, then returned to the book. "I will be staying here."

"Eh?"

"You no longer need me. We have found your Hero, and now you know where to take her."

"You began this, priestess! I would think—"

She touched a finger to my lips. "This is all part of the scheme of things, Korvas. It is a wheel that began turning long before the universe was born." She placed the amulet of Sabis around my neck and pointed at the god box. "You have everything you need." She held out her hands toward the countless books and scrolls. "I have what I need."

"But Syndia . . ." I faced Abrina. "Talk to her!"

Abrina smiled, and I turned to see the Nant priestess, Syndia, dissolve into thin air. I passed my hand through where she had been standing. Nothing was there that could be touched. That explained why I couldn't see her through the god box. "What about witnessing miracles, Syndia? You can't witness them if you're not there."

"She'll be there, Korvas."

"How can you know that?"

"When I see her I know Nanteria."

"The goddess? Syndia?" I frowned as I lowered myself into an uncomfortable chair. Near the surface of my thoughts were things I needed to consider. I glanced back at Abrina. "Let's close this place. Once we're out of here, call out your creature and pump him up. We're going to Kienosos to find passage to Ahmrita."

The giantess grinned. "Posing as husband and wife?"

I rubbed my eyes for a moment and decided to deal with questions of that sort once they were posed, and not a second before.

24

Between the stars and the shadow of the world, Abrina and I flew upon the winged lion toward the port city of Kienosos. She sat behind me, and when I was near mad from the cold, she put her arms around me. Once out of the mountains, gliding toward the southern coast, it was warmer and I could stop my shaking. As we flew, the giantess sang to her creature.

I didn't know the song, or the language in which it was sung, but it was a song of love. While she sang, I argued with myself.

Why was it that this expedition, beginning with so many, had been pared down to Abrina and me? If Syndia had indeed been Nanteria, goddess of smoke, what had been her purpose in being with us? Was it to gift me with the god box and Sabis's sapphire? Was it to test me? Was it both? Was it to find the Mankua faith's hidden library? But why would a goddess need help in finding such a thing? The gods may not be able to speak very clearly, but they are supposed to know everything.

Syndia was certainly a goddess, which placed an unbeliever such as myself into a very awkward position. The most awkward part of that position wasn't admitting that I might have been wrong. It was: just who is Korvas to be doing the work of the gods? Why would Nanteria, or the god of this god box, make me a necessary part of the inevitable path of the universe? It was a highly suspicious honor.

Was it not more likely that, through deception and trickery, I had been enlisted to do the work of the Destroyer? But, again, why would the Destroyer choose me? Why would he not, instead, find a man who was at least a competent sinner? Surely there must be a burgeoning young prince of evil somewhere with the appropriate skills who would like the work and appreciate the notice.

Abrina's hand pointed toward the distance. I squinted my eyes against the wind and saw the lights of Kienosos. As we came closer I could make out the navigation lights in the harbor, the sedate and orderly sheva's palace, temples, and government buildings, cupped by the final meander of the Great Serpent. Here, however, they called the river the Nepri after the last of the Kienosan kings.

The brightest section of the city, of course, was where the wealthy went to have their pockets cleaned. As we glided above it we could hear the chaos of music, singing, and bellowing that accompanied the separation of fools from their money.

"Korvas, where should Url put down?"

"It's late. Daybreak isn't too far away and Url can't take us across the ocean. While it's still dark we should get near the docks. That's where we hide you and look for passage to Ahmrita."

"Hide me?"

Her voice sounded hurt. "Abrina, Kienosos is supposed to be independent, but the Heterin Guard has a tentacle here. Do you see that large temple? The one next to the mouth of the river?"

"Yes."

"That's Kienosos's Heterin Temple—look, they're changing the guard." I looked back at her. "With your size and that ax, if you were seen Shadows would find out in no time that we were here. If he knew that, it wouldn't take long for him to find out where we went. His agents would be scouring the docks within moments."

The giantess was silent for a moment, then she patted my shoulder with surprising gentleness. "Where be the docks?"

"Across the river from the Heterin Temple are the old docks. It's a rough place, but we ought to be able to find a ship without being asked too many questions." I looked down at my god box. "Provided I can pay the going rate."

Abrina chattered and called at the winged lion and it swooped down past the lights and across the water toward the infamous waterfront district of Kienosos. It had been years since I had been there, and my feeling was that I could go the rest of my life without ever seeing it again.

As Abrina had Url come to roost on the dark roof of a deserted warehouse, my fingers sought out the scars on my left side that I had received upon my most recent visit to the waterfront's Blood Street Bazaar. A fellow with a knife, bad breath, and a remarkable lack of good taste had insisted that my purse belonged to him. Two local citizens held me while I was separated from my money, and, when I threatened to call in the city guard, the fellow with the knife ripped into my guts with a rather long blade. I remembered the look on his face. He seemed slightly amused, as though I should have learned the rules before walking into his corner of the underworld.

Url again became the size of my thumb, and I stood on the roof looking across the housetops of Bay Street toward the lights of the bazaar. Abrina knelt next to me. "Korvas?"

"What?"

"Are you afraid?"

"Afraid? Me?"

"Yes, you."

"Nonsense, my dear. I have been in my time thief, soldier, assassin, and more. I am not afraid. I am petrified."

"I will go with you."

"No. I have explained why. Just let me give my fear to my little friend here, and I will be fine." I turned to her and pointed at the roof. "Stay here. I don't want to have to worry about you."

"Worry about me?"

"Indulge me, please."

I picked up her hand, kissed it, and scooted over the rooftops until I found a stairway down to the street. Even at this hour it was overflowing with horse teams pulling huge vans, men and women scurrying around pushing carts, a few dark-eyed loiterers who were furtively waiting for opportunity to slither by. It was brutal, loud, and smelled of rot, spice, salt air, and dead fish.

Once on the street, I stayed back in the shadows and tried to get my heart to calm down. I had my knife in one hand and my god box in the other. I needed to make a choice. I opened a drawer on the god box and whispered into it, "I give you most of my fear, and while I'm at it, you can have a good piece of my bad luck." I decided to keep some of my fear. On one's way to the Blood Street Bazaar, a little fear is simply good sense. The river bottom is crowded with the foolish brave who entered Blood Street with trust in their hearts and a song on their lips.

The drawer closed on its own. I put the knife into the pocket of my robe, walked across Bay Street, and entered Blood Street. There was a shadow in a doorway talking to another shadow while eyes studied me and inventoried my pockets from a hundred dark corners.

A shadow stepped out in front of me. "Friend?"

My hand stole into my pocket and wrapped itself around the handle of my knife as my feet stopped and my knees turned to jelly. I could hardly speak as I fought with my tongue about what to say. I wanted to fire back with a clever remark that would show the utter contempt in which I held the fellow. Such a display would, perhaps, convince the fellow that, for unapparent reasons, I was too dangerous to attack. Another part of me wanted to scream and run. Hence, I stood there like a marble study in cowardice. The shadow walked around me and greeted another shadow. Together they walked toward the bazaar.

I found a portion of wall that was clear of threats. I leaned against it, inhaled and exhaled. I was at a loss as to how to proceed. Courage was foolhardy, yet fear was crippling. I held the god box in front of me and asked, "Why didn't you work this time?"

The box spoke to my mind. *"You took back your fear."*

"Then what do I do now?"

Just then, to the left, I saw a richly clad man walking quickly down my side of the street toward the bazaar. He was being followed by two hefty-looking shadows. He looked to be a man of substance—hardly a thief—hence, he would be the one to ask for information about securing passage to Ahmrita. I patted my god box and stepped away from the building, but before I could utter a word, the man yelped. The two toughs following him abruptly returned from whence they came, and the man himself pulled a purse from his belt and threw it into my hands.

"There," he said, "now just leave me be!"

He walked around me and continued toward the bazaar with a rapid pace. I felt the weight of the purse and had a moment of delicious temptation. However, the honesty of the Nants and the divine nature of my mission corrupted my instinct. I turned and began running after the man. "Sir, stop!"

His pace picked up a good deal and we dodged through and around the carts, camels, and donkeys crowding the way. As he came to where Blood Street widens and becomes the edge of the bazaar itself, a horse and wagon pulled in front of him, blocking his route.

I grabbed him by his shoulder and said, "Now I've got you," which even then struck me as a possibly poor choice of words.

The man turned about and had another, larger, purse in his hands. "Here. Take everything, just please spare me."

I laughed, which again struck me as being possibly unsettling to this man who thought he was my victim. "Fellow, I am not robbing you. Keep your purse, and take back this one, as well."

His glance darted around until he had examined every wheel and dung heap in this end of Blood Street. "Where are your two confederates?"

For a fear-filled moment I thought he was referring to Abrina and Url, but then I remembered the two shadows who had fled when I stepped out to talk to the man. "I never met them before. I simply wanted to ask you for directions."

"Directions?"

"Yes." I supposed that this fellow entering my life was what I needed right then from the god box. It gave me a view of my own panic. His face became very red and he angrily snatched the purses from my hand.

"I suppose you expect some kind of reward for your honesty."

"I would just like to know where I should go to obtain passage to Ahmrita."

He arched an eyebrow as he tied his purses to his belt. "What have you done?"

"Done?"

"Fellow, you wouldn't be seeking passage on Blood Street unless you were on the run. Who is after you?"

"Have you ever heard of Captain Shadows?"

Both of the man's eyebrows went up. "Of the Heterin Guard in Iskandar?"

"The same." I waited for further questions, but the man stood staring at me. "Aren't you going to ask me why Shadows is on my trail?"

The man shook his head. "I doubt if even you know that." He tapped the side of his head. "Captain Shadows doesn't exactly ride a four-legged horse, if you know what I mean."

"Can you help me?"

He nodded. "Perhaps, but not here. By what name are you called?"

"Korvas."

"I am called Delomas. Come with me, then, Korvas."

I followed the man called Delomas across the traffic at the edge of the marketplace into the bazaar itself. At this hour there were only a few customers, but the merchants appeared willing to keep their tents and stalls open. There was a clear place toward the center for farmers and less wealthy merchants who displayed their produce or merchandise from a rug or directly on the paving stones. My years in the Iskandar market came back to me, and it was with gratitude that I followed Delomas to the opposite side of the bazaar.

We came to a substantial building crowned with minarets and a gold and blue onion dome. There were two magnificent private guards flanking the doorway, resplendent in blue silks and silver-studded swords. They saluted as Delomas approached, but they seemed to be surprised. I was curious to know whether they were surprised to see him arrive on foot rather than on a litter of suitable distinction, or that he had arrived at all.

Once inside, my eyes were feasted by the rich goods that filled the huge room. Bolts of fabulous silks were draped across gold-worked furniture that stood upon carpets so rich and deep it tempted one to try and swim in them. Magnificent porcelain statues, ornate cases of gold and silver bracelets, rings, and chains, articles of blown and cast glass, and intricate tapestries hung all around.

I must admit, the inclination to review my refusal of a reward passed through my mind. It appeared that Delomas was a very wealthy fellow. Nevertheless, I followed him through a curtained doorway into another magnificent room, twice as large and filled with ten times the riches. In the center of these riches was a silk-covered hassock upon a raised platform of multicolored cushions. Delomas climbed up to the hassock, sat upon it, and crossed his legs.

"Muzto," he called.

"Your servant, master," came a voice from behind me. That was the first time I knew that we had been followed. It was frightening how quietly those huge guards could move.

Delomas held out his hand toward another hassock. "Please enjoy my poor hospitality, what there is of it, Korvas."

"My thanks." I sat upon the richness and made an effort to hide my shabby boots beneath my robe, which was also getting to feel a bit ragged.

Delomas pointed toward a doorway on the far side of

the room. "Muzto, when I walked through the door of my own business establishment, my own guards looked surprised to see me. Why is that?"

The guard held his hands to his sides and bowed. "Great master, it is just that we were told that you had been killed."

"Ah. Who passed on this bit of information?"

"Your commander of the household guard, master. Nigiza."

"I see." Delomas nodded quietly as his face became very cold. Through hooded eyes he looked at Muzto. "Take Bakku with you and bring Nigiza to me. Say nothing to him."

"As you wish, master."

"And send Eshkigal to me."

"As you wish, master." The guard bowed and left the room. No sooner had he gone through the doorway than he was replaced by a liveried servant who approached Delomas and bowed. "You wished to see me, master?"

"We have a guest, Eshkigal. Bring refreshments."

As the servant bowed out of the room, Delomas looked at me and smiled as he blushed. "I apologize for being brusque when we first met, Korvas. I fear I was terribly embarrassed by my display of fright. I've had a harrowing day, and dawn has yet to make an appearance. To begin, my litter never arrived at my home, my household staff all seemed to be elsewhere, and it was vital that I be here early today. I am to meet with an important person here in a few minutes to close a deal for a considerable sum. Of course, this meant that I would be carrying such a sum with me. There was only one person—Nigiza—who knew, and who could have arranged all of these mishaps, leaving me at the mercy of those two knife-artists you chased away. I'm certain that they were arranged by Nigiza, as well."

"My good Delomas, I'd hardly say that I chased them away."

"Nevertheless, when I noticed those two cutthroats sniffing at my heels, you can believe I sent an urgent prayer to my patron, Nalas, for her intervention. No sooner had I uttered my prayer than you appeared, friend Korvas."

"I fear I make an unlikely angel."

"Who can argue with the tools chosen by the gods? Remember what the great philosopher Zaqaros once said: 'If we could see as the gods and choose as the gods, we would be the gods.' "

I pondered the words of Zaqaros, since they did answer the question that had been worrying me. Is it then even possible for me to understand the reasons why I had been chosen to be the Guide of the ancient prophecy? As I was turning this over in my mind, the servant called Eshkigal brought in a tray with hot tea, wine, and tiny little delicious things. After Delomas had taken something for himself, the tray was held before me.

I took tea and was sampling one of the tasties when the two huge guards, Muzto and Bakku, entered dragging between them a fellow I suspected might be the ambitious Nigiza. Considering his station, Nigiza seemed inordinately clad in gold and silks. Judging from the smell that began to fill the room, he had been caught in midcelebration.

The trio came to a halt before Delomas's hassock, and the merchant motioned to the guards. "Not quite so close. Back up a bit."

"Master," called Nigiza, "you are wrong about me. I had no idea what those men were—"

"Back further," said Delomas to the guards. "Move him off the carpet."

"Master, I beg you, I am innocent. I—"

As Nigiza begged, the two guards pulled his feet off the carpet. Delomas reached into a hidden fold of his hassock, pulled out one of the new pistols, aimed, and fired, sending a gob of lead straight through Nigiza's heart.

"Muzto, dump him in the sewer and send in a girl to clean up the floor."

"As you wish, master."

As they were dragging out Nigiza, Delomas put down

his weapon and leaned to his right. There was a lap desk there and he picked it up and began writing a note.

"Delomas, I hesitate to interrupt such a decisive fellow, but wouldn't it have been more prudent to call in the city guard?"

"When a man strikes at me through the state, I retaliate through the state. When a man employs his own resources, I employ mine."

When he had finished his writing and had marked it with his ring, he handed it out to me. "I know of a ship sailing on this morning's tide for Ahmrita. This is a note to the captain of the *Silk Ghost* telling him to give you, and whoever you have with you, passage to Ahmrita and no questions. The captain's name is Abzu. You will find the ship moored at the last slip on Corner Pier. Just follow the alley off the corner of Bay where it joins West River."

I stood, and took the note. "Master Delomas, I . . ."

"Was there something else?"

"No." I shook my head. "Nothing except to give you my thanks."

"Don't bother. That note contains my thanks to you, and now all accounts are paid. The gods be with you."

"And with you, Delomas." I bowed deeply, walked around the puddle of blood, and left the room. When I was once again outside, crossing the bazaar, I placed my hand upon the god box. I whispered to it beneath my breath, "I wonder how many times I will have to see you split the continent before I believe in you without reservation."

A drawer opened and there was a note. I stopped by a lampmaker's stall and read it. It said, *"You already believe. You don't believe you believe."*

25

As I was crossing the warehouse rooftops to where I had left Abrina, the dawn elf was beginning his climb out of the bay. In the rosy half-light I saw Abrina looking toward the east in meditation. She appeared to be surrounded by rubbish. As I came closer I saw the rubbish for what it was: parts and pieces of mutilated humans. Fear for her closed my throat and I accidentally stepped upon a detached hand.

"I'm terribly sorry," I said to the hand's owner, wheresoever he or she might have been. There were half-robed torsos here, a leg or two there, here an arm, there an arm, everywhere—

"Abrina?" I stood looking up at her. I could see by her eyes that her mind was in another world. I reached out and touched her arm. "Abrina?"

She turned her head, looked down at me, and smiled. "Korvas. I wondered if a back-alley blade had found you."

"No, nothing like that. I've arranged passage on a ship that leaves for Ahmrita this morning." I swept my arm, indicating the human litter. "What happened here?"

"Do you mean the bodies?"

"Of course I mean the bodies!"

"A misunderstanding."

"Abrina, this had to be some misunderstanding."

"They assumed I be helpless." She closed her eyes and slowly shook her head. "So many dead. I never saw anyone dead before."

I pointed at a torso that had been ripped in two. "Did *you* do this?"

"What difference does it make?"

"Whoever did this thoroughly enjoyed the event. If it was you it might change things a bit."

"What things? How you look at me?"

"At least." I looked around at the pieces. "How many of them were there?"

She slowly shook her head. "I don't remember. I've tried counting torsos, but I have more pairs of legs than I have torsos." She turned her head toward the east. "Url saw them attacking me, and immediately he went for them. He be just a wild creature and he hasn't eaten anything since we be in the mountains, you know."

"Where is he now?"

"He took a live one with him and flew off into the night. Right now he be having a meal and a nap."

Sudden images leaped before my mind's eye, and just as suddenly I forced them out of my awareness. If there had been enough time to panic, I would have. There wan't, so I didn't.

"Abrina, our ship leaves soon."

She stood and rested her ax on her shoulder. "Where be the ship?"

I pointed north. "All of the way at the end of this row—it's the ship at the end of Corner Pier. It's called the *Silk Ghost*."

The giantess began walking across the rooftops toward Corner Pier. I looked above me for a sign of the winged lion, then looked around at the roof. There were eleven torsos. I saw several knives, even one still clutched by a hand that had long since lost its arm. Despite the horror of the scene around me, I felt my lips tug into a bit of a smile. With eleven or more blades dispatched to the underworld, the odds of one or more of the three who had cut me being among them really weren't all that bad. I did a quick search for an ownerless purse or two, but found nothing. After a chill tickled my bones, I left those parts and hastened to catch up with Abrina.

At the end of the rooftops we could see Corner Pier

extending north into the river. There were three slips that branched off to the right, and on the riverside edge of the last slip, a large, gray and white four-masted ship, the *Silk Ghost*, was tied up. The crew was preparing to get under way.

As we walked down the pier there were hoots and rude remarks from the various crews of the ships in port. The remarks, however, were directed not at the giantess, but at me. From a distance it must have looked as though a normal-sized beauty was walking next to a minor dwarf. As we came closer, however, the hoots ceased. At the end of the pier we turned and stopped next to a man at the bottom of the gangway. Abrina stood on the other side of the man, looking up at the ship. Several members of the crew were looking back.

The man at the bottom of the gangway was absorbed in some papers he was examining. He was in his thirties with a chunky build and a scrubby black beard.

"Captain Abzu?"

"Eh?" He raised his bushy black eyebrows, glanced at me, and looked back at his papers. "I'm not the captain. Captain's on board."

"Who are you?"

"First mate. My name's Lanthus."

"I have a note for Captain Abzu."

Lanthus held out a scarred hand. "Give it here."

I placed the note into the first mate's hand and watched as his eyebrows went up. "You know important people." He scowled at my clothes and boots. "Are you traveling in disguise?"

"Of course . . . not." This honesty business has its drawbacks, and I squirmed with anger as Lanthus grinned.

He jabbed the note with his finger. "What's this, then? Do you have someone with you?"

"Yes. A woman: Abrina, daughter of Shamas." There were a few chuckles from the crew.

"Then she is not your wife or daughter."

I shook my head. "What difference does it make?"

The mate's face grew a leer that could make stone

crawl. "Is she very pretty, friend?" There were more chuckles from the crew.

I glanced over his shoulder at Abrina and shrugged. "Yes. She is a great beauty."

"Is she your sweetheart?"

"Not exactly."

"She isn't Delomas's current bedwarmer, is she?"

My face grew red. "Sir, you teeter upon the brink of unpleasantness."

"I meant no offense." That leer came again. "I just inquired to see if she is fair game." The crew's laughter became very loud.

I pursed my lips. "You consider women to be game?"

"What else? Look, fellow, do you have a claim on her or not?"

A smile worked its way to the surface. "No. I have no claim on her. However, she can look out for herself." I took my note back, started up the gangway, and paused to look down at the giantess. She had her ax off her shoulder and was examining the ship's planking. "Come, Abrina. Let's get aboard."

She swung the flat of her blade against the ship's side with a whack that must have sprung a few joints and sent whoever may have been leaning against the inside of the hull on a trip to the other side of the ship. Lanthus turned around abruptly, looked at her left hip, and slowly let his gaze increase in elevation until he was looking at her face. The crew's laughter was deafening.

Abrina nodded, patted the mate on the top of his head, and said, "You have a solid ship." She walked around the mate and up the gangway.

Once we were aboard, I leaned over the railing and whispered to Lanthus, loudly enough for all to hear, "I think she's partial to flowers."

26

As we raised sail and the *Silk Ghost* glided out of the river's mouth into the bay, I watched the seasoned merchant crew climb among the rigging, resembling so many pirates. I checked the flag on the mast, but there was only the red, white, and gold diamond-star of Kienosos; nothing black and bone-littered.

The ship's deck was as spotless as a surgeon's theater, almost as though the blood had been recently scrubbed from it by leering crewmen who had cutlasses in their teeth while they wielded their scrub brushes.

Behind the quarterdeck railing stood First Mate Lanthus, his cruel face and shifty eyes probably plotting mutiny or some other outrage. Before we passed the New Dock light and turned at Grave's Point, however, he was joined by the captain. Captain Abzu was a powerful-looking man with gray hair and beard and fierce black eyes that seemed to shout their joy at observing hapless crewmen being picked apart by the lash.

He was a man of priorities. First he checked the position and speed of the ship against the navigation lights and the topmost wind pennants. As his gaze worked its way down the rigging I had the feeling that if there were one knot, nail, or thread out of place anywhere on board, Abzu's eyes would find it, and some poor wretch would be over the side to feed the fishes. Satisfied that his ship was afloat and headed in the correct direction, he looked up at Abrina and down at me.

"What have we here, then?"

Lanthus pointed at me. "Give the captain your note, lad."

I reluctantly handed the letter to Abzu, and the captain seemed to read with one eye while he watched his ship with the other. "You are Korvas."

It was a flat statement, but I felt as though it merited a response of some kind. "Yes."

"Ummm." He tapped the paper with his finger. "A powerful friend you have in Delomas—shorten sail a bit, Mate—"

"Aye, Captain."

"—and the friend of Delomas is the friend of Abzu."

Mate Lanthus returned to the railing and began screaming in what was possibly a foreign language. Immediately the men in the rigging performed countless complex tasks with the precision of a machine.

"Delomas's note says no questions, and I shall respect his wishes, although curiosity may get the better of my other passengers."

"You have other passengers?"

"Yes. Master Delomas's agent, Lem Vyle, and his bodyguard." Abzu handed the letter back to me and looked up at the giantess. "Lady, may I know by what name you are called?"

"I be Abrina. At home in the Valley of the Omergunts I be Abrina the Ax."

The captain looked at the ax in her hands. He held out his own hands. "May I?"

She grinned and held it out. Once Abzu had a grip on it, Abrina let go. I will say this much for Captain Abzu: although he may have sentenced himself to a life with his guts held in by trusses made of sailcloth, he held the ax. His face went red and he nodded toward the blade. "Heavy."

"I hammered it out from an anvil at my father's forge," she informed him.

"You may take it back now." As Abrina relieved the captain of his burden, he removed his cap and wiped the perspiration from his forehead. "Someday,

Abrina the Ax, I would very much like to see you swing that blade. It must be a magnificent sight to see."

"I would be happy, Captain Abzu."

"Is there anything I can do to make your stay on board more comfortable?"

"Yes. I cannot easily fit through the doors in this ship, all of the ceilings be too low, and the beds be too short and narrow."

Abzu's face winced. "Lady, they are hatchways, not doors; they are bunks, not beds; and they are overheads, not ceilings."

"My apologies. Your hatchways be too small, your bunks too short and narrow, and your overheads too much overhead."

The captain chuckled and turned to Lanthus. "As soon as we round Fort Chara, put some of the crew on fixing up the forward hold for her quarters. Scrub it until it smells like a forest. I want the hatchway to the deck built twelve feet high, and a bunk constructed with a sleeping surface of twelve by five."

"Aye, aye, Captain."

Abzu looked up at Abrina. "If you need anything else, please let me know."

He turned back to his business. I looked at Abrina's face and thought I detected a smile.

That evening, as the ship rounded Point Nepri and entered the Straits of Chara, I stood alone in the prow of the ship listening to the carpenters put the finishing touches on Abrina's quarters. I looked eastward and watched the endlessness of the ocean called Ilan after the father of oceans. Before we would see dry land again, there were over five thousand miles of water to cross. The smaller swells of the Sea of Chara grew to become the watery hills and valleys of Ilan.

The Straits of Chara were named after the ancient Itkah sea goddess, patroness of those who go down to the sea to do battle with water monsters. It struck me as strange how what we know to be rank superstition in the daylight on land can become tenable theory as night falls on the ocean.

Since this was my first time at sea, I had entertained thoughts about becoming seasick. I was grateful to find out that, although my stomach was sour, at least this experience wasn't going to cost me any dinners. That it was going to cost me somehow, however, I had no doubt.

There was a knot in my guts. The sky was darkening, as was the water, and we were heading directly into the dark. I was used to trusting to my own devices to keep alive, and now my existence depended upon Captain Abzu's honor, judgment, and skill, the performance of his crew, and the dependability of the *Silk Ghost*. Once I began to appreciate the size of Ilan, Captain Abzu's magnificent ship began looking rather small and leaky, and he and his crew a band of incompetent buccaneers.

"With your fear upon your shoulder, Korvas, you may as well be ridden by a demon." I turned abruptly but could see no one. I strained my eyes and, against the deck and the house that they had built to cover the forward hold for Abrina, there was a shadow. The moon was behind a cloud and could cast no shadow.

"Syndia? Nanteria?" I studied the shadow but it didn't seem to move, which was strange because the ship was moving. "Are you the goddess of shadows and smoke? Or am I seasick, seeing things, and unaware of the fact?"

"How many times must you see the continent split, Korvas?"

"Bah!" I turned my face back toward the sea. "Talking with shadows!" It was very silent, and I turned to see if the shadow was still there. It was. "Why do you remain silent?"

"You wanted silence."

"This is maddening. I—how do I know that I am not hallucinating? I haven't slept for days. I could be seeing and hearing things."

"Yes. Or you could be seeing my shadow and hearing my words."

I fumed at the shadow for a moment, then asked the question that the goddess had wanted me to ask in the first place. "What did you mean about the demon? I knew a fellow who had one of those invisible curses that never left him. He used to complain about the thing. He said that it constantly called him names and ridiculed him. I don't believe in demons, myself. I'm convinced it was the beggar's conscience."

The shadow laughed. "Korvas, I thought you believed in mean little spirits."

I wrapped my robe about me against the sea's chill. "I suppose I do. But I don't have a demon myself, and I've never seen one."

"You have a mean little spirit of your own, Korvas. It's called fear. It rides you harder than any demon and enslaves you more harshly than any master."

I felt the anger rising within me. "I give my fear to the god box when it's necessary."

"No, Korvas. You have yet to give your fear to the god box."

"Well, shadow, what is it that I have been doing?"

"When the fear becomes too crippling, you loan the box a small piece of your fear. As soon as you can, you take your fear back."

"I don't like being afraid, Nanteria. Why would I do such a foolish thing as take back fear? I would just as soon take back a sour stomach or a headache."

"You have done all three."

"Oh, have I?"

The shadow against the wall seemed to change shape, becoming a silhouette of . . . Captain Shadows, the cut-throats and their knives in the Blood Street Bazaar, the wings, teeth, and talons of Abrina's great winged lion. "Korvas, do you have a headache?"

"Yes."

"How is your stomach?"

"Sour."

"And your fears?"

"I have them back. These are all fears I had given the god box and now I have them back." I looked back at the water. "Why do I take them back? I don't like being afraid. I hate it."

"Fear is how you attempt to control the future. You

don't understand that the future is not yours to control. That belongs to the gods."

I snorted out a cynical laugh. "That's not a great recommendation, Nanteria!"

The shadow grew until it covered the wall, until it covered the ship, the ocean, the universe. I could not see my fingers in front of my face. Did Nanteria cut me off from all light? Did she blind me? Fear grabbed me by the legs and threatened to run me off the ship, over the railing, into the bottomless ocean.

I held onto my god box with one hand and the railing with the other. I thought, why would Nanteria bring me this far only to blind and drown me as some kind of object lesson? I could turn over my fear to the god box, but what did Nanteria say I needed from the god box?

Trust. I picked up the god box in both hands and said, "To you I give my fear. Do with it what you will. From you I ask that you grant me trust."

I waited in the darkness, confident that what was happening was what was supposed to happen, and that when I was ready it would become light again. It amused me to find out that patience is a result of trust. That was when the shadow-goddess returned the shades of night to me. The blues, blacks, whites, and grays of the ocean, the black lines of the rigging against the moonlit clouds, the tiny pools of warmth made by the few oil lamps on deck.

I saw First Mate Lanthus walking toward me, and I marveled at how different he looked. Instead of a cruel face and shifty eyes, he was a fine figure of an officer.

"We have finished with the lady's quarters, and the captain has moved his table there. I have the watch right now, so I can't be with you tonight. However, I'm extending Captain Abzu's invitation."

"Thank you."

He turned and I began to follow until, out of the corner of my eye, I caught sight of a long neck with spiked fins coming out of the water supporting a ferocious head. It towered there higher than the tallest mast of the world's tallest ship. I stopped and looked over the railing. The shadows and waves continued to play among themselves, but the monster I thought I saw had vanished.

"Is there something wrong?" asked Lanthus.

"No." Somewhere my brand-new trust had slipped away. Had I only borrowed it from the box, returning it when the shadows returned the light? I pushed away from the railing and followed Lanthus, pondering shadow-goddesses, fear, pirates, sea monsters, trust, and such.

27

Lanthus and the crew had done an excellent job of turning a damp, smelly cargo hold into a lady's cabin. A curtained bunk large enough for Abrina had been built into one side, leaving the area directly beneath the hatches open. A ladder led to the deck and to the special doorway that had been ordered by the captain. The table for dinner was located upon a platform that was three or more feet above deck level. Abrina sat in her special chair on the deck while the rest of us sat with our chairs on the platform. It was something of a novelty to be looking at the giantess at almost eye level.

The rest of the table's occupants were an odd lot. Captain Abzu was there, of course. To his left sat his second mate, Dentaat, who hailed from the barbarian kingdom of Ounri. He had unusually dark skin which contrasted sharply with his startling blue eyes and white-blond hair. His hair must have been very long, but he kept it braided and wrapped around his head. There were long bone needles through his hair to keep it in place, and he ate from the point of a knife.

To Dentaat's left was Lem Vyle, a former teacher and magician of note who was Delomas's agent on this voyage. Vyle had pale skin, a black beard salted with gray, and the most disconcerting gray eyes. They seemed to see all while revealing nothing.

At the foot of the table was Abrina. I was to her left, and between me and the captain sat possibly the most beautiful and mysterious woman I had ever seen. Her long black hair framed her face with wispy curls. She was dressed in black trousers, slippers, and jacket topped by a deep purple, lacy robe. She was known only as Tah, and she was Lem Vyle's bodyguard.

One of the crew members, introduced to us as Mahvat, sat off to one side strumming an Ahmritan stringed instrument called an utai. He played the thing quietly, and he seemed to be an expert. At least he seemed so to me, having only seen one other person—my father—attempt the forty-stringed guitar.

Abzu raised his cup and said, "To Chara and to Ilan: may she protect us on our voyage, and may he forgive our trespass."

In response Lem Vyle, Tah, and Abrina held up their cups, while the Ounrian second mate, Dentaat, held up his knife. I held up a leg of chicken. Together we toasted, "To Chara and to Ilan." When we were settled, Abrina spoke. "Captain Abzu, I thank you, Mate Lanthus, and your crew for preparing this cabin for me."

"It was our pleasure, lady; however, I will pass on your thanks to my first officer and the crew." He quickly looked over the inside of the hold with that same practiced eye. When he concluded his inspection, he returned his gaze to Abrina. "It is to your liking, then?"

"I find it quite comfortable."

Tah sat back in her chair, her lips parted in a bit of a smile. "That bed is magnificent, Captain. There is enough room there for some highly fascinating games."

The captain's face reddened. "We did our best, lady."

"On such a bed," said Tah, "I could do my best."

Abzu's face was redder than the Grave's Point light as Lem Vyle, without looking up, quietly said one word: "Tah."

Tah returned to her dinner as Vyle addressed Abzu. "You must forgive my bodyguard, Captain. I fear her frankness is one of the penalties for too long an association with me." Seeing the confused looks from those at the table, he explained. "Among my poor gifts, I am a *ziusu*."

He looked toward me as though I should know what a *ziusu* was. "I am not familiar with the term."

"It is Ahmritan, and it means 'seer of lies.' It simply means that when someone tells me something that departs from the truth, I know it."

"I take it you are not invited to many parties," said Abzu with a smile.

Vyle faced the captain. "My gift does not require me to be a boor. Knowing that a man is lying does not necessarily obligate me to point it out to him." He raised his eyebrows and chuckled. "However, you are correct. I am not invited to many parties." Those at the table laughed. "Nevertheless, my gift does make me a very valuable agent to Delomas."

"Do you read minds?" I asked.

"No. That is a different discipline. The mind reader sees substance—the 'what' of a thought. I see only true and false when thoughts are put to words and gestures. It is often the same thing in practical application, however."

I kept my gaze on Tah, but asked Lem Vyle, "How did you two get together? Do you mind me asking?"

Vyle nodded at his bodyguard, and Tah looked at me with the damnedest eyes I have ever felt—something between fear and lust. She parted her lips and spoke. "I don't mind. Three years ago my master, an enemy of Delomas, ordered me to kill Lem Vyle. Vyle watched as I took on and dispatched the two bodyguards he then employed. He hired me on the spot."

As a minor chill danced upon my spine, I looked at Delomas's agent. "If you don't mind me asking, she betrayed her former master. How do you know she won't betray you for the right price?"

Vyle smiled. "I am a *ziusu*, and I have already paid the right price."

"What if she is offered more money?"

"My dear Korvas, you find it difficult to trust, don't you?"

"That's a strange sentiment from someone who employs a bodyguard and deals on behalf of a merchant of the Blood Street Bazaar."

The agent wiped his mouth, leaned back in his chair, and studied me. I felt that, beneath his stare, every lie I had ever told was displaying itself upon my face like so many pimples. "A certain amount of caution is necessary from wherever one hails, my dear Korvas. A life dedicated to caution, however, is fear-ridden insanity." He held his hand open toward Tah. "I asked her how much money she would need to have to wish no longer for more. She answered, I saw that it was the truth, and it was a price I was able and willing to pay to obtain her services. She now has all of the money she needs, and I provide her with the rest of what she needs."

"Which is?"

"Action," completed Tah. "Master Vyle always takes me with him wherever he goes, and there are few persons in the world who have the price on his head that Lem Vyle does. I discourage those who would, through some misguided sense of greed, attempt to collect that price."

"I don't understand. Why is there a price on your head? Are you a criminal?"

"Quite the opposite. I'm so honest, some persons—mostly those in business and government—find it painful. Those who would rather not be hurt by my honesty put up the price. Merchants, not city magistrates, called down the bounty hunters on me. You see, there are those who would rather not deal with an agent who is a *ziusu*, hence the price—"

"—and the action," Tah completed.

"Enough about us," Vyle said as he faced toward Abrina. "What is your story?"

Abrina glanced at me, then looked back at Vyle. "I would tell, but I be but a part of a larger tale. Did I tell the truth?"

"Yes."

Abrina looked at me. "Be there a reason not?"

Abzu cleared his throat for attention. "I do have instructions from Master Delomas not to subject this lady and gentleman to questioning."

Vyle grinned. "Why, I wonder? Friend Korvas, are you in trouble with the King's Guard?"

Before the protest even made it to my lips, Vyle nodded. "I see. Now, with your dark skin and straight hair, I detect an Ahmritan in your family tree, yes?"

"Yes."

"But I sense that you know little or nothing of the language. Your speech comes from the less fashionable districts of Iskandar. It is intended to sound educated, however; thus we pose the question: Why is an overblown street git from Iskandar coming from the Valley of the Omergunts—lady Abrina's speech, of course—with a giantess, on a ship bound for Ahmrita under Delomas's protection, payment, and instructions of silence?" He leaned forward. "There are two of you?"

The steam fairly shrieked from my collar. "First I'd like to finish up this matter of the overblown street git."

"I meant no offense, friend Korvas."

"I certainly took no offense, friend Vyle," said I as I wrapped my fingers around the handle of my knife. Before I could move my blade an inch from my pocket, I felt a pointed something pricking my neck. I looked, and the lovely Tah had the needle point of a dagger ready to zip through my jugular.

"Please don't," she said.

I removed my hand from my pocket, without the blade of course. Tah nodded her approval and put her knife back in its hiding place. At times, I thought, fear is a useful thing for one who plans on surviving a meal at this table.

"Now," Vyle continued, "there are two of you?"

Thinking of Nanteria and my god box, I held out my hands. "Well—"

"More, then? Five? Three? Four of you. Very good. In our close company, the other two must be personages of a more spiritual character. Is that peculiar box one of them?"

"I—"

"I see." Vyle held up his hand and nodded. "The other, then, is a ghost, demon, troll, god, goddess—

goddess, then." Lem Vyle turned his head slowly until he was looking Abrina full in the face. His eyebrows went up as he said, "The Hero and the Destroyer?" Abrina smiled, and Vyle looked at me. "You are the Guide?"

"Now—"

"Yes, now it all makes sense." He held up a finger. "Tretia—the Heterin Guard—no, Captain Shadows is on your trail; hence the no-questions caution from Delomas." Delomas's agent leaned back in his chair and clasped his hands over his belly. "I always thought the prophecy about the Hero and the Destroyer was a myth."

Both Abzu and Abrina laughed out loud. "Excellent, Vyle," said the captain.

Lem Vyle rubbed his temples and said, "Let me see if I can remember the oracle. 'Guided by the Mirror of the Second, the Hero will be found by the Second, who will be chosen by a father's hand, kept by the First, loved by the Mirror, and burned by the Mirror to be gathered by the Smoke.' "

He opened his eyes, lowered his hand, and stared at me with those gray eyes. "There is more? No. Something different." He smiled. "With enough time and patience, friend Korvas, I could get the exact wording of the oracle and the reasons why it is different from the version we all know. Could you spare me the effort?"

I slowly shook my head. "You are a frightening person, Lem Vyle. I am not surprised that you find few invitations to parties."

"Actually, friend Korvas, I am not a frightening person. You are scared of me. There's a difference."

I glanced at Tah. "I can see how being around this . . . person could affect you." Her lips filled my sight. "Now that I think about it, being around you could affect a person, too."

She smiled and nodded toward me. "Is there any reason why we can't hear what you think is the real version of the oracle?"

I looked around at my dinner companions. "I can't think of a single reason." I thought for a moment, then recited what I had seen in the book:

"The Child, orphaned by the cult,
Is charged by the Smoke
To protect the Seeker from harm
Until the Smoke releases the Child
To hand the Seeker to its Reflection.
The Seeker shall find the Blade,
And more, himself, beside the one
Before Manku in Land-beyond-the-Sunrise
All is Manku.
At the tip of Ihtar's hand,
Where float the lavender leaves,
The Destroyer shall meet the Blade,
Leaving only one.
All is Manku."

As I finished, Lem Vyle was filtering the words of the oracle through his special gifts. I felt Tah's hand upon my left arm. "The Blade is not a man?"

"It doesn't say."

Vyle's lips moved silently as his eyes looked upward. " '. . . the Seeker to its Reflection./ The Seeker shall find the Blade,/ And more, himself, beside the one. . . .' Friend Korvas, there is no Guide in this version, unless you are both the Seeker and the Seeker's Reflection."

"What a pleasure it is to know something about myself that you don't."

"The Seeker was your twin brother, then? My condolences for your loss."

I folded my arms and scowled, wondering where one might contribute to the bounty fund on Lem Vyle's head.

Vyle placed his elbows on the table and rested his chin upon his clasped fists. "Do you believe in the prophecy, Korvas? Do you believe in Manku? Do you believe the world will end unless someone kills the Destroyer?"

I looked deeply within myself. "No. I don't really believe in any of it. I do believe that Captain Shadows believes in it enough to kill Abrina and me."

"You spoke the truth as you saw it, friend Korvas. Yet there is a part of you that thinks you are lying."

I raised my arms in despair. "What would you have me do? I have spent my life not believing in the gods. Yet these past few days have shown me things that can be explained only by the existence of the gods."

I placed the god box on the table. "This, for just one example. Is it just magic, or is there a god inside? It acts and talks like a god, and it is certainly as confusing as one. On the other hand, it's only a box. I have made god boxes that work as well as this one out of candy bowls. I have had a goddess stand next to me and talk to me, yet I would rather believe that I am overtired or have gone insane. I am at my wits' end."

"Korvas, a *ziusu* can see lies that the teller of the lie believes to be true. I think you have a lie such as that."

"I have been wrong about a great many things in my time, and I will probably be wrong about a few more before I rest my bones. Which mistake do you have in mind?"

"What I see is that you did not spend your life not believing in the gods. In fact, you believe in them very strongly."

I issued an involuntary laugh. "I'm almost inclined to call you a liar, Vyle." I held up a finger toward Tah. "Almost."

Tah shrugged and said, "You may call him anything you wish. I am his bodyguard, not his censor. Just remember to leave it at pointed words. Pointed instruments are another matter."

I looked at Vyle. "You were saying?"

"The lies we tell ourselves," said Vyle, "are the most damaging. In you is much pain, yes?"

"No."

"Indeed, that much?" He pursed his lips, nodded, and stroked his beard. "Did you know your parents?"

"Of course I did," I answered hotly.

"Only one, then—your father?"

"How can you know that?"

Vyle waved an impatient hand. "The important thing is this lie that is strangling your present."

"I want to know."

"Very well. You part-lied when I asked you if you knew your parents, hence you knew only one of them. It had to be your father, since you are the Mirror." He saw the puzzled look on my face. "You are the Mirror of the Second, his twin brother, and the Second 'will be chosen by a father's hand.' Now, let us continue. Your mother died in childbirth?"

"Yes."

"And something more. Your brother—your twin?"

"What of him?"

Lem Vyle rubbed his chin as he studied me. "You feel that he died—no, that he was murdered? Your father killed him—allowed him to be killed. Yet he was not dead, otherwise the Seeker never could have found the Blade. But your brother is dead now." He took a sip of tea and continued. "When we put the pieces together, we have a motherless child who is separated from his twin brother soon after birth. With his father being Ahmritan, the child's skin was very dark and he was raised in the Ahmritan faith, the Ihtari.

"The child was called by many cruel names, and was beaten by the other children. Not understanding his father's service to an ancient prophecy, the child blamed his father for the persecution, for his brother's death, even for his skin. He blamed his father for it all. Hence, at a young age the child ran away from home and took to the streets. How young were you, Korvas?"

"Eight," I whispered.

Vyle sadly shook his head. "There are many horrors awaiting the innocent alone on the streets, and the back streets were where you had to survive. You stole whatever you had to steal to survive. You sold everything from your body to your soul, to survive. You even killed to survive. You have many scars, but most of the scars you carry are on your heart. While you were collecting them upon the street, your father was no longer there to blame. That's when you blamed the universe and, hence, the gods who were responsible for it. You believed the gods hated you, and you wanted your revenge. How does one take revenge upon the gods, Korvas?"

I felt the hot tears slip down my cheeks. It didn't matter whether they were hidden tears or in my eyes.

Lem Vyle could see through the wall I had built about myself. I thought about his question. How does one take revenge against the gods?

"The only way I could strike back was to kill them with the only weapon I had. I refused to believe in them."

Vyle nodded and said, "That is the lie that is crippling your soul, my friend."

I pushed back my chair, stood up, and without excusing myself, I climbed the ladder to the deck. It had begun to rain and the wind had coaxed up the swells into whitecaps. I stood in the prow and let the rain wash the tears from my face as I cried for the first time in twenty-two years.

28

Late that night, as the storm rocked me back and forth in my bunk, I searched the dark corners of the compartment I shared with the Ounri, Dentaat. The second mate was on watch, which removed much of the discomfort I felt about the fellow's sleeping habits. Before he went on watch he rested by sitting cross-legged on the deck and staring directly at me, never blinking. A few hours of that could give the shakes to Mount Eternity.

I drove the image out of my mind, closed my eyes, and tried to sleep. Sleep, however, was a thousand miles away. The words of Lem Vyle kept teasing the back of my head. The lie that was crippling my soul. Perhaps I had been wrong about everything, but what could I do about it now? Once your last dart leaves your hand, what good is it to know that it was thrown with a foul aim?

I thought I saw a green light coming from the porthole. I pulled myself naked from my bunk, braced myself against the tossing deck, and went to the porthole. For a moment nothing was visible except for the white tops of the waves. A pale green, glowing mist began forming above the waves, and it swirled, parted, and became as a hundred specters at the King's Ball, dancing against the storm.

I had seen the glowmist once before, as a child of ten condemned to the evil-smelling fisher shacks in Shantytown on the coast north of Iskandar. For twenty hours a day I cleaned fish for a brute named Halpus who kept me and four other children prisoner.

There was a storm one night that boiled the Sea of Chara. Through the door of Halpus's shack, I saw the glowmist ghosts dancing above the waves. The other children saw me looking, and they stopped what they were doing and looked. The glowmist was the kind of happening that lifted my heart from the world of mundane brutality long enough to taste the possibility of mystery, romance, and adventure.

Suddenly Halpus was standing in the doorway. With a bellow of rage he stormed into us with a barrel stave. We had been beaten many times before, but always one at a time. The ones who were not being beaten would always concentrate upon their work, thankful that the beating was happening to someone else. This time, however, Halpus lit into all five of us at once. All five of us had our gutting knives, and we jumped him at the same time. We gutted and cleaned Halpus and packed him in his own salt. Then we watched him scream himself to death.

As I stood in that cabin on the *Silk Ghost*, I remembered the faces of my four accomplices. The eldest one, a boy named Jopo, drowned that night in the storm, trying to escape in a small boat. The two other boys, Ciutvi and Lasc, were beheaded three years later for a robbery that resulted in the death of a minor bureaucrat. The girl, Tanza, was twelve when we gutted Halpus. She began selling herself to the very old and wealthy. Only last year I saw her begging for half-coppers in an alley, her teeth gone, her skin wrinkled, and her back bent at the age of thirty-one. Her hands shook with the ravages of some horror of a disease.

"Is it any wonder," I said to the glowmist, "that I hate the gods? Look at this world of yours!"

The greenish glow above the waves formed into the face I had seen while looking through the god box at the Shrine of Manku. Was that the face of the Destroyer? There was something of the same face when I looked deeply into the image of Captain Shadows. Was Shadows the Destroyer?

I shook my head at my own foolishness. Why would a god, any god, wish to become Captain Shadows? He was evil, that's true. However, that is only on a human scale. His dungeon tortures affected only a tiny part of the whole of the world's peoples. An evil god, I thought, would want to wreak havoc on a larger scale. Perhaps all of the gods are evil, and we convince ourselves of the existence of a few good ones in an attempt to wrest a bit of peace and sanity from reality.

I felt a bit of a chill and pulled the blanket from my bunk and wrapped myself as a thought ate its way into my awareness. Perhaps the gods had no more of a hand in creating this world than did I. Perhaps they do not punish, but were, instead, like Syndia said of the god box. They are there to help avoid or endure calamity. If I choose to do without their help, it is not they, but reality, that punishes. I had done without the help of the gods for many years, and during those years I had been punished a great deal.

I sat on the edge of my bunk and listened to the ship's wooden beams creak and groan in the storm. "But what to do about it now?" I whispered.

There was scratching—no, a quiet knock—on my cabin door. Dentaat wouldn't knock. I stood up, my blanket wrapped about me, and pulled my knife out from beneath my pillow.

"Who is it?"

The door opened, and a standing figure was cast into silhouette by the dim oil light from the passageway. Despite the almost nonexistent cobweb of a sleeping gown she wore, I knew it was Lem Vyle's bodyguard, Tah.

"Korvas, it is Tah," she spoke with a low voice as she closed the door behind her.

Tah entering my cabin in such a state of dress was a fantasy that I possessed neither the time nor the courage to entertain. Before I panicked completely, I decided to ask a really stupid question.

"What is it?"

She laughed, and I felt rather than heard her silent

footsteps across the cabin's deck. When I could feel the warmth radiating from her entire length, I wheezed my lungs into a semblance of action. "Tah, why are you here?"

"You are the Guide, Korvas. The one who will lead the Hero to challenge and defeat the Destroyer. I am the Blade you want." Her arms stole beneath my blanket and gently pulled it from me. "Choose me," she said as her hands danced here and there on my person.

"The choice has already been made—" I cannot quite describe the moves she made, but the lights flashing in front of my eyes were quite startling.

"No one—man, woman, creature, or god—can defeat me. I have lived off of the tale of the Hero and the Destroyer since I was old enough to swing a blade. This is the challenge I need, Korvas. Lead me to fight the Destroyer."

My own hands evolved a life of their own, and I noticed right away that her gown, what there had been of it, was now gone. It is Angh's guess where she kept her weapons, but I had no doubt that she was armed.

Honesty, with regret, fought its way to the surface. I managed to hold her at arm's length and retrieve my blanket. "If it was up to me, Tah, I'd be happy to choose you. But the Seeker, my brother, found the Blade. Somehow I'm supposed to guide Abrina to the battle, but my brother Tayu chose the Blade."

I expected her either to walk out or slit my throat. Instead she pushed me back toward my bunk. "As you seek the Destroyer, Korvas, may I tag along?"

The back of my legs hit the bunk and I sat down rather more abruptly than I thought dignified. "What about your master?"

She laughed with the sound of a million silver bells as she straddled me with her knees and bent me back until I was flat on the bed. "Lem Vyle would witness a fight between the Destroyer and a human. He admires a good fight."

"If Manku won the contest, would Vyle hire the god for his bodyguard?"

She laughed again as her breasts brushed my chest and her lips prowled around my left ear. "I'm certain he would try. He's wealthy enough to buy a god. But you needn't worry about Lem Vyle. He will want to be there because, as I have heard him say, 'Wherever a god touches the world, money is to be made there.' "

"You master sounds . . . very spiritual—" By Angh's nose hairs, I was beginning to gibber. Passion, guilt, duty, honesty, and the strange feeling of not knowing whether I did or didn't want Tah—

—I'm cackling like a painted fool. Of course I wanted her. But what—oh, the demons of the underworld be damned, which is a silly thing to say, because by definition the demons are damned and—

I reached out my hand and touched the god box. In my mind I asked, "What do I need right now?"

In my mind it answered, *"You're getting it."*

Just before I released my hold upon the edge of reality and let myself fall into this chasm of passion, there was a thought. My head said to itself, "Perhaps there are gods after all."

29

The next morning I awakened, smiled, and reached out my hand. There was nothing in the bunk with me except a memory. Had it been real? Had it been a dream? I opened my eyes, and there was Dentaat sitting on the floor staring at me with those unblinking eyes. I turned my back to him, tried to go back to sleep and recapture my images of Tah, but Dentaat's eyes made the back of my neck itch. After a few moments of that nonsense, I got out of bed, dressed myself, and made my way to the deck.

The storm hadn't abated, but it seemed less fearsome in the gray daylight. Between the whistles of the wind in the rigging and the crashing of the waves against the hull, it promised to be a noisy morning. Above that noise, however, I heard cheering and laughing. Using rigging and railings for handholds, I pulled my way to the center of the deck, where there was a small crowd.

The captain was there, as was Lem Vyle. In addition there were about fifteen members of the crew. I found an opening and wormed my way through until I could see Tah, dressed in a loincloth of minor imagination. She had a three-foot stick in each hand and was grinning at the five crewmen who surrounded her. Each crewman had a similar stick. All of the sticks had been dipped in some black sticky substance. I knew that because I could see five black-striped crewmen without sticks who were nursing their bruises. Tah was starting on her second batch of the morning.

I made my way over to Lem Vyle and asked, "Why is she wearing out the good captain's crew?"

Vyle laughed and pointed at Tah. "This is her exercise. She finds exercise partners by promising herself for the night to anyone who can stripe her." He turned to Abzu. "I believe they are ready, Captain."

Abzu nodded and said, "Begin."

In less time than it takes to tell about it, Tah pounded the five crewmen into the deck. As she fought, I detected something strange in Vyle's eyes. He looked worried, afraid for her. It would have made more sense for him, however, to have been worried for the crew.

"Next five," she called as she laughed. A wave broke over the bow and sprayed everyone on deck. Tah glistening wet was an incredible sight. "Come, pick up a tar stick and play for a night with me."

Abzu held up his hands. "Dear lady, I am afraid I must call off this sport. The storm seems determined to pick up, and I will be needing the sad remains of my sorry crew." He faced his crew, gave them a sad shake of his head, and said, "Back to your stations, lads, and lend a hand to the halt and lame."

Tah swung her sticks and said, "I hardly have my breath up!" As the crew departed, she continued swinging at her shadow opponents until Abrina walked from behind me and asked, "May I?"

Tah stopped and held out one of her sticks to the giantess. "Take this."

Abrina lifted her ax. "I have mine." She unlaced and removed her leather blouse, went to a cast-iron capstan, drove in the head of her ax down the handle, and turned to face Tah. "I'm ready."

Yes, the sight was magnificent, but now I was afraid for both of them. I shook Lem Vyle's sleeve. "Is this such a good idea?"

Without removing his gaze from Tah, he nodded and said, "Tah has a devil in her. This may be what she needs."

They circled each other on the deck. Sheer power was with the giantess, while agility went with the bodyguard. Tah pointed at Abrina's ax handle. "You should dip it in the tar. How else will I know when you've touched me?"

Abrina smacked her hand with the log-sized handle. "You'll know."

Again I shook Vyle's sleeve. "Master Vyle, this is insanity. You must stop it."

He looked at me, and as his lips smiled, his eyes did not. "My dear Korvas, they are fighting over you."

"Me?" I fear I only mouthed the word, for I hadn't the breath to speak it.

Vyle nodded and returned his gaze to the two women. "I know my Tah, Korvas. To do battle with a god, she would do anything."

"Even if that includes betraying you?"

"Anything." He nodded. "Tah is not a butcher, Korvas. She craves worthy competition."

Tah struck with her stick at Abrina's leg, and more quickly than I believed possible the giantess blocked the swing with her ax handle and swung at Tah's head. The bodyguard ducked and returned by thrusting her stick at Abrina's face, another block, another return. Abrina was fast enough and her arms long enough to keep Tah and her stick at a distance, but she was too slow to land a telling blow. On the other hand, Tah was all over the dome of Abrina's defensive reach like an angry hornet, too fast to be killed, but not strong enough to fight her way through the screen.

As the storm increased, the pair kept at it. More than an hour must have passed. It seemed like forever. While crewmen were shortening sail and using safety lines to cross the wave-washed deck, Abrina and Tah continued the battle. Some blows that had been too quick for me to see must have been landed, for there was a bleeding bruise high on Tah's left thigh, while Abrina's left forearm had a bleeding black stripe.

I turned to Lem Vyle. "When will they end it?"

"When one of them drops, it seems." He was hanging onto the rigging to keep from being swept away. He forced his gaze away from the conflict and looked toward the ocean. "I could swear we've been driven off course." He pointed with his finger. "Look. It's the masts of a sunken ship."

It was true. The great sticks reached out of the depths like the horns of Angh. "Where do you think we are?"

"I would wager my commissions for the next ten years that we're in Ilan's Graveyard."

"That doesn't sound good."

Vyle began pulling himself forward, and I looked to see if the contest between Tah and Abrina had been decided. It had not. I called to Vyle's back. "Why don't you order Tah to stop?"

"I have to see the captain," he shouted in return.

With my concentration torn between the sunken ship and the battle on deck, all I could do was stand there as they swung at each other. Neither one seemed as close to dropping as I was. The deck heaved beneath me and I was thrown down. Suddenly I was underwater and felt myself being washed overboard. I reached for anything, grabbed a rope, and held on. My head came above water, and the first thing I saw was Abrina and Tah still whacking away at each other.

"It pleases me," I shouted, "to know that you two have the ability to maintain a sense of priority." I don't think they heard me.

I took hold of a safety line and began pulling myself toward my cabin. That's when I heard a tremendous crack. Above us one of the masts was coming down in a tangle of ropes and a rain of splinters.

Where Tah and Abrina had been, there was nothing but wreckage. I climbed over the shattered mast and pulled aside the shredded sailcloth. In the center of the tangle of rigging, Abrina and Tah were still fighting.

"This is madness," I hollered as I climbed down to them. I walked in between them and held out my hands. "Stop! Both of you, stop!"

Mate Lanthus climbed to the top of the wreckage. "Is anyone hurt?"

"Not yet," I answered.

"Get out of there. We have to clear this mess off the deck. The topmast and sails are dragging in the water, and if we don't get clear soon, we go down."

Abrina held up her ax handle. "Can I help?"

Lanthus nodded. "Find the blade for that thing and you can." He pointed. "Up forward."

Another wave crashed down on my head, driving my face into the deck. Things became very confused about then. Crewmen with axes were on the wreckage cutting away at ropes while strong hands pulled at my shoulders. My back was leaned up against something and coils of rope were tied around my waist. Another wave, what seemed to be an eternity before my next breath, and I saw Tah squatting in front of me. She slapped my face.

"Ow."

"Good, you're alive."

She still had nothing on but her tiny loincloth. I noticed that she was carrying a single-edged sword with a curved blade. "Aren't you cold?" I asked her.

She laughed and leaped into the wreckage with her blade and went at the ropes as though she was fighting an army. Another wave came, I heard another tremendous snap, then I felt it in my back. The mast to which I had been tied had just broken. Just before everything landed on my head, I noticed that the waves were coming at the ship sideways.

Things became very dark, and the noises of the storm and the crew silenced. I felt the deck split open beneath me and I sank into the chill bosom of Father Ilan.

As I tumbled into the darkness below, I prayed for either the life or the soul of Korvas, whichever the gods found worthy of their attention.

30

Going to the afterworld was like no dreampath I had ever witnessed before. With the blackness of Universe all about me, I saw a bright light ahead. I could hardly flex my arms and legs when I tried to move toward it. I felt like a fly caught in a bowl of honey.

The light came closer, and the face of Nanteria was before me. Some part of me asked her, "Goddess, am I doing the work of the evil gods or the good?"

She answered, "Yes."

"The good or the evil?"

"Yes. Both. The smoke cannot live for long without the fire, and the fire cannot live without the smoke. How can there be Heteris without Nanteria, Nanteria without Heteris?"

"Why was I chosen, goddess?"

"That you were, is all."

The universe filled with stars as I pondered yet one more example of divine clarity. I always thought that after I died these things would make some sort of sense. I was quite disappointed.

I felt as though I was floating on the water, but when I opened my eyes all of the way I could see men and women dressed in cream-colored tights flying all around me against a sparkling background of bright green stars. I thought they must be angels, but they had no wings and wore necklaces made of fangs. They had long, black swords slung on their backs.

Upon closer examination, they weren't flying, but swimming. I saw that what I had thought to be tight-fitting clothing was, instead, naked skin with countless white markings, almost as though their dark skins had been tattooed with white paint.

Farther away were more men and women riding long-necked fish that looked like giant winged eels. The swimmers and riders wore filmy white coverings over their heads, and the stars turned out to be thousands of fish that gave off an intense, greenish white glow. We seemed to be silently moving through a forest of rotten masts and hulls—hundreds of sunken ships.

When it finally came through to my awareness that I was underwater, I put my elbows down to push myself into a sitting position. My elbows sank into something. I looked as I reached out a hand. I was on some kind of membrane. It surrounded me. Although it smelled a bit of fish and ocean, the air was sweet enough. I turned my head to see where I was being taken, and that was when I realized that I was inside a great transparent fish. I could see its head, tail, and fins, but I could only feel the rest.

One of the swimmers, a man, smiled and waved at me, and I waved back. He had only a little of the white tattooing on his body, mostly on his upper chest and arms. The six fangs dangling from his necklace were huge enough to belong in a nightmare.

I hoped that I would not have cause to meet the kind of creature that sported such ivory. Far to my right I could see Tah in another fish. I closed my eyes, certain that this was a bad dream. I felt around for my god box, but it was gone.

Panic placed a strong hand around my throat. I reached for the amulet of Sabis, and to my relief I felt its shape through my soaking-wet robe. I pulled it out, shielded it with my hand, and turned around. The closer I turned toward the head of the fish, the brighter it glowed. Hence, we were heading in the correct direction to find what I was seeking. Of course, the flaw in the sapphire's magic was the possibility that what I was seeking and what I thought I was seeking were different critters.

I dropped the amulet back inside my robe and watched the procession. After awhile I saw three of the fish ganged together to provide a breathing chamber for Abrina. She appeared to be missing her ax. In a moment more I saw Lem Vyle in yet another fish, although he did not appear to be conscious.

Two hundred men had been on the *Silk Ghost*. What had happened to them? I turned and looked toward the front of the fish. Ahead I could make out a huge shape in the water. It was brightly lit and resembled a monstrous clam, except that it appeared to be loosely woven out of some kind of green fiber.

The inside of it looked to be crammed with the transparent fish as well as the fish that glowed, and it was being towed by more than a hundred of the long-necked serpent fishes. My bubble fish and its escorts began descending, and soon we were beneath an opening in the clam. I feared to know what the object was.

A voice came clearly into my head: *"It is the palace of the Water Queen."*

It seemed as though the voice even came from a particular direction. I looked in that direction, and one of the swimmers was smiling at me. She was a very beautiful woman with short, dark brown hair and one of those black swords slung upon her back. Only her wrists and ankles were tattooed.

"Did you say something?"

The swimmer nodded. *"Yes."*

I looked back at the palace, and we were almost in the opening. The bubble fish broke the surface, rapidly unfolded its membranes, dived, and left me splashing in the water. My escorts broke the surface, their bubble fish removed themselves and dived, and then strong arms lifted me from the water and deposited me on a strangely squishy deck. The bottom surface of the shell was lined with those bubble fish.

"They are vatos."

I pointed at the bubble fish. "Vatos?"

The woman who had sort of spoken to me nodded. I looked at her and, as attractive as she was in all of her nakedness, I remembered the chill of the sea. "Don't you ever wear any clothing?"

This caused an enormous explosion of mental laughter accompanied by honking and braying sounds coming from their throats. The woman indicated the length of her body with her hands. *"Look at me. Already I am beginning to dry. Look at you."*

My robe was dripping, and the woman's comment provoked yet another outburst of laughter. As I self-consciously wrung out my robe, Abrina's herd of vatos broke the surface followed by Tah. They were pulled aboard, as was Lem Vyle, who was unconscious. He had an ugly dark mark upon his forehead. Tah knelt next to him. I went to Abrina and knelt next to her. She smiled at me, stood, and I felt like a fool. We all held our breaths as we watched the entrance to the chamber. No one else came to break the surface.

The woman who had laughed at me earlier placed her hand upon my arm. *"Father Ilan claimed the rest. By what name are you called?"*

"Korvas."

"Do you know of a tiny cask with drawers set into its ends?"

"Yes! That's my g—" I nodded. "Yes."

"The queen would see you."

I held out my hands toward the others. "What about my friends?"

"In time. My name is Lan Ota," said the woman. *"Follow me."*

I gave another twist to the hem of my robe and followed her, wondering what in the name of Heaven any of this had to do with doing the work of the gods.

31

With her current state of dress, following Lan Ota was not the most burdensome task I have ever faced. She was very beautiful, as were all of her comrades, both male and female. They were darker than the usual run of Iskandaran, with luxuriously thick black hair kept short. There was something that puzzled me, however. Lan Ota's skin was beautiful, while mine was beginning to resemble that of a prune.

We passed many small rooms down below, then climbed some stairs into the huge upper chamber of the clam. The entire roof was lined with vatos and glowfish and the floor was made of woven grasses. Near the center of the dome were a raised platform and throne, also woven from grasses. Seated on the floor and standing about the platform were two or three dozen men and women, half of whom were rubbing sweet-smelling oil into the other half. Judging from the looks on their faces and the motions their bodies made, the ceremony must have been a shade on the sensuous side.

Seated upon the throne was an unusually tall woman with reddish black hair and dark eyes. Upon the right armrest of her throne sat the god box.

Lan Ota nodded toward the throne and said, *"That is Her Majesty, Alya Am Ti, Queen of Ocean, Queen of Ilanyia. The one standing next to her is Zean Am, her uncle and first advisor. When I present you to the queen, bow."*

Zean Am was tattooed all over, including his ears and nose. The queen was not tattooed at all. Her sole raiment was her necklace of fangs. We approached the throne, and Lan Ota bowed, which fairly took away my breath. *"My Queen,"* said Lan Ota, *"I present the one called Korvas."*

I bowed deeply, and when I was again standing upright, the queen was examining me from head to toe. In fact the entire court was examining me. Everyone seemed very amused. I was amazed at how quickly one can become uncomfortable having clothes on in a crowd.

"Master Korvas," said the queen, *"from where do you hail?"*

"I come from Iskandar—"

My head filled with a dozen angry hisses. The faces in the queen's court were suddenly stone cold. "I do not understand. What have I done?"

Zean Am bowed toward the queen and turned to me. *"Korvas, our people were conquered by the Zivenese seven hundred years ago. Those who were not killed or enslaved escaped here. The city you call Iskandar was our city of Itkah."*

I faced the queen. "Your Majesty, that was seven hundred years ago. I had nothing to do with it."

"The debts of the father are the debts of the son," answered the queen.

"My father was not born in Iskandar. He came from Ahmrita." There were confused looks around the court. I held up my finger as I remembered the ancient version of the prophecy. "Kahnalru, Land-beyond-the-Sunrise."

As one person, queen and court repeated *"Kahnalru."*

The queen placed her right hand upon the god box. *"Korvas, this magical artifact says that you have all of the power of the gods at your fingertips."*

"I do?" Again, the humor of the gods. I held out my hands toward Alya Am Ti. "Great Queen, I confess that often the god box confuses me. Through it I have discovered things about myself that I never suspected. As to the power of the gods," I lowered my hands and shrugged, "even I do not believe the gods to be that feeble."

"Perhaps the artifact was referring to something other than your physical prowess."

"Your Majesty, according to the goddess Nanteria—or who I was told was Nanteria—I am the Guide, the reflection of the Seeker, in the Oracle of Heteris concerning the Blade and the Destroyer."

"Do you know the prophecy?"

"Yes."

"Then recite it please."

I did a fair rendition of the original Itkah version, with what I hoped was a touch of flair.

"Is that all?"

"That is all that I know."

The queen got to her feet and turned to her advisor. *"Zean Am."*

He bowed. *"Your Majesty."*

"Bring the Librarian."

"Yes, Your Majesty."

Zean Am stepped down and quickly crossed the floor to the staircase I had recently climbed. It seemed strange for the queen's first advisor not to send a servant for such a task, but I kept silent. While we waited, the queen patted the god box with her hand. *"Korvas."*

"Yes, Your Majesty?"

"What is the secret to this?"

I held out my hands. "I do not know. Perhaps it is a god."

"It would have to be a very small god." The queen's court filled with that strange laughing. When the jocularity had ended, the queen asked, *"How does this work?"*

"You simply give it what you do not need and ask it for what you do need."

The underwater monarch gave an almost imperceptible nod. *"That is what my advisor told me. That is why I asked this artifact for what I needed. Its answer was that I needed you. Why is it, do you suppose, that I need you?"*

"I have found, Your Majesty, that what the god box perceives as my needs differs somewhat from my own perception."

The queen looked up, then motioned for me to stand aside. I looked back toward the stairs and saw Zean Am leading an ancient toward the queen. Following them were close to a dozen bald children. Neither the old man nor the children wore fangs at their throats.

A chair woven out of grass was placed at the foot of the queen's throne and the old man was led to it by the queen's advisor. The old man nodded at the queen and was lowered into the chair. All of the bald children gathered around him in a circle and squatted.

"It is good to see you looking so well, Sahtu Es."

The librarian dismissed the pleasantry with a wave of his hand. *"Why have you called me, Your Majesty?"*

The queen seemed to take no offense at the old fellow's crust. Instead she pointed at me and said, *"This one is called Korvas. He claims to be the reflection of the Seeker in the Oracle of the Blade and the Destroyer."*

The librarian chuckled and slowly shook his head. *"It is but an ancient myth, my queen."* He pointed at my clothes. *"Look at his coverings."* The old man tapped the side of his head. *"Perhaps he has an eel in his ear."*

The audience chamber again burst out in that braying laughter. When it quieted down, the queen nodded and smiled at the librarian. *"Perhaps it is as you say, Sahtu. However, I am queen. I cannot place my trust in probabilities. I must know."*

"This is why you have summoned me, Your Majesty?"

"It is."

The librarian gave me a dirty look. *"Very well. I suppose you wish to consult everything written concerning the oracle."*

"Yes."

He clapped his hands twice, and the bald children began walking like ducks around him. He bent over and examined each scalp as it passed. When the scalp he wanted reached him, he clapped once and the children stopped. Sahtu Es ran his finger down a column of those tattoos, stopped and read a particular line, and leaned back to see the face of the little girl whose scalp he had been reading.

"Pruti?"

"Yes, master?" the child answered.

"Where is Yuva Im Ko?"

The child stood, closed her eyes, and recited, *"Yuva Im Ko, servant to Hunt Leader Havaak Os, is now with the hunt just north of the Great Divide in the Taan Mountains."*

The librarian patted the child on her head and looked at the queen. *"It will take some time to bring this man here all of the way from the Taan."*

The queen pointed at Pruti. *"There is something she is not saying. What is it?"*

Sahtu Es smiled and closed his eyes. *"The troubles of a baby are of no concern to a queen, Your Majesty."*

Queen Alya came down from her throne. She grabbed the child by her chin. *What are you keeping from us, child?"*

The child's face looked frightened. *"Yuva . . ."*

"Yes?"

"Yuva Im Ko is bavatos."

There was a mental gasp from the court, and I looked at the queen, hoping this turn of events didn't require my mortal sacrifice to remedy. The queen looked down her nose at the librarian. *"Sahtu es, how could you?"*

The old man had been caught doing something obviously disgraceful. His shoulders sagged. *"It was his turn, Your Majesty. His father was the index of prophecies before him, and we did not know until later that he was bavatos."* The old man slumped back in his chair.

"I didn't know until it was too late. By then there was no one else to take the information." He shrugged and held out his hands in a deprecating gesture. *"After all, Your Majesty, it is only a myth."*

"Sahtu Es, it seems that the Oracle of the Blade and the Destroyer may be, in fact, true prophecy. Let us hope for all of our sakes that you are right and it is only a myth."

Alya Am Ti, Queen of Ilanyia, dismissed the old man with a wave of her hand. In moments the old man and the children had been helped down the stairs and the chair removed. She turned to her advisor, Zean Am, and mentally whispered something to him. He nodded, bowed, and walked off to talk with Lan Ota.

The queen looked down at me. *"Master Korvas, you will come with us to the hunt to find the bavatos, Yuva Im Ko. There we shall find whether to honor you or to give you to the dirahnos."*

I bowed and Lan Ota led me toward the stairs. When we reached the stairs I asked her, "What are bavatos?"

"It means without vatos; without the breathing fish. The bavatos breathe in the water like the fish."

"Is there something wrong with that?"

"Why do you ask?"

"I sort of got the feeling that there was something wrong with being a bavatos."

A sad look came to Lan Ota's eyes. *"Because the bavatos can flout the tradition of using vatos in the water, they think they can flout all tradition. They are unruly, ill-mannered, and hateful."*

It has always been my policy to avoid entanglements in local politics, Oghar and the Omergunts notwithstanding. Hence, I pried no further into the matter of bavatos. There was one other thing, however, and I asked as we reached the bottom of the stairs:

"Lan Ota, what are dirahnos? The queen said something about giving me to the dirahnos."

The captain of the Queen's Guard smiled at me, and it was a lovely smile. *"They are tiny sea crabs."*

"Crabs?"

"Yes. They can eat a full-grown man down to his bones in less time than a child can hold its breath—except for the brain."

"Except for the brain?"

"Yes. You see, the crabs enter the brain through the eye sockets. Have you ever seen a skull picked clean?"

"Once or twice." I was beginning to feel a bit ill.

"Then you know that the holes in back of the eyes are very small. It takes some time for the dirahnos to widen them sufficiently to enter and eat the brain."

"Fascinating."

"It really is. Many believe that the body is eaten so

*quickly that the brain has a moment where it is still alive
and awake when the rest of the body is nothing but bones.
It is a subject of much debate among the priests."*

"I don't imagine that anyone who is in a position to
know for certain is in any condition to say."

Lan Ota laughed at my little witticism. She pointed at
the water and said, *"Simply dive in. A vatos will attach
itself."*

"About going in the water again . . ." I held out my
hands. "Look at my skin."

She looked, her eyebrows rose, and she began untying
a thong from around her waist. *"Take off your coverings,
Korvas. I need to oil you."*

"Oil me?"

*"Yes, and hurry. The queen will be wanting to leave as
soon as she dismisses her court."*

I wrapped my robe about me more tightly. "Under
normal circumstances, Lan Ota, your offer of lubrication
would bring a ray of sunlight to an otherwise dark and
dismal future. However, I've decided that I like my skin
wrinkled like this. It—"

*"Take off your clothing. It is not just the oil. You
cannot wear robes like that while riding a ratier. The water
would catch in those sails and drag you off in a moment.
Hurry."*

"But I will freeze."

"The oil will keep you warm." She grinned with just a
little bit of mischief. *"As will the memory of its application."*

I sent another urgent message skyward to Ehbot, patron of the pitiful, and began undressing.

32

Upon the back of a sword-nosed fish that sped through and around sharp coral crevices with such rapidity that it was all I could do to hang on to its harness, I entertained certain theological thoughts. I had a great desire to give my fears to my god box. I kept imagining the bubble fish on my head getting snagged and ripping open on some outcropping and drowning before anyone could notice. However, Queen Alya, riding the ratier fish next to me, had my god box tied to her waist.

I remembered from my experience with Oghar, high chief of the Omergunts, how to make a god box of my own, and I pondered the simple steps. I needed a container that could close. I had nothing save the pockets of my undervest. Those and my undershorts were all that I could keep in the way of clothing.

Next I needed to inscribe the name of my patron upon the container. And just who was my patron? There were all of the gods of the wicked and pitiful that I had angrily invoked as curses, but I could imagine no kind deity who wasn't at war with me. Hence the theological thoughts.

My fish was between the queen's and Lan Ota's, and we were being followed by forty guards. With all of those sword-nosed fish swimming at top speed directly behind me, perhaps it had been foolish of me to fear drowning. After all, had I fallen off of my racing fish, I would have been impaled a dozen times by the mounts of the Queen's

Guard. With luck one of the swords would get me through the brain before the crabs got me.

The procession dipped beneath a coral bridge, turned left around a jagged knife of rock that jutted straight up from the murky depths, and streaked for the darkness beyond. It was time to resume my theological musings.

As I hugged my mount, I pondered the god box that Queen Alya had at her waist. It had no name upon it, yet it had worked for me as well as Oghar's bowl marked with the name of Yulus. Perhaps the deity that served me had no name. Perhaps it just didn't need to be named. Perhaps putting a name on it would limit the god, as a word limits any thought to which it is applied. Perhaps, I thought, I am going insane. What else could a person who is about to pray to his pocket think of himself? It had worked before, but only in a dream. Nevertheless, I had gotten what I needed: I had awakened.

I gave my fear to my pocket, and as I felt the burden of terror lift from my heart, I wondered which of the many gods I had regularly cursed had deigned to favor me with his, her, or its forgiveness. As the distant glow of oros brightened the water with their glow, I put the subject to rest, hoping that I wouldn't forget which pocket I had used.

"*Korvas.*" I turned to my left and Lan Ota pointed toward the glow. "*The Taan Mountains. That is Hunt Leader Havaak Os and his party of fishers. His servant, Yuva Im Ko, should be with him.*"

Beyond the glow and surrounding it, tremendously tall mountains rose from the darkness below to become lost in the darkness above. As we came closer I could see a party of perhaps twenty spear-carrying riders mounted on the sword-nosed ratiers. As we approached, the ratiers slowed down and the fishers and their leader bowed.

"*Father Ilan's bounty upon you, Havaak Os,*" greeted the queen.

A muscular fellow in his middle years raised his spear and answered, "*Only through your prayers, Alya Am Ti.*" He lowered his spear, glanced at me, and turned again to the queen. "*How may I help you, Your Majesty?*"

"*It is your servant, Yuva Im Ko. We have an important reading to complete, and he is the Index of Prophecies.*"

The hunt leader frowned for a moment, then looked over his shoulder and gestured with his head. One of the fishers coaxed his ratier until it was next to Havaak. The fellow, true enough, had no vatos upon his head.

"*Master?*"

The hunt leader stared at his servant for a long time and then said, "*Why do you choose this moment to shame me in front of my queen?*"

"*Master I do not shame—*"

"*Be still!*" Havaak turned toward the queen. "*Your Majesty, please accept my most humble apologies for my servant's insolence.*"

The queen nodded. "*I know how it is, Hunt Leader Havaak. As always with the young, it is a way to attract attention.*"

The hunt leader angrily gestured with his head toward his servant. "*Present yourself, idiot!*"

The servant bowed toward Queen Alya and said, "*I am your servant, Your Majesty.*"

The queen studied Havaak's servant with obvious scorn. "*Yuva Im Ko?*"

"*Yes, Your Majesty?*"

"*What is it that you hope to accomplish with this bold display of rudeness?*"

"*With respect, my queen, it is not rudeness.*"

"*You contradict me?*"

"*But with respect, Your Majesty.*"

The queen glanced at Lan Ota, then looked back at Yuva. "*You are less then eel dung to me, bavatos. In my mother's time your shreds would already be feeding the water mites while the dirahnos ate your brains. And pity the poor dirahnos, for your brain would be a pauper's meal, indeed.*" She fumed for a moment, shook her head, and continued. "*This is my reward for trying to treat the bavatos with kindness and justice. I will be honest with you, bavatos. It would take nothing to move me to have you skinned and your record given to another.*"

"Even so, Your Majesty, I am not being rude."

Havaak Os jabbed the butt of his spear into his servant's back. *"I shall skin you myself, Xaxos's gift to the world!"*

After jabbing his servant again, the hunt leader faced his queen. *"Your Majesty, I would be honored if you would allow me the pleasure of feeding my servant to the dirahnos."*

"I am quite tempted. However, he is a servant, not a slave. Thanks to my misguided sense of fair play, there are no more slaves in Ilanyia. He cannot be put to death unless he murders."

"Great Queen," I interrupted, "before things get any further out of hand, might I step in with a possible solution?"

"Solution?"

"Yes. You see, it doesn't matter to me one way or the other. Vatos or no vatos, it's all the same to me." Judging from the expressions on the faces surrounding me, not to mention the half-dozen spear points aimed at my throat, I had said exactly the wrong thing. "If I might clarify—"

"Briefly," the queen amended. The spear points did not come down.

"If you would allow me to consult my god box that you have so considerately kept tied to your waist, I think this problem with the vatos fishes can be resolved."

"Nonsense. There is only one solution. That is for the bavatos to return to our honored ways and stop trying to be different just for the sake of being different."

"We are different," Yuva Im Ko insisted.

The queen arched her eyebrows at me as if to say she told me so, but I had the courage of my vest pocket. "Your Majesty, we all know that the first step in solving a problem is recognizing that there is a problem. The second step, I suspect, is wanting the problem solved. Perhaps you do not want this problem solved."

"After I am done skinning my servant," said the hunt leader as he held his spear point beneath my chin, *"I shall feed you to the dirahnos one limb at a time."*

The queen held up her hand, palm facing Havaak. *"Hold."* She lowered her hand and faced me. *"You don't seem to be the type who would have a great deal of courage, Korvas, but that was a dangerous thing to say to any queen, even without spears at your throat. Does courage come from your god box, as well?"*

"That, and other things."

With an amused expression on her face, Queen Alya untied the god box and held it out toward me. *"Very well."*

I took the box, and I confess that I was relieved to have it in my grasp again. Although the pocket worked well enough, it required just a little more faith than I could gather at a moment's notice.

"God box," I whispered to myself, "what do these people need?"

I waited for a drawer to open, but none did. Instead, I noticed Havaak Os's vatos fish slowly lift from his head and swim away. The hunt leader waited patiently for another vatos to take its place, but none came. His face filled with panic, and I told him the message that came into my mind. "Just breathe, Havaak."

He tried, coughed, and tried again. He breathed in and out a few times, his face stunned at the wonder of breathing. The transparent vatos lifted from the fishers, the Queen's Guard and even from the queen herself. They lifted from everyone's head, except mine. There was some panic, but soon they were all bavatos.

"You are all the same," I said to the queen and Yuva. "Some of you only had to resist wearing the fish."

The queen practiced breathing for a moment, then she slowly shook her head. *"Vatos were a gift from Father Ilan. When we were driven from Iskandar, the god gave them to us and offered to hide us behind his face. But now—"*

"But now," I interrupted, "you no longer need them. It is time to thank Father Ilan for his help and return the vatos."

The queen looked at Yuva. Havaak's servant looked

sullen. *"Is that look because of the beating you took for being rude to your queen?"* The servant didn't answer. Alya laughed. *"I see. Yuva Im Ko, you did not want this problem solved any more than did I. Is that not true?"*

"Perhaps I am confused, Your Majesty."

"Perhaps, Yuva, it is nothing more than the fact that you are no longer special." She faced me. *"Korvas, you may keep your god box."*

"Thank you, Your Majesty."

"Have the vatos lifted from all the Ilanyians?"

"I don't know."

Queen Alya smiled. *"If they haven't, it will be an interesting time in court when I return. Now to why we are here."* She faced Havaak's servant. *"Where is the prophecy of the Blade and the Destroyer?"*

Yuva consulted the inside of his right thigh. *"Your Majesty, it is with Vio Ta. He is a driver with the hunt."*

The queen looked at Havaak. The hunt leader was searching the distant darkness. *"We should see their lights soon. We were waiting for them to drive the school in this direction."* He held out a spear to the queen. *"Would you join us, Your Majesty?"*

"You tempt me again, Hunt Leader. It has been a few years." She took the spear and tested her grip and its balance. She turned to Havaak's servant. *"Yuva Im Ko, would you guard my back?"*

The servant was speechless for a moment. He smiled and sat upright. *"I would be honored, Your Majesty."*

Nodding with satisfaction, the queen looked at Havaak. *"When you give the signal, Hunt Leader."*

I spoke to Lan Ota. "Is this a dangerous sport?"

"Why do you ask?"

"The queen asked for a guard at her back."

"This is no sport, Korvas." She and her guards pulled out their swords and held them at the ready. *"We harvest tiwi. Very tasty."*

"Lan Ota, you were about to explain why she needs a guard at her back."

"The tiwi is a very agile creature. While you are concen-

trating on putting your spear into one, another will get behind you and give you a little nip. That's why we team up in pairs. The fishers use spears and the back guards use swords."

Lan Ota gestured with her sword, and the Queen's Guard spread out among the fishers, half of whom returned their own swords to their belts and withdrew spears. The captain of the guard held out her hand toward Yuva Im Ko.

"The loan of your spear?"

"My pleasure, Captain."

Yuva flipped it through the water at her. She caught it and held it out to me as she held up her own sword. *"I will guard your back, Korvas."*

Personally I didn't much like the idea of being in the middle of a bunch of weapon-slinging hunters, however tasty the game. Besides, racing around on a ratier was still something that I needed to practice. I looked at the weapon in my hands. The point on it was well over two hands long and edged with wicked-looking barbs. I began to suspect that the tiwi fish might have a bit more spunk than I had originally thought.

"Lan Ota . . ." I lowered my spear. "Do you think it would be permissible for me to stay here?"

"Of course, although you'll miss all of the fun."

Havaak pointed with his spear and called, *"The lights of the drivers!"*

I squinted my eyes and could just barely make out a pale green glow in the distance. The glow became brighter, and soon I could see huge black silhouettes against the glow accompanied by a faint chattering sound. The shadows were some monstrous kind of fish with fleshy ribbons hanging from the corners of fang-littered maws. A row of jagged spines crowned each head like a cockscomb, and I do believe their eyes glowed red.

"Lan Ota, are those tiwi fish?"

"Yes. The sounds you hear are the drivers hitting together their stones."

"The name 'tiwi' sounds like it would belong to a much smaller fish."

The hunt leader held up his spear and said, *"To Chara!"*

The remainder of the company held up either spear or sword and answered, *"To Chara!"*

Recalling that Chara is the patron of those who do battle with sea monsters, I was just congratulating myself for not participating in this insanity when Havaak brought down his spear and the entire school of ratiers, including mine, bolted toward the approaching nightmare.

I pulled upon my ratier's fins, his gills, his antennae, each time screaming "Whoa!"

It was not necessary to ask the god box for what I needed right then; what I needed was a miracle.

"Whoa! Please whoa."

As we streaked toward the school of perhaps a hundred tiwi, I saw that each was almost three times as long as a ratier including the sworded snout. The chattering sound became deafening as I saw the queen raise her spear and lead her ratier just beneath the lead tiwi, leaving her spear in the fish's gut.

It seemed simple enough. I placed my fear in the god box, and I vowed to retrieve the remnants of my dignity and get me a fish. My mount seemed to know what it was doing, so I gave the ratier its head. . . .

To be truthful, which I must, ever since it had carried me off I hadn't been steering the racing fish. Thus, by "giving the ratier its head," I didn't mean that I had stopped steering it. What I meant was that I continued to let the fish go where it wanted to go and stopped worrying about it.

My mount seemed to be aiming for a particular tiwi, so I raised my spear and braced myself to drive it in the tiwi's gut. In half a moment the huge fish filled my vision and I drove the spear into it with all of my might.

Suddenly my ratier was no longer between my legs and I was being dragged toward the darkness below by my intended victim. It's difficult to know what to do in such situations. I was already out of sight of the hunting party. Hence, if I let go of the spear, who would know where to look for me? The tiwi and I together could be seen more easily than I alone. However, the tiwi kept speeding straight down.

I could see nothing and I imagined that if I ever did let go of that spear, the tiwi would thrash around until it gobbled at my legs with its fearsome jaws. It was quite disconcerting, especially after my vatos fish disagreed with the depth and left me.

I released my hold upon the spear and hung suspended in the blackness, horrible choking silence replacing the sound of my heart pounding in my ears.

Soon I floated upon the air, sailing among the black clouds of my mind. I held my god box outstretched in my hands before me and began kicking.

I heard a voice in my mind, and it was the god box. *"Where would you have me lead you, Korvas?"*

"Lead me? I do not know, nameless spirit. Where do you think I should go?"

"What do you need more than anything else in the universe?"

My desire to live, my greed, my lust, my mission, all of them clamored for my attention. In the midst of this noise was the spirit of the god box, which made me hesitate.

What did I want?

What did I need?

What should I ask for?

What jokes do the gods have left to play upon a poor honest carpet merchant?

I didn't know what I should say. If I said nothing, I would go nowhere. I would end my moments there in the blackness. Could I risk making one more wrong choice to end a life of wrong choices? It was too much for me to decide.

"Spirit, take me to where you would have me be."

The blackness grew until it was as complete inside my head as it was in the surrounding waters. I felt my mind slipping away as I said to myself, "Again the great Korvas dies."

Among dreamy billows I flitted among my possible

futures like a fly in the marketplace buzzing from apple to sausage to rug to onion, wondering where to land to make the most of voluptuous opportunity.

I took a deep breath, and as I stopped kicking, all of the sweet and ragged agonies of the underworld seared my lungs. I opened my eyes and saw that I had another vatos upon my head. Coming toward me were four riders. The queen led them and just behind her were Lan Ota and Havaak. Yuva Im Ko followed, leading what I suspected was my ratier.

"I am glad to find you alive," said the queen with a grim tone to her thoughts. *"Once you have thrust your spear, Korvas, you must let go of the shaft."*

"Words to live by, my queen. However, that is advice that would have been much more useful if I had received it before the hunt." The queen smiled thinly, which is better, I suppose, than her taking offense. I settled on the ratier held by Havaak's servant.

"Congratulations, Korvas," said Yuva Im Ko.

"On what? On being alive?"

"On your kill." He pointed behind me and there was my tiwi, stone-cold dead, floating in the water.

Yuva maneuvered his mount until he was next to the tiwi. He withdrew the spear and used its point to pry six of the fanglike teeth from the tiwi's jaws. He cut one of those fleshy ribbons and used it to tie the teeth together into a necklace. When he was finished he put the necklace over my head.

"For your first kill. It gives you the strength of the tiwi to add to your own. When you marry, this must go to your bride. For as long as she wears it your family will never want for food."

I fingered one of the fangs and looked up at Lan Ota. "I do not feel much like a mighty hunter."

"Korvas, in life it is not necessary that you face the monster with dignity and carry away perfect victory. It is only necessary that you face the monster. All you can ever do is try. Outcomes belong to the gods."

I looked around. "Where is the fellow we wanted? The driver, Vio Ta."

"*He is dead. A tiwi turned and charged him.*"

"What about the prophecy?" I faced Queen Alya. "What about the prophecy?"

"*What is left of Vio Ta's skin is being removed for the librarian. We know the remains do not contain the prophecy.*"

"What now?"

"*As my captain said to you, Korvas: All we can do is try. Outcomes belong to the gods.*"

33

All we can do is try. Outcomes belong to the gods.

The words teased at my mind as we returned to the queen's palace. Who would have thought that the ancient Itkahs, who fled before the invaders who founded Iskandar, would survive to create this underwater kingdom? If I was truly doing the work of the gods, might it not make sense that the gods foresaw the wreck of the *Silk Ghost* and created Ilanyia to save Abrina and her Guide?

No, that didn't make any sense at all. Granted, the gods could do such things, but why would they? It didn't seem very efficient. Wouldn't it have made more sense to give the *Silk Ghost* safe passage? To my mind it would have been less trouble to calm the sea or to grant the Kienosan shipbuilders a better design. Of course, I was thinking in terms of money; the gods do not concern themselves with such trivialities, which is one of the reasons why I once decided they didn't have much practical value to the living.

The existence of Ilanyia had answered the prayer I uttered as the *Silk Ghost* sank, but all of this couldn't be just for me. The refugees fleeing from their ancient city seven hundred years ago must have prayed to their gods to save them.

I watched the backs of the queen and her guards. Ilanyia was the answer to many prayers, and the sinking

of the *Silk Ghost* was, as well. I, Korvas, had been the
answer to the prayers of those deviled by the bavatos
problem. But wasn't it the spirits who caused the bavatos
problem in the first place? Is life simply a series of trials
designed to force the hapless to turn to the gods? Now,
what would be the point of that?

I had to begin again. Did the spirits who allowed the
possibility of Ilanyia see seven hundred years ago the
sinking of the *Silk Ghost*? That would mean that all of
this thing I called my life was planned out in advance.
Considering how that life had gone, that seemed to make
even less sense. That would mean that the gods, perhaps
in moments of boredom or spite, occasionally peeked
over the edges of their clouds, spied poor Korvas in a
rare moment of serenity, and flung down calamities upon
him to brighten up otherwise dull moments.

"Here is another test, Korvas. Try and do better this
time."

Then I remembered the words of Zaqaros quoted to
me by the trader Delomas. "If we could see as the gods
and choose as the gods, we would be the gods."

It was time to put the subject to rest. I suspected that
what I was attempting to understand about the gods
might be beyond my ability even to imagine, much less
understand.

When we had given our ratiers to the servants and had
entered the lower part of the queen's palace, we all received another massage with the sweet-smelling oil. I
hardly noticed mine, except that when it was finished I
couldn't bear the thought of putting my wet clothes back
on again. I supposed one could get used to anything
given enough time and a sufficient supply of other
persons who were doing the same thing. I didn't begin
feeling uncomfortable again until I was returned to my
shipmates, all of whom save Tah were still dressed.

Awake, recovering, and propped up on cushions of
grass, Lem Vyle was amused at my lack of attire. "Have
you become an Ilanyian, Korvas?"

"No. I am, however, quite warm and dry. That is more

than I can say for the rest of you." I glanced at Tah
in her patch of a loincloth. "With one possible excep-
tion."

Tah, of course, was out of her loincloth in a second.
She was like a jungle animal that had been forced
to wear silly costumes in a traveling carnival, suddenly
freed.

"Tah," called Lem Vyle. "All modesty aside, the re-
moval of these wet rags does appear to be the sensible
thing to do." The agent's bodyguard assisted him in
removing his robes. After he had been shucked, he
looked to his left. I turned to see what he was looking
at.

Abrina was removing the last of her clothing. Already
undressed from the waist up, she peeled down her wet
trousers and slipped off her boots. When I realized that I
had forgotten to breathe for a minute or so, I took a
deep breath and looked at Lem Vyle. Vyle turned and
looked back at me, his eyes wide and his eyebrows raised.
"Well, Korvas?"

"Well, Lem Vyle?"

"That's what I thought."

"That's what I thought, too."

He held out a hand toward Abrina and looked at her.
"That sight does seem to merit at least a round of ap-
plause, doesn't it?"

Curiously enough, it was Tah, not Abrina, who blushed.
Abrina only smiled and began running her fingers through
her short black hair to dry it. Tah's blush ceased as
quickly as it had begun, to be replaced by her sly smile
and cold eyes.

Something very important became clear to me. Tah
loved her employer yet kept it from him; which, because
of his powers, was pointless. Pointless, that is, unless
Lem Vyle could lie to himself. An ironic flaw for a *ziusu*.

A thought seemed to entertain Vyle for a moment,
then he returned his gaze to me. "Where have you been
for all of this time, Korvas?"

"The queen took me in search of someone who had

the story of the Blade and the Destroyer tattooed on his body. I killed a fish and the fish killed me." I held up my fang necklace.

"What about the fellow you wanted to find?"

"We didn't get there in time. One of this fish's relatives took a rather large bite out of him"

"Sad." He glanced at Tah and looked back at me. "You know the prophecy. I heard you recite it."

I nodded. "I know the oracle, not the story that grew around the oracle."

"Perhaps, Korvas, it is only a myth."

"Wouldn't we all look foolish on the last day of the world if it is not? I do not want to defend myself to the beings who will make my final judgment by saying, 'Silly me! Wrong again!' "

"On the last day of the world, I doubt that I would waste my remaining time worrying on how I might look to others, divine or not." He glanced toward the grass room's doorway. "Why are there armed guards on our quarters?" He gestured toward the doorway. "Korvas, ask one of the guards to come in."

As soon as I stood in the doorway, two guards armed with swords blocked the entrance. Eight more armed guards stood behind them.

The first guard to my right lifted his sword and said, *"No one is allowed to leave the room."*

"Why?"

"It is the order of the queen."

I turned toward Vyle. "I don't understand. Just a short time ago I was quite popular. It must be something you people did in my absence."

"Ask the guard in, Korvas."

I cocked my head at the guard and he entered followed by another guard who stood just inside the door. Lem Vyle held up his hand. "Come here, fellow. What is your name?"

"Rhal Ivak."

"Tell me, Rhal Ivak. Why are we being held as prisoners?"

"I cannot."

Lem Vyle nodded. "I see. Are we to be executed?"

"*I cannot—*"

"Why are we to be executed? Has it to do with the prophecy?"

"*I—*"

"No? But we would have been spared had the queen found the lad with the prophecy tattooed upon him?"

The guard stood silent and glared at Lem Vyle. Vyle nodded. "I see. That clears up the entire matter." He faced me. "It is simple, really. We are to be executed to protect the secret of Ilanyia—its existence."

Abrina's expression did not change, while Tah looked at the guard's sword with frightening relish. "That is insane," I answered. "What about the prophecy?" The guard glanced at me, returned his glower to Lem Vyle, and folded his arms across his chest.

"Vyle," I said, "it doesn't take a *ziusu* to see that the only reason we were kept alive was because the prophecy just might be true."

He nodded. "Now that it cannot be proven one way or the other, we are about to be done." He raised his eyebrows at the guard. "By what method?" The guard's expression did not change. "I see. Since we are not criminals, we will not be thrown to the crabs. Instead we will have our heads removed with one of those formidable-looking blades."

The guard began to back toward the door. In a flash Tah leaped across the space that separated them, knocked him silly with one of her lovely feet, and armed herself with his sword. The guard on the door sprang forward and an unseen hand had me jump in between them. "No!"

"Korvas," spat Tah, "get out of the way!"

"No! Hold there, Tah." I looked at her opponent. The man was about to bring his sword down upon my head. I held my hands over my eyes. "No!"

For a terrified moment I tensed every muscle in my body, awaiting the sensation of having my head split like a melon. I opened my fingers a bit and took a peek at the

Ilanyian guard. He still had his sword raised, but he was lowering it.

"Why do you interfere?" he demanded.

"I don't know." I lowered my hands from my face. "I don't know why I am here doing this. I hardly know why I do anything. Does anyone?" I laughed like a maniac and the guard began bringing his sword up again. The guard named Ivak pushed himself up from the grass mats. I calmed down a little and the sword came down again.

"I understand you wanting to protect your lady," said the guard, nodding toward Tah.

My maniacal laugh escaped once more. "You don't understand, fellow. I'm not protecting her. I'm protecting you and the rest of the Queen's Guard from her."

This time the guard laughed. Rhal Ivak got to his feet and shouted at the door, *"In here!"*

The remaining six guards came into the room. Rhal Ivak took a sword from one of them and joined the arc of soldiers facing me. I turned around and saw Tah's face flushed with anticipation.

She said, "You are in the way, Korvas."

I looked back at the guards. "Friends, it will be no end of trouble trying to sort this thing out should I let lovely Tah have her way with you."

Rhal Ivak nodded. *"She is right on one matter. You are in the way. Step aside and let us finish with that tiny scrap."*

"Korvas," called Lem Vyle, "let Tah have them. She will enjoy the exercise and we can use the weapons."

Abruptly I faced Vyle. "Can't you think of anything other than blood?" I placed my hand upon the god box and looked at Tah. "You are an excellent fighter. I believe you could slay all of these guards and a hundred more besides. I don't believe you could slay the queen's entire army. A fight at this point will accomplish nothing but a lot of unnecessary dead." I lifted my hand and touched her cheek. "I cannot bear the thought of you dead."

Tah's lower lip trembled as her dark eyes filled with tears. She slapped away my hand. "Korvas, I could kill you for that. I could rip open your belly and dance in your guts."

Ah, true love. I could feel a streak of light coming from the god box through my arm and into my mind. Understanding filled me. I spoke to lovely Tah. "How many have you slain simply because you cannot pronounce a single word? How many have you killed just because you cannot tell your master that—"

The tip of her black blade was instantly pricking my throat. Lem Vyle pulled himself to his feet and limped over to Tah's side. "Look at me, Tah." Her head didn't move. "Look at me!"

He reached out his hand and turned her face toward his. He looked deeply into her eyes. "Don't do this for me, Tah. Give Korvas the sword."

She was frozen for a long moment. Then she lowered the blade and held its handle toward me. I took it and watched as Vyle and his lady returned to his couch. As they reached it, they faced each other and embraced. A very strange pain entered my heart.

"Indeed, you are the Guide, Korvas."

"Eh?" I looked around as the walls of the room divided into a hundred panels and were carried off by Ilanyian servants. I saw that what had transpired in the room had been observed by the entire queen's court. Queen Alya and her uncle were grinning at me, as was the entire retinue. The one who had spoken was the librarian, old Sahtu Es. He was seated in his chair surrounded by his rotary file of bald children.

"Another test, then?"

"Observed through the eyes of wisdom," said the librarian, *"everything is a test."*

"I take it that I did well."

"As you did during the test before: well enough."

I debated a moment whether I should behead the librarian before returning the sword to the guard. In the end, I just gave it back to Rhal Ivak. "Try and hang onto this." I looked back at Sahtu Es. "Why test me? If the prophecy is true, then these tests only waste time. Why bother with them at all?"

"Only you can answer that, Korvas," answered the old man as the light grew dim and the floor of the underworld opened beneath me. *"Only you are testing you."*

It became all black. With my hand upon the god box, I waited for the end to the blackness, confident that it would come.

34

When it became light I found myself standing upon a wide sandy beach. To my left was a garden filled with ornate shrubs and naked trees that filled the air with a heady perfume. To my right was a body of water. On the beach and floating on the water were the leaves from the garden. They were the color of lavender. I let the final words of the Oracle of Heteris come into my mind.

> At the tip of Ihtar's hand,
> Where float the lavender leaves,
> The Destroyer shall meet the Blade,
> Leaving only one.
> All is Manku.

This then was the Sea of Manku, and I was standing on the edge of the holy city of Givida in the Empire of Ahmrita. Here was where the Blade would meet the Destroyer to decide the fate of the world. They would meet and only one would remain.

"Abrina?"

"Yes, Korvas." Her voice came from behind me.

I turned around. The giantess was dressed in a filmy golden gown that went from her neck to her ankles. Golden slippers were on her feet, and in her hands she carried her ax. "You look beautiful, Abrina."

She smiled widely and pointed at me. "You look very handsome, my Guide."

215

I looked down at my own attire and found myself clad in robes of pale blue silk. Upon my feet were soft new boots of matching leather. It was curious how unimportant they seemed just then. I looked back at Abrina. "Are we alone?"

"For the moment."

I looked up and down the deserted beach. "Did Tah even exist? Did she ever live?"

"She lives in your heart, Korvas. It be a precious place."

"You are in my heart as well, Abrina."

"I know."

"I do not love you as a friend or brother."

"I know."

I looked across the sea of Manku, hoping to see a piece of reality upon which I could anchor myself. "I move though time and across distances with more ease than I dream."

"Korvas, the real world has many levels. Somewhere Tah be real. Somewhere she and Lem Vyle be wed. Somewhere she and you be lovers. Somewhere you and I be lovers. But not here; not now."

"What of you, Abrina? Are you real?"

"Here and now. There are places in the universe where I be not. But that does not make me any the less real here."

I glanced at Abrina's amber eyes and immediately turned away. "I don't want you to fight Manku."

"Why?"

"I just don't."

"Do you find it as difficult as Tah to pronounce the word 'love'?"

I reached up and took her ax, surprised that I could do so. I looked up at her and said, "I love you."

I threw the ax away. "It is silly, I know. Together we would make a preposterous-looking couple. I can't even imagine how we could have children, and if we did they would probably bounce me on *their* knees. But I don't care. If the only way to save this world is to sacrifice you in some contest with evil, then the world be damned." I frowned at her expression. "You don't seem surprised."

"I think you have finally finished testing yourself, Korvas." She reached down her hand and stroked my cheek. "I be proud that you love me. Especially proud that you love me in that way. But in this place, my friend, I be meant for another." She withdrew her hand and stood up. "Turn around."

I turned around. Before me stood a huge foot. I could hardly look over the top of the big toenail. I craned back my neck and looked up and up and up.

High in the sky looking down at me was that strangely compassionate face of Manku. I looked at Abrina's ax and almost cried at what a pitiful weapon it was. I turned to tell Abrina to run, and what faced me was the toe of Abrina's golden slipper. It was every bit as tall as the toe of Manku. I looked up and up and up and Abrina's face was among the clouds next to Manku's.

There were sweet sounds of singing, bells ringing, crowds raising their voices in celebration. I felt myself rising, growing, expanding, and soon I could face Manku eye to eye.

"Am I . . . am I a god, too?"

"We are all slaves, we are all gods, somewhere," answered Manku.

Garlands of flowers carried by golden birds streamed through the air as the clouds filled with other faces. There were Nanteria, Heteris, Ahjrah, Tayu, my father.

I looked at Manku. "This is a wedding," I said to the god.

"Yes."

"There is to be no battle for the world?"

"Not in the heavens. The battle for the world will be on the world and will be fought by those who still need to test themselves."

"Why am I here?" I looked at Abrina. "Why?"

"Korvas, the gods saw your need, and your need was to know of the gods and of the gods' love for you. For you, Korvas, the gods have split the continent again and again." She smiled. "There is a second reason." She took me by the hand. "You are to give away the bride."

I held her hand with both of mine, not wishing to give her up. I loved her and now I could look her in the eye. Was I not also a god? I looked at Manku. "They call you the Destroyer. What kind for work is that for a future husband?"

The god laughed, as did Abrina. Then Manku looked me in the eyes. "The Destroyer is the one who clears the way for new life, new beginnings. Without me there would be no worlds, no life. Without me the universe ends."

I thought upon it and cocked my head to one side. "I suppose it's useful." I looked at Abrina. "Is this what you want? Is this who you want?"

"Yes."

I realized I was still holding her hand. At that moment I could look her in the face and love her as a man to a woman, and at that same moment I had to give her to another. I held out her hand to Manku, and the god took it. "Take care of her."

"I always have," said the god.

Inside my chest was a horribly dreadful pain. I gave Abrina to a god, it is true. It didn't make any difference to my heart.

Abrina reached to my waist and held the god box. "All of the gods and goddesses, all of the powers of life and the universe are in here, Korvas. Always it will take what you don't need and will give you what you do need. But you must ask. If you take back what you turn over to the box, we will give it back to you."

She kissed my cheek and handed the god box back to me. I held it in my hands as she released it. "My dear friend, all of the power of the universe is at the fingertips of those humble enough and brave enough to use it. Tell the people."

The gods kissed and the skies filled with blinding light. At the center of the light the couple embraced, the edges softened, and they seemed to meld into one another until there was a single sunbeam that withdrew to its father in the sky.

Suddenly I found myself shrunken to my usual size and standing in the center of Iskandar's marketplace. I turned around, and turned around again. As the god box had said, "You cannot return to where you have never left."

The marketplace at Iskandar. The smells, the noises, the bustle—all the same. I looked down and saw my carpets. I sat down, stunned. After a moment I seemed to get a handle on my current reality. I still had my god box, my threadbare rags and sorry rugs. I turned over my top rug and saw the spots left from Dorc falling down and crushing my beetles. I hadn't been away from my place at all. I was back at the beginning—back at one beginning. Realities within realities. It made my head spin. What of Syndia, Tah? And Abrina. What of her?

"Master Korvas!" I could hear the fool Dorc shouting from a distance. I had no time for the idiot. Somehow I had to sort out things. Had I never left the bazaar? Had I gone and come back? This was a considerable amount of time for the gods to mulch for one little carpet merchant.

What of the Omergunts? In this reality do they exist? What of the Ilanyians, the crew of the *Silk Ghost*?

I had the god box, so that much had changed. It still had that *X* carved into its finish, so Ker dropping dead in Fort Braw and me being murdered . . . and everything else had happened—or not. I supposed it depended upon where and when one was standing.

Somewhere, somewhen, I was with Abrina. "Korvas," I muttered to the inhabitant of that reality, "you'll never even guess how fortunate you are."

I looked again at the box, then up at the Nant Temple high on its hill. What about Syndia? What about the priestess at the Nant Temple? Had she existed? Did she exist? Will she exist? Was she a goddess, a phantom, a case of indigestion, or in this reality just a person? I needed to talk to someone.

I felt a movement within my robe. My three surviving mahrzak beetles were still in my pocket. I took them out and placed them on the pile of rugs. "Forgive me, my friends, but I think we are out of business. Find some respectable work."

Amram, Tiram, and Iramiram simply stood there with their front legs crossed and their antennae drooping. "Very well." I put out my hand and they climbed aboard. "Perhaps I'll start a stud farm with a herd of those slick-looking mahrzak beetles from Desivida—if they exist in this reality."

I climbed to my feet as I remembered. "I must be going. The magician Jorkis will be here any moment with the King's Guard."

I turned to go to the Nant Temple to find Syndia. There was a warp in the image of the market before my eyes, almost like the shimmering of heat from paving stones on a summer day. Through the warp came three men in red uniforms. They blocked my path, and two of them grabbed my arms. The third grinned with the face of Captain Shadows.

As soon as I saw that ugly face I remembered the prayer I had uttered in the Nant Temple soon after Syndia had informed me that the magician to which I had tried to sell a crawling carpet was Jorkis, father-in-law to Captain Shadows. *May the gods save me.* All of that which followed was in answer to that prayer.

"You have led me quite a chase, Korvas. My master must have bled half the wizards in Iskandar for the powers to keep up with you. But now you are mine."

I shrugged and answered, "By now you must know how hopeless your task is."

"The power you possess is a gift for my master."

"The only power I possess, Shadows, everyone possesses."

"It's more power than I possess."

"No. It's more power than you have the humility and courage to ask for."

The captain snorted his amusement. "It must be more than this box you wear." He took the box and lifted the strap over my head. He nodded. "I will get this power from you, Korvas. Slowly and painfully. I have an excellent torturer named Quaag who is so skilled and patient he can find and destroy with his instruments every single nerve in your body, one at a time."

"Well," I laughed, "how many of them can there be?"

"Millions. It will take more than a year to get them all."

Shadows turned and walked toward a horse carriage and the two guards dragged me along behind. No one in the market interfered or even looked at us for fear of drawing attention to themselves. I was thrown into the carriage, face down on the floor. Shadows and his two thugs put their boots on me and laughed as the wagon lurched and began moving.

I wondered how the gods were going to get me out of this one. On the other hand, I thought, they may not. The tender mercies of Quaag might just be the kind of eye-opener the gods think I need to enlighten some corner of my life. Could I find the strength to endure a year of unendurable pain? Could I find the strength to ask the gods for the strength?

Oh well, I thought, faith that hasn't been tested isn't really faith at all; it's just an opinion.

35

In the dungeons beneath the king's palace, the smell of hot irons in my nostrils, I stood facing the most feared person in the world, the woman responsible for my father's death: the bloody horror herself, First Priestess of the Heterin Temple, First Priestess of the Sacred Flame, Tretia, advisor to the king and all-around wicked soul. Although her face brooked no hint of kindness, it carried a beauty of a different sort. It made me think of the beauty of a tiger or a serpent. Admirable in the distance with an edge of sheer terror at close range.

It was kind of curious to let play through my mind that somewhere and somewhen I was her husband, father, brother, lover, judge, slave, god, and executioner. Whatever happened to me in this reality, there were still a great many moves that would be made.

She sat in a chair examining the god box as an aide whispered in her ear. When the whispering was concluded, the aide slinked off with all of the dignity of a weasel.

Every now and then the priestess would frown. She looked up at me and said, "Speak to me, dog. I want to know the power behind this instrument."

"I would be happy to tell you what I know, Your Eminence."

"Proceed. If you lie once I will have your tongue drawn from your mouth with infinite patience."

I suspected that she meant she would have my tongue

ripped out very, *very* slowly. "Please, Your Eminence. I am happy to tell you all that I know. If asked the god box will take from you what you don't need, and it will grant you what you do need. However, there is a warning: what you need and what you think you need are different creatures."

She nodded at someone behind me and my right arm was pulled up until I could touch the nape of my neck. Liquid fire poured through my shoulder.

"Again, dog. Tell me of the power of this instrument."

"I did!" Then I screamed.

The priestess crossed her legs as she continued to examine the god box. Directly to the gods I turned over my pain. It then became bearable.

"My man Shadows, there, had to chase you not only halfway around the world, thousands of miles at an instant, he had to chase you through time. Are you saying that this is what this instrument granted you?"

"Yes."

"Traveling through time was your request?"

"No, Eminence. I simply asked for what I needed. The choice was left to the god box."

She examined the tiny chest of drawers. "This is what this box did for you?"

"Yes, Your Eminence. Or at least it is what the gods did through the box."

"The gods? Then this is magic?"

"How do you mean, Your Eminence?"

"Magic is the power that coerces the gods to do the magician's bidding. Is this box of yours magic?"

"Then it is not magic, Your Eminence. It does not coerce the gods but only gives them a means through which they can do for you what you need."

"Need? Who determines these needs?"

"The gods, Your Eminence."

"By what lights? What one needs for what?"

"I know not, Your Eminence. The gods have lights of their own."

"Why did the gods do all of these things for you? If I am to believe Captain Shadows, you were brought back from death any number of times. Not just from the edge of death, mind you, but back from the stone-cold variety."

"I suppose, Your Eminence, it is what the gods determined I needed each time, and I can't argue with that."

"Dog, who are you? What are you? A petty criminal, part of the underwashed and unscented underclass of Iskandar. Why would the gods favor you?"

"The gods favor all of us, Your Eminence. Doesn't the Heterin faith teach that to be so?"

"You presume to instruct me in my own faith?"

"Of course not, Your Eminence. I only—"

"Be silent." She looked again at the box. "What you needed was a trip through time, eh?"

"Several, actually—" The pain in my shoulder became a crowd.

She stood up and looked me in the face. "Dog, I doubt if you have any idea of the significance of the events you have experienced. Let it suffice to say that the only true faith in this world is faced with a grave danger. Unless you immediately place all that you know in my care, there may be no tomorrow for any of us."

"I beg you to believe me, Eminence. I will do whatever you wish."

"Will you answer my questions fully, holding nothing back?"

"I swear it, Your Eminence."

Another bureaucratic creature slithered out of the masonry and whispered in Tretia's ear. She nodded, whispered something back, and dismissed the thing with a wave of her hand. Her eyes aimed in my direction.

"You have heard of the Hero and the Destroyer, haven't you, dog?"

"Yes, Eminence. In the oracle, I am the Mirror of the Second. In the Itkah version—"

"Enough of this sacrilege!" interrupted Tretia as the crowd of pain in my shoulder became a population.

"No! I speak the truth! I swear it!"

She nodded at the guard who was making a twist-pastry out of my arm, and the pressure in my shoulder eased a bit. "Answer me, then, Mirror, a few questions."

"As you command, Your Eminence."

"Who is the Second?"

"He was my twin brother, Tayu."

"Was?"

"He died shortly after naming the Hero—or Heroine. She is the Blade in the original version of the oracle. I have seen the original version—"

"Her name, dog."

"Abrina. Abrina, daughter of Shamas of the Omergunts." Everyone laughed at the thought of an Omergunt being able to do anything but stink. Perhaps they were also laughing at Abrina being a woman. That made me mad, and I looked around at the guards. "She could slay the lot of you in an eyeblink."

"Where is she now, dog?"

"I last saw her in Ahmrita as she was becoming wed to the Destroyer, Manku."

"Sacrilege again," declared Tretia. She looked at Shadows. "Captain, what of this?"

"Chasing him, Your Eminence, I rode the limit of the powers at your command all of the way to the shores of the Sea of Manku before catching up with him in Iskandar. I saw no wedding."

"Did you see this woman?"

"I saw no woman."

Tretia handed the god box to a servant and folded her arms as she looked at me with eyes as gray as any storm at sea. "You are wasting my time, dog. What can you say to prove to me that any of this you say is true?"

"Ahjrah was the First."

The priestess sat up. "That again?"

"Ahjrah, the Nant priestess whose father and mother were killed by the agents of Pherris, First Priest of the Heterin Temple before you, Great Tretia. Ahjrah was the First of the Oracle of Heteris."

The priestess studied me for a long time. "There is no way you could have known that. It is the most closely guarded secret of the Heterin faith."

"Who can keep secrets from the gods, Your Eminence?"

"Indeed." She glanced at Captain Shadows for a moment, then nodded at the guards who were holding me. "Release him for the time being." I wiggled my fingers as the blood returned to them. "Was your name Gorbas?" asked Tretia.

"Korvas, Your Eminence."

"Korvas, the Heterin faith honors the goddess Heteris, and it is through her revelations that we have come to know of the great test of mankind through the battle with the Destroyer. We know that if the destroyer fails, our goddess Heteris, the goddess of flame and goodness, will die. We will all die with her as did the Elassans and the Mankuas when their gods deserted them."

"I have learned this much, Your Eminence. The gods never desert us; when we find ourselves alone, we have deserted the gods."

"The test of mankind? What of that?"

"As I said, Your Eminence, my task was to give away the bride at a wedding. There was no test of mankind invented by the gods. We invented our own tests. If the end of the world comes, we will be the ones who bring it."

The Heterin priestess laughed. "If that is so, then what purpose do the gods serve?"

"If we ask for their help, they grant us what we need and relieve us of what we don't need."

Tretia held up the god box. "The same as this?"

"Yes, Your Eminence. It is the same for any god box, not just that one. You may even make one of your own."

"Make my own?"

"Any kind of container will work, Your Eminence. Once I even used my vest pocket."

"That time did you receive what you needed?"

"Every time, Your Eminence. It didn't always look like what I needed at the time it happened, but eventually I saw the need."

She held the box in both of her hands and turned it over. "I will be frank with you, Korvas. It seems too simple. I've studied formulas, stars, charts, and scriptures for decades to obtain the power of the gods. You have as much as said that I am holding exactly that in my hands right now, and that I need nothing more than to ask for it."

"Your Eminence, I think I mentioned that what you need and what you think you need are different."

She nodded. "I remember." She smiled with sly lips and held out the box. "Shadows, ask it for what you need."

Captain Shadows bowed before the Heterin priestess. "Your Eminence, with all of this talk we are wasting time with this gutter rat. Let me turn him over to Quaag and his hot needles."

"All in good time, Captain. First, ask the box for what you need."

Shadows snorted angrily and took the god box in his hands. He laughed through his black beard, and the sound gave my spine a chill. "Little box, little box, this is Pagas Shadows. Give me what I need—"

The entire room filled with that strange heat shimmer as warps opened on all sides. Through the warps came three, then four, five Captain Shadowses! All of the Heterin captains who had been chasing me through this time and that dimension caught up to this Shadows at the same time.

They saw each other and froze for an instant. The dungeon then filled with moaning and screaming more hideous than anything ever imported from the underworld. They all drew their swords and waded into each other cursing, screaming, and hacking. In a moment all of them were down save for the one who had asked for what he needed. He stared at the decapitated bodies on the dungeon floor. All of the heads were still alive, rolling their eyes and snapping their teeth.

The original Pagas Shadows just stood there, the god box in his hands, his eyes staring blankly at the floor. Tretia came from behind her chair and stood next to the captain. She snapped her fingers in front of Shadows's face.

"Captain? Captain Shadows?" She pushed the captain, and Shadows tipped over backwards and fell flat on the floor. "His mind has gone." The priestess looked at me. "What do you suppose the gods thought he needed?"

I held out my hands. "If I could think as the gods, I would be the gods." I rubbed my chin and chuckled as a thought entered my mind. "Maybe they thought what the captain needed was a good look at himself."

The priestess gestured with her hand, and one of the guards picked up the god box and handed it to her. Tretia held the box and looked at me. "If I should ask it for what I need, would I too be destroyed?"

I shook my head. "I do not know, Your Eminence. I have seen everything from love and diamonds to death and insanity come from the box. In asking it for what one needs, one might receive a judgment upon one's life. But I am beginning to believe that only men judge. The gods are there to forgive, to pick up the pieces, and to pull together lives. The box never punishes, however all of this butchery might look."

Tretia resumed her seat, crossed her legs, and looked at the god box. "What do I . . ." She shook her head. "No. That would be selfish, to ask only for myself. After all, I am the first priestess of the Heterin Temple and the close advisor to the king." She stroked the box and with a sly smile said, "What do I *and* the people of Iskandar need?" Her sly smile grew into a wide grin. "This way, if I am destroyed, so too will be the people of Iskandar."

As I was silently thinking how generous her request had been, a drawer opened. I and the two guards craned our necks to see what was in it. Tretia looked up, a puzzled look upon her face. "Korvas, what is this?"

I took a step forward and looked. Immediately I praised the wisdom of the gods as well as cursed them for making me almost break my ribs trying to suppress a laugh. There would be no more palace intrigue, for no one would ever whisper to the priestess again. Neither would she be able to approach the king. Hence her power over the king would evaporate. As her ability to exercise clandestine power ended, the yoke of fear would lift from the neck of Iskandar, and the people would get what they needed.

As her power eroded, her opportunities to develop personal humility would increase. Thus both the people and the priestess would get what they needed. "They are delicious. Try one, Your Eminence. They are called butnuts."

She held the god box toward me. "You first."

"With pleasure, Your Eminence." I reached toward the drawer.

"Close your eyes, dog."

"Of course." I closed my eyes, plucked a nut from the drawer, and popped it into my mouth. When she saw me chewing, the priestess tried one herself. Her eyebrows arched. "These are amazingly delicious!"

She popped another into her mouth as the two guards began edging away. "This is indeed the food of the gods!" She emptied the tiny drawer into her hand and began tossing them into her mouth. "I must have more, Korvas." She opened another drawer, and it too was filled with butnuts.

"Bring me a large bowl," she ordered. Both guards left the dungeon at a dead run. When they didn't return immediately, I collected the helmets from the snapping heads at my feet and helped the priestess fill them. The god box produced enough nuts to fill four of the helmets. Tretia shook the god box. "It's empty." She looked at me as she stuffed more of the nuts into her mouth. "This will not last me! I must have more!"

"Your Eminence, if you are very very frugal with those nuts, I know where I can obtain more. It will take several weeks."

"Go." She pulled a purse from the folds of her robe and threw it at me. "Spare no expense." She tossed down another handful as one of her whispering lizards slithered into the dungeon. He came within ten feet of the priestess and stopped as though his face had been smacked with a griddle stone. Tretia snapped at him, "Well? What do you want?"

The man looked at me as the yellow-green color worked its way up from his throat to his face. "My most . . . humble apologies, Your Eminence." He backed away a few feet as he said, "I seem to have forgotten what it was I was going to say." He ran from the room.

"How strange," the priestess remarked. Tretia nodded at me. "Never mind about that. Get going. If you fail to bring me the nuts, there will be no place in this world where you can hide from me."

"I will bring them, Your Eminence. You may depend on me. May I have my god box?"

"You are certain that one of my own manufacture will work as well?"

"Yes. You have my word on that."

"If your word proves to be false, I'll have your tongue." Tretia thought for a moment, then nodded and clasped her hands as she tried to force herself to slow down with the butnuts. "Take it. I'll have one made that isn't quite so drab. Would a god box of hammered gold work?"

"Certainly, Your Eminence."

The priestess raised her eyebrows. "Is there anything else?"

As I remarked at the beginning of my story, I am always looking for more efficient ways to increase my fortune. There I was in the center of opportunity, and I could not resist. I pointed at the floor. "Would I be too bold if I asked for one of these snapping heads?"

She glanced at the floor, ate another butnut, and gave a tiny shrug. "Not at all. I'll have it pickled for you so it will keep until you return. If you fail to return, I'll have you pickled."

"Thank you, Your Eminence."

"I will even throw in one of the bodies as well. Just bring me more of those nuts."

"I will, Your Eminence."

With an annoyed expression she looked about the chamber. "Where are my guards? Find one of my guards, if you can, and have him show you out."

"Thank you, Your Eminence." I bowed and backed from the room.

Certainly Tretia stank. Just as certainly everyone but the priestess will know it. Who will ever grow the courage to shout this information to Tretia, for no one will ever get close enough to whisper? And now I was Korvas the wealthy importer of exotic delicacies, by special appointment to the king's advisor.

Of course she was responsible for my father's death and the deaths of many others. Her sudden death, however, wouldn't bring my father back or bring freedom to Iskandar. Her murder would probably only raise another serpent from the slime. This way Tretia was curbed, the people could rise above their fears, and I suddenly found myself with a new line of profitable work. I have learned not to question the will of the gods.

When I stepped through the gated entrance to the king's palace and was once again in the sunshine, I began laughing. I was well into the Mystic Mountains three days later before I could stop. My ribs hurt like sin itself.

AFTERWORD

Here I stand before you, my patient listeners, and soon my assistant Ruuter will open the doors and set you free, for I am at the end of my tale of *The God Box*.

What did you say, fellow? Yes, I imagine there are more than a few of you who are wondering about loose ends. This fellow asks why the commander of the Nant Guard, Meru, paid the Dagas storyteller fifty gold reels to keep his secrets? This one down front wants to know why Sergeant Rosh didn't warn us that Shadows was coming when we were in the Blackwood? That lady in back wants to know what of the *Silk Ghost* and the underwater empire of Ilanyia?

I cannot answer your questions. To be honest, which I must, I do not know the answers. In one reality Ilanyia and its beautiful queen exist. In another reality the Itkah refugees drowned as they were driven into the sea. In still a third reality, the Itkahs defeated the invaders from the north and there never was a city called Iskandar. Ah, you laugh, but I speak the truth.

You see, when I returned to the Dagas to complete the story for Bachudowah, she put the story before her people and went down in legend as a goddess. Every single one of the Dagas carries a god box now. But in another reality they hissed and laughed at her. In still another I never returned to complete the tale because I died.

It is not important to snip off these loose ends. Too firm a grip upon what one calls reality, and being too grasping for exact answers to every little this and that, makes one very dull. More than that, it places one in a self-constructed and self-maintained prison.

Somewhere I am a king, and this knowledge makes me more tolerant of the kings I see in this world. Somewhere I am a slave, and this knowledge makes me treat the slaves I meet in this world with kindness and dignity. Somewhere I am still selling crawling carpets to stupid magicians, and somewhere else I am a god waiting patiently for someone to ask for what he or she needs so I can help.

We are all of us all of these things. If you do not believe me, that is your choice. However, for those of you with a bit of daring and the humility to open your mind to the possibility that you alone are not the power of the universe, make yourself a god box, place the power of the universe at your fingertips, and discover all of your many selves. Whether you name your patron on the box or leave it blank as I do, always you will get what you need.

When I began my tale I said that I would tell you about a great hero, a beautiful maiden, a great villain, and how Captain Shadows came to be in these jugs. Although there were several beautiful maidens in my story, the one to which I referred in my opening was, of course, the divine Abrina. I fear that I am not the hero. The hero is this little box, and the god or gods that work through its drawers, for the villain was neither Shadows nor the Heterin horror who held his leash. The villain was fear. Hence, the villain was defeated and the hero got the girl. But wait, there is more.

You may often question why you need what you receive from your god box. I did many times as I traveled from the Dagas's lair past the no-longer-extant Shrine to Mankua to the Valley of the Omergunts to obtain more butnuts to keep the world free. I questioned because I still felt a pain in my heart where Abrina's love should have been.

While Coul and his companions cried the nuts off the trees, I turned my horse up the Blackwood Trail. That was where I met my former guide and current assistant Ruuter working at the sawmill. He had no memory of our time together, or of guiding us through the mountains. That was when I had the idea of putting Captain Shadows on display for the people. I would need an assistant, and Ruuter accepted the post.

Leaving him behind at the sawmill, I felt myself being drawn irresistibly toward the Blackwood treehouse of Shamas. When I reached the place where the house had been, there was nothing there, not even a stump. The huge tree was not a part of this world, and neither was Shamas, father of Abrina.

I dismounted, gave the horse its head, and stood looking into the woods, my hand upon the god box, as I filled with sadness. I remember thinking that I didn't understand the pain, why the pain was necessary, or if it would ever end. I felt I knew what I needed, but even then I was not arrogant enough to ask for a goddess. All I could ask for was what I needed.

No drawers opened, but I heard the sound of an ax coming from a great distance. My heart threatened to burst through my ribs, and as I mounted my horse I reminded myself of the humor of the gods. I snickered out a laugh before the terrors and hopes of chance dangled before me.

Soon I was at that clearing where I had met Abrina in another world. At the far end a logger was limbing a fallen blackwood. I dismounted, tied my horse to a bit of brush, and walked toward her. She had short black hair, amber eyes, full red lips, and the body of a goddess held in by a laced vest, brown trousers, and boots.

She stood up as I approached the log. She was only a head taller than I, but she didn't look smaller. Perhaps I had grown. She looked down at me. "Who are you?"

"My name is Korvas." My lips became very dry. "Is your name Abrina?"

"Yes, it is. Is something wrong? Shamas, my father?"

"No." I shook my head. "There is nothing wrong in the entire world. I want to ask you a question."

She placed a hand on her hip. "What question?"

I held out my hand toward a stump. "May I sit and watch you work?"

Her eyebrows went up. She laughed and prepared to take another swing with her ax. "It's a free country."

"Yes, it is."

I sat down on the stump and watched my goddess swing her blade as I patted the god box and praised the wisdom of the gods. Abrina's cheeks were rosy. She was blushing.

ABOUT THE AUTHOR

Barry B. Longyear is the author of over a dozen science fiction novels, including the Hugo, Nebula, and John W. Campbell award-winning *Enemy Mine*. Born in 1942 in Harrisburg, Pennsylvania, Barry is a graduate of Wayne State University. He currently resides in Farmington and New Sharon, Maine, with his wife, Jean, and their three cats and dog. *The God Box* is his first fantasy novel.

There's an epidemic with 27 million victims. And no visible symptoms.

It's an epidemic of people who can't read.

Believe it or not, 27 million Americans are functionally illiterate, about one adult in five.

The solution to this problem is you... when you join the fight against illiteracy. So call the Coalition for Literacy at toll-free **1-800-228-8813** and volunteer.

Volunteer Against Illiteracy. The only degree you need is a degree of caring.